KNIGHT GAMES BOOK 5

A GAME OF HEARTS

USA TODAY BESTSELLING AUTHOR

GENEVIEVE JACK

A Game of Hearts: Knight Games Book 5

Copyright © 2023 Carpe Luna Publishing
Published by Carpe Luna, Ltd., Bloomington, IL 61701

SECOND EDITION: June 2016
*V*3.4

eISBN: 978-1-940675-21-3

ISBN: 978-1-940675-22-0

CASH BAR

"Crazy-ass witches." Logan Valentine leaned his elbows against the bar, swirling the ice and lime in his almost-empty cocktail. The vodka and tonic was doing its dirty work. His nose tingled with the numbing effect, and his mind teetered on the edge of a good solid buzz. He needed it. It wasn't every day you attended a witch's wedding, let alone one who had effectively saved your soul.

On the dance floor, said witch, Grateful Knight, was getting cozy with her new husband, Rick, the white lace of her wedding dress pressed against his black tux, her forehead tucked into the side of his neck. Logan couldn't look away. Entranced, he barely registered his friend Silas Flynn hopping onto the barstool next to him.

"Attractive couple," Silas said, his bushy hair and eyebrows giving his face a decidedly wolfish appearance. Fitting for someone who sprouted a snout and tail every full moon.

"Yup." Logan sipped his drink.

"Can I ask you something?"

"Shoot."

"How are you handling all this?"

"What do you mean?"

Silas glanced down into his bourbon, scratching behind his ear with suspiciously long fingernails. "I heard you and Grateful have a history."

Logan shook his head. "Not really. I was in a car accident over a year ago. My soul was knocked out of my body. Grateful put me back in. While I was, shall we say, corporeally challenged, we had something, but it wasn't real. She sorts lost souls; I was a lost soul. Our attraction was misdirected magic."

"So that look on your face isn't jealousy?"

Draining the rest of his cocktail, Logan contemplated the question. He wasn't jealous exactly. He loved Grateful as a friend and nothing more. Although, there was a time when he'd thought he loved her in the romantic sense. Maybe that was the problem. He was another year older and no closer to having what she had, what he truly wanted. Not for lack of trying.

"It's not her specifically," he tried to explain. "I want *this*, Silas."

"This."

"The whole thing. A wife, children, the house with the yard. To be in love with a flesh-and-blood human woman who can love me back." He frowned into his empty drink. "I guess weddings make me sentimental."

"I get it, man. I'd marry Soleil in a minute if she'd have me."

With a snort, Logan turned toward his friend. "Are you saying she won't have you? Have you asked her?"

He tipped his head from side to side. "Not in so many

words. She's fae and I'm a werewolf. There's still a lot of prejudice in the supernatural community." He chuckled. "To her kind, I'm one step up from hu—"

"Human," Logan finished. "Like me."

"Sorry, buddy. I didn't mean it like that."

Logan shrugged. He was used to it. As one of the few humans who were aware of the supernatural community living among them, he'd discovered quickly that humans were not respected as equals. He supposed he should be happy for relative benevolence considering any one of them could make his life a living hell if they were so inclined.

"Can I buy you another?" Silas asked, obviously wanting to make up for his earlier faux pas.

"Naw. I better get my human ass back to the restaurant. I'm training new kitchen staff. My assistant manager can hold down the fort, but he can't cook worth a damn."

"Aww, come on, Logan. Don't go on my account. It was a slip of the tongue. You're my best friend. I forget you're human sometimes, you know?"

"I know. I'm just feeling a little... out of place."

Silas slung an arm over his shoulder. "You belong here as much as I do. Plus, I'm sorry, but you can't leave. As a member of the Carlton City police force, I can't let you drive in your current inebriated state."

Logan groaned. He *had* been drinking. Silas was right; he shouldn't drive. He set his glass on the bar and shook his head when the bartender offered another.

"They just cut the cake. Have a slice and a cup of coffee with me. You should be good to go in an hour or two."

"I don't want a slice of ca..." Logan trailed off as Silas turned him toward the cake table. What had he been saying? His mind blinked like a cursor on a blank screen. A vision in gold had officially wiped his mental hard drive. Long waves of intensely red hair. Creamy skin. Full breasts that mounded over a beaded gold corset. Long, muscular legs. High heels. And sapphire blue eyes that drifted absently over the small group of wedding guests.

"Who's the warrior princess?" Silas whispered into his ear.

Logan snapped out of it. He blinked a few times before answering his friend. "You've never met Polina?"

"That's the Smuggler's Notch witch? Soleil told me about her, but I've never seen her in person. She looks like a badass."

"She's got a personality to match."

"I'm not looking at her personality."

Logan punched him in the side. "What would Soleil say?"

Silas smirked. "She's the madam of a fae bordello, Logan. She'd be looking with me, perhaps asking Polina to join us later." He jostled Logan's shoulders roughly. "Besides, I'm not interested for me. I'm only thinking of you. Come on."

"Oh no." Logan struggled, shaking his head, as Silas forced him toward the cake table. "Silas, she's... we... witch." It was no use. Although Silas was slightly shorter than Logan and no more muscular, his werewolf constitution gave him superhuman strength. Tripping forward, Logan fought against the man's viselike grip until Polina's gaze flicked from her slice of chocolate cake to him. The moment those sapphire blues locked on, Logan stopped struggling and floated toward her. It wasn't magic but attraction that drew him in.

He should leave. A smart man would turn and run, sober up at a safe distance, maybe locked inside his car.

"Hello." Her voice was confident but somehow sweet, as youthful as the straight-toothed smile that spread her lips. That smile cut through his sternum, her stare seeming to weigh his soul.

"Polina." Why did his heart have to race when he looked at her? From the first time Grateful had introduced them, she'd seemed familiar, like her face was a long-forgotten memory. Part of him was sure that if he could stare at her long enough, he would figure it out. Maybe she held a resemblance to a celebrity or distant family member.

She fidgeted with the side of her plate. Awkward. He'd stared too long. Now, she knew he was staring. Fuck. Polina never let him forget he was a mere human. She probably thought he worshiped her. He turned to Silas to break the tension.

"Polina, I'd like to introduce you to my friend Silas," Logan announced formally.

"A pleasure," Silas said, extending his hand. "Any friend of Logan's is a friend of mine. Now, if you'll excuse me..." Silas released her hand and with a nod of his head, disappeared into the crowd of wedding guests.

"Silas!" Logan called, sending death rays in his general direction.

"Was it something I said?" Polina asked.

"How could it be something you said? You said, 'Hello.' That couldn't have possibly been offensive."

"Why would he leave so abruptly?" She motioned in the direction of Silas's disappearance with her delicate hand.

Truth was, Logan suspected that Silas wanted to play matchmaker and had abandoned the two of them on purpose. He couldn't say that. For one, Logan understood something Silas did not: Polina hated humans, and Logan was more than slightly wary of witches.

"Who knows?" He shrugged. Oddly nervous, he reached for a piece of cake, trying not to notice how close his arm came to her hip. A circle of heat formed on the inside of his elbow where it brushed past her. What was wrong with him?

"Werewolves," she said with a weak laugh. "Cheeky bastards."

"How did you know he was a werewolf? You just met him."

"I can taste it on his aura. It's unmistakable. Along with the hint of wet dog he leaves in his wake."

Logan poked his cake with his fork. The chocolate was a wretched orangish brown and it crumbled like sand under the pressure of the tines. Along with the oil separating from the frosting, Logan deemed the dessert an inedible disaster.

"Do you hate werewolves, too?" he asked.

"Too?"

"Like you hate humans?"

She leaned a hip against the table and cocked an eyebrow at him. "I never said I hated humans or werewolves. I don't hate anyone."

"Oh, that's right. You said my kind was inferior. That's different than hate."

Her face screwed up. "Are you baiting me?" The hand holding her fork turned palm up in question. "It is a simple fact that witches are the more durable species. Humans can't do any sort of magic and are physically fragile. But I appreciate your race's many accomplishments, all things considered. I'm not a human-phobe or anything. I've had plenty of human friends over the years." She pointed a finger at his face. "Franklin...

Benjamin Franklin. We spent time together once. Good times."

Logan's chin dropped as his jaw popped open. After a moment, his spine straightened with offense.

"Don't look at me like that," she said. "I'm not trying to be arrogant or elitist. I saved your life, after all."

It was true. She'd saved him from drowning a few weeks earlier when he'd gone on the road to help Grateful with her mission. A water witch almost turned him into fish food. If Polina hadn't intervened on his behalf, he'd probably be dead.

"I guess I owe you one," he said flatly. Why was he letting her do this to him? The longer he talked to her, the more he felt inferior. It was always the same with witches. He seriously needed to start hanging out with his own kind. "Nice seeing you, Polina," he mumbled, turning to leave.

Her perfectly manicured fingers landed on his upper arm. "Wait. Stay. I wasn't trying to be unkind. I simply—"

"You needed me to know the truth." Logan's eyes fixated on the cake and something snapped. His mind pictured another witch, another pastry. No way would he allow her or any other witch to tell him what to do. Never again. Acting on a deep instinct, he stepped into her so that his chest was almost touching hers. In this position, her petite stature made it impossible for her to look him in the eye without wrenching her neck back. He wrapped his hands around her upper arms.

"You think you're out of my league, don't you? That pretty little head of yours is so big under that beauty queen hairdo that you know without a doubt you could never stoop to associate with a guy like me." He shook her slightly.

She didn't try to pull away, but focused on his mouth, her forehead furrowing.

Logan continued, "Well, I need to tell *you* the truth. I've been with your kind and it was a major head fuck. I've been fed potions and had thoughts thrust into my brain to manipulate me. I've been forced to do things I didn't want to do. I may be the more fragile species, sweetheart, but I'm also the more trustworthy. You don't have to worry about making sure I know how superior you are. I couldn't care less."

He released her with a little push. With only a small space between them, he expected her to back away. A human woman would storm off after a tirade like that. Not Polina. She stared at him like a bug under a microscope. Even leaned forward, narrowing her eyes in scrutiny. "Are you finished?"

"Yeah," Logan drawled.

"Good." She loaded her fork with the nasty brown cake on her plate. "I know Salem's witch, Tabetha, misused you before Grateful and I killed her. I can understand why you are traumatized. But don't take your human tantrum out on me. I've been quite generous with my abilities when it comes to you. The least you can do is show your gratitude." The dry crumbles coasted toward her luscious mouth. Despite his anger, he couldn't watch her full, red lips wrap around that disaster of a baked good.

"Gratitu—" He slapped her fork away. "Don't eat that."

"Why ever not?"

Grunting with frustration, he broke off a chunk and ground it to dust between his fingers. "I'm a chef, okay? Chocolate cake should be moist. It should be sweet perfection nestled in whipped heaven. This is a travesty."

"A travesty? Why?"

"It's under emulsified."

She shook her head.

"An emulsifier distributes and stabilizes fats with

liquids. Not only does this chocolate cake not have enough fat, it's been overcooked and over processed." He stepped in closer, lowered his voice to a sultry whisper. "Chocolate cake should melt in your mouth. When you eat a slice of Valentine's chocolate cake, the cocoa hits your tongue first, followed by a burst of subtle sweetness. The consistency is loose but almost fudgy. It comes apart and permeates every corner of your mouth. And when you swallow..."

"Yes?" Her eyes darted between his. One thing he'd learned about witches was that they couldn't cook. It was the curse of their species and left them persistently obsessed with epicurean delights.

"When you swallow well-made chocolate cake, there should be a buttery finish. Savory to balance the sweet. It leaves you longing for the next bite." She leaned forward, lips parting. He could feel her breath on his chin.

"Sounds delicious." Her hand pressed into her stomach. All at once, she seemed to realize how close they were and she took a step back.

"It is. You should come into Valentine's sometime and try a slice."

"Do you make it yourself?"

He nodded slowly. "Along with a positively wicked buttercream frosting."

He watched her throat contract with a swallow and her beautiful pink tongue dart along her bottom lip. He had her. She was practically drooling.

The corner of his mouth quirked, and he backed away from her. "Oh, wait, you can conjure your own damn chocolate cake, can't you? Being that you're the superior species and all."

Her face twisted and her mouth gaped like a fish out of water.

Logan turned on his heel and headed for the exit, giving a small wave over his shoulder. "Have a nice immortal existence, Polina."

Her mouth was still hanging open when the door closed behind him.

2
THE VISITOR

"Chocolate cake, he says. Like I would eat his chocolate cake." Polina huffed over her cauldron, stirring like a madwoman, the human way. She could have used magic instead of elbow grease to do the job, but the latter was more therapeutic. Therapy was exactly what she needed. Only an unbalanced mind would still be thinking about the human.

"Are you still fussing about that man Logan?" her owl familiar, Hildegard, asked. The bird sat on one of the many carved wooden perches that adorned their home, watching Polina's flurry of activity with curiosity. "It's been almost a month since the wedding. I'd think you'd be over it by now."

Polina straightened, placing one hand on her hip. "It's confounding, Hildegard. The man approaches me in a crowded reception hall, obviously attracted to me."

Hildegard rolled her eyes.

"Don't make that face. I know when a male is attracted to me, especially a human male. He was the spitting image of Pepe Le Pew with his tongue hanging out. I could see the outline of his heart throbbing through the wall of his chest."

The owl laughed. "All right. All right. He was attracted to you. What happened next?"

"He crossed the room and entered my personal space with the familiarity of a friend—"

"He should think of you as a friend after how you saved him from the water witch. Not to mention the other reason." She lowered her voice to a whisper on the last.

"Regardless, he approached me, and I thought, sure, he's human, no better than a dog, but even a dog might be a welcome diversion from the strange human wedding formalities. Do you know there is a thing called the Chicken Dance?"

Hildegard shook her head. "Do they dance with poultry?"

Polina inhaled deeply. "No. Heavy drinking and flailing of arms. Very disconcerting."

"So, you thought you would tolerate some mild entertainment by the human."

"Indeed. He was with that werewolf friend of Grateful's. What's his name again?"

"Silas. Silas Flynn."

"Ah, yes. The detective. They were together and as we've had little experience with werewolves in Smuggler's Notch, I thought the conversation might be enlightening. But no sooner were they in my company as the wolf wandered off, leaving me with the human, who immediately accused me of supernatural elitism."

"How did you respond?"

"Honestly, of course. I suggested that although witches were the more powerful species, I respected humans for their many accomplishments over the centuries and had met quite a few reputable members of his race. I even admitted that his company was rather enjoyable at times."

Hildegard snorted. "Why on earth would he take offense?"

"By your tone, I assume you're being facetious."

"I'm simply suggesting that your comments may have been a bit heavy handed."

Polina grunted.

"What was all that about the chocolate cake?"

"He told me to go bake my own."

Hildegard inhaled sharply and then broke into a fit of laughter. "A sharp tongue on that one. Does he know what an insult that is to a witch?"

"He knew exactly what he was saying," Polina said. "That's why it was so infuriating. The man was a ghost in Grateful's attic for months. He's annoyingly knowledgeable about all things witch."

"And he can cook." Hildegard raised the arched feathers that served as her eyebrows skyward, her massive yellow eyes twinkling. "I see the problem here. You like Logan, more than you want to admit."

"Humph," Polina said. "You don't know what you're talking about."

"Mmmhmm."

Polina stirred her cauldron absently. "Although, there is something about the man. He knows I can destroy him with a wink of my eye but still he challenges me with his sharp wit. Plus, he's a medium. He receives messages from the human heaven, a thing no witch can ever do. A creature with such a tenuous existence should be timid, but he charges into the world, flags flying. The way he helped Grateful was nothing short of selfless."

"So you do like him."

Polina's stirring strokes became violent. "Pshaw. Even if

my attraction to him was authentic and not a side effect of the incident—"

"Rare if it were…"

"Even if it weren't, there's a reason humans and supernaturals don't mix. It's a recipe for disaster. I've been down that road before. I know how it ends."

"Ronin? He's long dead, my lady. Perhaps it's time you let him go?"

Angrily, Polina twisted the knob to turn the burner off under the cauldron and slapped the wooden spoon on the counter. Potion sprayed across the granite. Snatching a mug from the cupboard, she poured herself a cup of the brew.

"I've had to let Ronin go, Hildie. He's dead. Dead, because that's what humans do. They die."

"I am sorry to dredge up the past," Hildegard said contritely.

"It's all right." Polina waved a hand dismissively. "It's a good reminder. I have no business having feelings for a human." She sipped the concoction in her cup. "It's not real. It's soul magic. Nothing more."

Hildie's deep sigh filled the kitchen. "What's in the cauldron, my lady?"

Polina shook her head.

Hildegard crossed the small space to the grimoire open on the counter. The book was covered in solid gold and inscribed with the title *Elemental Alchemy*. "Queen Mary's brew. Essence of peace lily and lavender. This elixir calms the mind and eases strong emotions," Hildie read.

Polina shrugged. "It's either this or vodka, and I can't do magic drunk."

"Aye," Hildegard said softly.

Polina drained the mug and slammed the empty on the stone counter. "Sun is setting. Time to get to work."

"As you wish."

Polina hastened into the bedroom to a large looking glass inside a crafted pewter stand, what they called a cheval mirror in furniture catalogs. Only this particular piece of furniture held an important secret. Without pause, Polina walked directly into the center of the glass. The mirrored silver accommodated her body, flowing in a ripple across her skin before allowing her access to her sanctuary.

At the heart of Aurorean House, the large Tudor mansion she called home, Polina's seat of concentrated power was a multifaceted silver structure—the room of reflections. The mirrored walls shifted around her, their interlocking geometric formation constantly changing to meet her needs. With Hildegard on her shoulder, she crossed to the center of the living metal gem to a giant, table-height stretch of silver—a *lucubratus*—a magic mirror she used to monitor her realm.

Polina wasn't just a witch; she was a Hecate, a sorceress of the dead. A Hecate's duty was to police the supernatural. The mirror was enchanted to show her possible futures, anyone or anything with malicious intent within her realm. Her job was to predict and prevent evil deeds from occurring. In Smuggler's Notch, Polina was judge, jury, and executioner. Supernaturals who evaded or ignored her intervention were sentenced to her hellmouth, the small mountain cemetery behind her home that served as a supernatural prison after dark.

In a loud, clear voice, she passed one hand over the silver and said, "Reveal." The mirror melted to the consistency of liquid mercury, bubbling to a three-dimensional peak before settling into a reflective pool of molten metal. She leaned over it, her reflection dulling, replaced by the vision she was meant to see.

At the base of her mountain was a human campsite. The silver depicted a man Polina had never seen before walking toward the trail opposite her property. This was to be expected. The enchantment surrounding Silver Sparrow Mountain not only made it effectively invisible to humans but produced a sense of dread that steered any who wandered too close toward the human trail. It was the natural alternative to the base of her dark forest.

"Surprise, surprise," she said as the silver continued its revelation. At the head of the trail, the man stripped off his clothes and bent over, limbs twisting in an agonizing display of metamorphosis. A moment later, a humungous wolf stood in the man's place. Werewolf.

The wolf looked hungry and clearly had a mind of its own separate from its human counterpart. Instead of continuing down the trail or running into the forest, it turned around and headed for the human camp. Interacting with humans in supernatural form was forbidden. Injuring a human was a sentenceable offense. When the mirror showed the wolf attacking a human family in their tent, Polina had to take action.

"Time to go," Polina said.

"There might be more tonight," Hildegard replied, nodding at the silver.

"Later. The sun has already set. If this wolf is in camp, he's shifting now." She grabbed her wand from the side of the *lucubratus* and hurried for the door. "I don't think he means to injure anyone, but my understanding is that shifted wolves are extremely impulsive. An ounce of redirection is in order."

"After you, my lady."

The problem with using a *lucubratus* to see the future was the magic mirror often left out important details. In this case, it was the rain. As Polina made her way down her mountain to the human camp, thunder rumbled overhead, lightning tore across the sky, and rain sheeted, soaking her fitted yellow dress and leather slippers.

At the boundary of Silver Sparrow, she circled her wand above her head, dropping a hoop of purple magic down her body. By the time she set foot in the human camp, she was dressed in the brown uniform of a Smuggler's Notch State Park ranger, wide-brimmed hat and all. Not a moment too soon. Man shifted into beast across the camp-site from her. She concealed her wand along the inside of her forearm and hurried to the head of the trail.

The red wolf was enormous, not the natural variety. Its lion-sized head came mid-chest, and its shoulders were wider than hers. Amber eyes zeroed in on Polina, and leathery nostrils twitched with the effort of a good sniff of air and rain.

Through the sheet of water running off the brim of her hat, Polina met the werewolf's stare. Its claws sank into the mud, ears twitching, teeth bared.

"Easy, fella. I'm here to help." Polina showed the wolf her wand and made her eyes glow gold to reveal her iden-tity. Although she suspected her scent was enough of a clue, it never hurt to show a supernatural what they were up against. In response, the wolf stopped and whined like a chastened dog.

"Now, if you promise to be a good werewolf, I have a place for you, safe from these nasty humans. Plenty of rabbits and deer to keep you busy for the night. Would you like that?"

The red wolf made a high-pitched sound of consent.

"Very well. Follow me." She walked toward Sparrow Mountain, the wolf heeling to her side. Glancing toward the campsite, she was relieved the humans were snug inside their tents and campers due to the rain. No eyes. No ears.

The wolf cried as they broke the foggy barrier that was her enchantment. Mist hung permanently at the mountain's base, and Sparrow Mountain appeared out of nowhere like a page in a giant pop-up book. The mountain cut through the illusion in a headache-inducing act of magic. The wolf hesitated, the protective wards no doubt making his skin crawl. He paced the border.

"Keep walking. You'll feel better in a hundred yards or so."

The wolf refused. It crouched and growled, baring its teeth. Fine. She'd hoped to do this the easy way, but she was nothing if not adaptable. Drawing her wand, she positioned herself behind the wolf and sent a shower of sparks toward its tail, an attempt to scare the beast deeper into her realm. The plan backfired. The wolf spun and leapt, jaws snapping. She avoided the teeth, but one massive red paw tore through her shoulder. With a blast of magic, she sent the wolf tumbling.

"Fuck! Bastard, I'm trying to help you." Polina pressed a hand into the bloody wound. A few more sparks and she drove the beast farther up the mountain, the wolf snarling and snapping all the way. Thankfully, they were far enough into her realm to be hidden from human view.

With a few jogging steps, she caught up to the wolf, who seemed less agitated now that he was beyond the enchanted border. Polina's brown uniform glittered gold, then faded away, replaced by the yellow dress and slippers. She raised her wand and pointed it toward the mountain.

"Go on," she said. "Stay away from humans. I'd hate to have to hurt you."

The wolf bowed his head slightly, then turned to advance into the trees.

Hildegard hooted overhead. "I believe we have our realm's first werewolf."

Polina smiled at the owl. "Well, I'm not going to suggest that wolf stay after tonight." She was soaking wet and couldn't wait to get home. "He must have a pack somewhere. Don't they usually belong to packs? Let's hope he's just passing through. My enchantment should keep him safely away from the humans for the night."

Hildegard bobbed her head. "You're a good witch."

Polina was about to say thank you when a man's scream ripped through the night.

3

NIGHTMARE

Something warm and wet streamed down Logan's outstretched arms, forming dark tributaries against his pale skin. He tried to focus, but his vision blurred and adjusted as if he were rousing from a deep sleep or the effects of anesthesia. When his vision did clear, panic set in. The dark rivulets running down his arms were blood. His blood.

The cause of the bleeding was two thorny vines that constricted and cut into his wrists. He was strung to the ceiling, spread eagle. Another two of the woody-stemmed plants held his ankles apart. Naked, exposed, he waited in the middle of a bedroom. The walls, the floor, the ceiling, even the four-poster bed crawled with living, growing green tendrils covered in red roses. Their scent permeated the air, thick and floral to the extent he would retch if he had anything in his stomach.

He gave a cursory tug against the vines but they were strong as steel cables. No give at all. How long had he been standing here with his arms strung up over his head? Long enough for his entire body to ache. Long enough for him to fear what his captor might do to him next.

He didn't remember how he'd gotten there, but he sure as hell remembered who was responsible.

"Is my toy awake again?" Tabetha, Salem's witch, strolled into the room stark naked. The rose blossoms turned their heads, following her progress. Her blunt-cut black hair reminded him of Cleopatra, as did the gold scarab beetle she wore around her neck. He flinched and struggled against his bindings. Tabetha was a wood witch, as evil as they came.

"Why are you doing this to me?" Logan asked.

She gave a wicked grin. "Because your pain pleases me, human."

"My name is Logan."

"Not here it's not. Here you are what I say you are. Right now, you are my amusement." She picked up a silver hairbrush from the vanity near the window. With a *crack*, the etched back connected with her palm. "Call me Queen Tabetha."

"Let me go," he said, clenching his jaw.

Her arm slashed and the brush smacked Logan's ass. Pain shot up his already aching backside.

"Queen Tabetha," she demanded.

"Fuck you."

Smack. This time the brush slapped his jaw, knocking his face into his outstretched bicep.

"Say it."

"Queen bitch." Logan spat in her face.

Whack. The brush connected with his ribs. *Bam.* Ass again. *Smack.* The back of his thighs. The vines tightened with her anger, and Logan feared he'd lose control of his bladder if the pain got much worse.

"I tire of this diversion." She left Logan's field of vision and returned with a bite-sized purple tart between her fingers, the green seeds a dead giveaway that the filling was persigranate fruit.

Logan shook his head vigorously. "No. I won't eat it this time." The stuff got into his brain, made him do things he didn't want to do.

"Open." She pinched his nose and tipped his head. When he opened his mouth to breathe, she shoved the tart to the back of his throat. He coughed and choked and eventually nature took its course; the pastry slid down to his stomach. The disorienting dizziness came on almost immediately.

"More," she commanded, another tart in her hand. Head spinning, he was helpless to resist. He chewed and swallowed like a good little robot, the hate giving way to the floaty feeling of intoxication.

"Call me Queen Tabetha."

"Queen Tabetha," Logan murmured.

"You will serve me."

"Serve you."

"You love me."

Logan did not answer.

"Never mind. On your knees." At the wave of her hand the vines retracted, and Logan collapsed onto the hardwood floor. She pulled over the chair from the vanity. He thought she meant it for him and began to rise, but she forced him down to his knees by the shoulder.

Propping one foot on the chair, she grabbed his head. "You exist for my pleasure, human."

A prisoner inside his own body, his brain became a swirling mess of contradicting emotions that had nowhere to go. He closed his eyes, opened his mouth and...

In total darkness, Logan woke to his own scream. He opened his eyes and sat bolt upright. He was in his bed in his penthouse condominium in Carlton City, New Hampshire. Covered in sweat and heart thumping like a bass drum, he swung his legs over the side and lowered his head between his knees.

"Pull yourself together," he said to himself. "She's dead. She's fucking dead." Logan sprang up, running his fingers through his hair. This was ridiculous. He needed his sleep. A stiff drink and he'd go back to bed.

He stalked from the bedroom toward the kitchen for a nightcap, passing by the floor-to-ceiling windows that overlooked Carlton City. When he glanced toward his balcony, two sapphire blue eyes glowed back at him. He grabbed his chest and stumbled into the sofa. The visitor was a horrific sight, wild red hair, pale skin, a yellow dress stained with blood like something out of that Carrie movie. But as his eyes adjusted to the dark, he recognized the figure standing on his balcony. Polina.

"Are you hurt? Do you need a doctor?" he yelled through the glass.

Polina furrowed her brow and then followed his stare to her right shoulder. "Oh, this? No. No. I'm fine. Here, I didn't mean to frighten you." She waved her wand and the blood was gone.

Logan rubbed his chin. Thankfully, it had stopped raining and he didn't feel obligated to invite her inside. Grateful had placed a protective enchantment around his condo. Nothing supernatural could cross his threshold without an invitation. But once permission was given, there was no taking it back.

"What are you doing here?" he demanded.

"I heard you scream."

"You... what?"

Polina licked her lips. "Do we have to talk through this window?"

Logan thought about his options and decided he wouldn't give her the satisfaction of believing he was scared of her. He unlocked the sliding glass door and joined her on the balcony. "Better?"

"Yes."

"Why are you here?" Logan repeated.

"I was in the area, and I heard you scream. Are you all right?"

Logan paused. She must be joking. Sure, his nightmare had made him scream, but how could she have heard that? Why was she in Carlton City anyway? She lived in Vermont.

"I was having a nightmare about Tabetha," he said, surprised at his own candor. She'd probably think he was weak, make some crack about him being a helpless human.

Polina leaned against the railing, her usually ballerina-straight posture sagging slightly. "I have them too."

"You do?"

"She buried me alive. I fertilized a tree lining her driveway for almost a year. Can you imagine what it must be like to be immortal, conscious, and unable to move for three hundred and sixty-two days?"

Logan swallowed and shook his head. "No, I can't. But Tabetha made the Wicked Witch of the West look harmless."

"Who's the Wicked Witch of the West?" Polina asked. There was no hint of levity in her voice.

"Never mind." Logan rubbed his gray T-shirt awkwardly. "Thanks for stopping by, but I really am fine."

"What did Tabetha do to you?" Polina asked.

Logan didn't want to answer that question. He walked to the railing and looked out over the city. Polina didn't say a word. She stood next to him as if she could have waited a lifetime for his answer, silent and smelling of chrysanthemums and pumpkin spice. Why was she here?

"She used me," he said, again surprised at himself for sharing. "For sex and cooking mostly. To be honest, I don't remember much. She loaded me up with persigranate fruit and pulled my strings like a puppet. I'm glad she's dead."

"Me too," Polina said.

Logan had to admit, it felt good to talk about it. Being able to share what happened to him with someone who understood was a relief. Tightness he didn't know he carried bled from his shoulders.

"Why are you here, Polina?"

"I told you, I heard you scream and thought you might need my help."

He turned toward her. A late-summer breeze whispered through her red hair. In the poofy yellow dress she was wearing and carrying her wand, she looked like someone's fairy godmother.

"I can take care of myself," he said.

She rolled her eyes. Big mistake. There was nothing Logan liked more than a challenge. He stepped in closer. Powerful witch or not, he was bigger and, worse, he had something to prove.

"I think you came for the chocolate cake."

"What?"

"You're still hoping I feed you a slice of my chocolate cake. You've been thinking about it since the day you saw me at the wedding." He narrowed his eyes and lifted the corner of his mouth salaciously.

Her cheeks reddened. "I want no such thing."

"Liar. As much as you say I'm a weak, fragile human, you know that there is something I can give you that no one else can, and I'm not just talking about the cake." He placed his hands on the railing on either side of her hips, causing her to arch her back to keep from pressing into him. How far could he push her? He'd seen the way she looked at him. As powerful as she was, the attraction between them was not one sided. He wouldn't let her sit on her high horse. No way was she standing on his porch in the middle of the night for his protection.

"You know, watching someone through their window in the middle of the night doesn't make you a hero. It makes you a stalker," he said.

"Stalk—" She gasped in offense. Her hand landed in the middle of his chest, and she pushed him away with enough power to knock him back a good foot. "What are you implying?"

"I'm not implying anything. I'm saying outright that I think you're flying your broom past my condo real slow because you're interested in me. It's okay." He flashed her his most lascivious grin. "Most women react that way to this." He patted his chest with two open hands. He was being an asshole and every word was intentional.

She snorted. "Don't flatter yourself. I don't want you or your chocolate cake."

It was exactly the reaction he wanted. He'd pushed her to the brink, tore through that aloof demeanor, and rattled her cage. The smug satisfaction he'd expected to feel, however, didn't deliver on its promise. On the contrary, he had a strong desire to pull her into his arms and tell her he was just teasing. But he didn't.

"Then why are you still here?" he asked.

Her face turned impassive. She bent over and lifted her

skirt to her thigh, giving Logan a heart-stopping view of one perfect, creamy-skinned leg. What had he been saying? He wasn't sure. All the blood had rushed from his brain to a spot lower on his anatomy.

She pulled a pinch of gold dust from a pouch in a leather garter she wore before dropping the hem of the yellow dress. Her eyes raked down Logan's body to the evidence of his arousal. It was her turn to flash him a smug grin.

"You are absolutely right. I shouldn't be here at all." Releasing the gold dust above her head, she came apart, swirling around his body before her molecules melded with the metal railing. She was gone.

"Fucking witch!" Logan slammed a fist into his palm. With a shake of his head, he moved inside and continued his quest for a much-needed drink.

4

HALLOWEEN PARTY

"This had better be important." Two months later, Polina glared at her familiar as she approached Valentine's restaurant. "Did Grateful give you any hint what this was all about?"

"No, mistress," Hildegard answered. "According to Poe, she has important news to share with you. If there's more, he didn't make it known."

"Ah. Seems like a strange venue for sharing important news." Polina sulked.

"Aye." Hildegard bobbed her head. "The Monk's Hill witch is young. Barely in her mid-twenties in this life. Perhaps her choices are based on inexperience."

With a sigh, Polina faced the heart-shaped sign on the door. Valentine's restaurant. In place of Cupid's arrow, a fork protruded from the lower left of the heart, a spoon extending from the upper right. Valentine's was scrolled across the center. It had been eight weeks since she'd visited Logan on his veranda. Eight weeks since she felt the heat of his body next to hers, heard the quick pace of his human heart. That was the thing about humans. Everything about them was intense. The shortness of their lives made their emotions sharp compared to the jaded reactions of most immortals. Seeing his body react to the simple flash of her leg had been a satisfying conclusion to their banter. The problem was, she wanted more. For some reason, the human haunted her dreams, a wayward attraction she'd fought to deny these weeks. Even now, she felt a rush at her core. It was senseless.

"The last thing I want to do is see this human again, and here I am walking into his restaurant."

"Don't fret," Hildegard said. "It's been months since that god-awful conversation at the wedding, and the place is brimming with partygoers. You may not see him at all."

She'd never told Hildegard about the conversation on Logan's balcony. Some things she wouldn't even share with her familiar. Waving a dismissive hand, Polina said, "Go enjoy yourself with your male suitor. Poe is waiting for you." She pointed to Grateful's raven familiar waiting patiently on a lamppost across the street. "I'll be fine. Whatever Grateful has to tell me won't take long, I'm sure. I'll be home before you've caught your first mouse."

"That's the spirit." The owl spread her wings, and in the eerily silent fashion only barn owls are capable of, soared from her shoulder to join Poe for the evening. Polina straightened her spine, gathered her courage, and opened the door.

Humans had the strangest perceptions of All Hallows Eve. The guttural utterance of an automated zombie greeted her, its rubber arms flailing and its glowing eyes as red as Christmas lights. A small table with a bowl of miniature chocolates rested in front of its crotch.

"Scream your brains out. Eat sweets," Polina said dryly, turning her gaze to the spiderwebs stretched across the ceiling. Apparently, arachnid infestation was a Samhain tradition as well among Homo sapiens.

"Nice coconuts."

Polina lowered her gaze and came face to face with the one person she'd hoped she wouldn't see—Logan. His green eyes twinkled over a wry grin. He was dressed in an old-fashioned chef's outfit, his sandy brown hair peeking from under the tall white toque.

"Oh, uh, I'm the Little Mermaid." Her eyes darted to her coconut bra.

"Like the Disney movie?" He shook a finger and nodded. "Totally works with the red hair. You're missing the purple seashell necklace though."

Despite herself, she gave him a small smile. "Actually, I'm supposed to be the Hans Christian Andersen version."

"Isn't that version a tragedy?"

"Depends how you look at it. The mermaid returns to the sea, and the prince marries someone else. It's only a tragedy if you believe they were meant for each other."

He made a deep, disapproving sound. "She turns into sea foam. I think I prefer the Disney version."

"I find it amusing that a man without children knows the Little Mermaid at all. Do you watch cartoons in your spare time?"

He shrugged. "Guilty as charged."

"What about you? Why didn't you dress up for your own costume party?" she asked.

"I did. I'm Chef Boyardee." He pointed to a patch in the shape of a can on his breast pocket.

She snorted. "The canned ravioli man?"

"I wanted to dress as Julia Child, but I couldn't find the right skirt." He met her eyes and winked.

As much as she'd wanted to avoid him, she felt it

happening again, that magnetic draw of attraction. She laughed at his joke, authentically, a worrying warmth spreading in her chest. She had to find Grateful and get out of here. Her eyes drifted across the crowd, and she forced the smile from her face.

"I wasn't expecting to see you here tonight. I thought you'd be above human Halloween parties," Logan said, his formerly personable grin fading to a sharper expression.

"Grateful asked me to meet her here. She said she had news."

"Yeah." He nodded. "She does. Big news. And here I thought you'd come for my chocolate cake."

Not this again. She frowned. "Have you seen her?"

"She's here." Logan gestured across the restaurant. "Check the billiards room. She and Rick were having a game a few minutes ago."

Polina nodded her thanks and drifted across the restaurant, relieved to break from Logan's charm. Within the hunter green walls and stained glass lighting of the billiards room, she found Rick leaning across the pool table dressed in a *traje de luces*, complete with gold embroidery and montera for his head. With his straight back and formal air, he made a convincing matador.

"Polina! You came!" Grateful's blond head bobbed into her vision, and Polina was squeezed around the neck before she could even say hello. The Monk's Hill witch was dressed as a bull, horns protruding from the sides of her head and hoof-shaped gloves attached to the sleeves of brown onesie pajamas. Only, the couple's costume had a twist. Grateful was wearing Nightshade, her enchanted blade, at her hip, and the matador's red cape was tied around her neck.

Polina grinned. "Who is slaying whom? Clever."

"It was Grateful's idea," Rick said, sounding slightly embarrassed, although when the caretaker looked at his witch, there was nothing but reverence in his expression.

"Poe delivered your message," Polina said. "What's this big news?"

Rick sidled up to Grateful, handing her the pool cue and pulling his wife into his side. A grin to rival the Cheshire Cat's spread across his face. Grateful exchanged glances with him, giving Polina the distinct impression they were communicating, although neither said a word. Finally, Grateful gave a high-pitched, bouncing squeal before blurting, "We're pregnant!"

With a snort, Polina laughed the statement away. "Don't tease me, Grateful. What's the real news?"

The smile faded from Grateful's face, and she stopped bouncing. She placed a steady hoof-covered hand on Polina's arm. "I am pregnant," she said quite seriously, holding eye contact.

Polina shook her head. "How is that possible? Immortals cannot reproduce."

"I am not technically immortal anymore, because when I made Rick my caretaker, I gave him my immortality. And while he is immortal, before I lost access to the wood witch's power, I used Tabetha's grimoire to make a few humanity candles. We used one to temporarily make Rick human." She lowered her voice. "It worked, Polina. I'm pregnant."

Mouth agape, Polina tried to process this revelation. What Grateful was describing had never been accomplished as far as she knew. It was a miracle. "How far along?" she asked.

"Three months. Honeymoon baby," Grateful said, the ridiculous grin back on her face.

Polina's eyebrows crept toward her hairline and she

pressed a hand against the space between her coconut bra and her fish-scale green skirt. "This is... wonderful news. I'm so happy for you. It's practically a miracle. First you unite the elements, then you hold a beautiful wedding, and now this." Polina was babbling. She always babbled when she was nervous. She forced her lips to stop. "Congratulations," she said firmly, then gave her friend a quick hug, and Rick a congratulatory pat on the shoulder.

"Are you okay?" Grateful asked. "You look a little pale."

Polina swallowed hard. "I traveled here by gold dust. It can be disorienting."

Grateful winced. "I remember."

"I think I need a drink and to collect myself."

"I don't know how you survive traveling like that all the time. Come on, I'll buy you a drink."

Polina shook her head. "Don't trouble yourself. Finish your game."

Grateful must've read the insistence in her voice because she backed toward Rick, nodding. "Okay."

"Again, congratulations. I'm so happy for you. Please excuse me." Polina left the billiards room, the tears in her eyes blurring her vision. In a state of near blindness, she turned a corner and made her way down a hall to what she thought was the bathroom. But when she turned the brass knob and shouldered open the door, she found herself in an office. Logan's office. She'd been here once before with Grateful. Luckily, Logan wasn't in it, and a box of Kleenex rested conveniently on the edge of the big mahogany desk. She helped herself to one as the tears fell in earnest.

Exhausted, she sank into one of the two padded chairs facing the desk.

"Am I responsible for this?" Logan said from behind her. "That chocolate cake crack... I was just teasing."

She hadn't heard the door open over her sobbing. She shook her head in answer to his question, wishing he would leave, but then, she was the one who shouldn't be here. She was in his office.

The door closed and she heard the lock engage. He lowered himself into the seat across from her and offered her the drink in his hand. "Vodka and tonic. It's fresh. Dustin just made it for me. I haven't even had a sip."

She should leave. Against her better judgment, she lifted the drink from his hand and tossed a large swig to the back of her throat. "Thank you."

"Do you want to talk about it?" Logan's face held genuine concern.

She wiped under her eyes. "You are probably loving this, aren't you? The witch who claimed superiority to humans brought to her knees in front of one."

"No. I suppose I should enjoy it more, but believe it or not, it's hard for me to see you cry."

His eyes were green, like the first leaf of spring, and she found herself leaning toward him, drawn by the calm she saw in their depths.

"Immortals can't have children," she said. The admittance surprised her, the words leaping from her mouth before she could stop herself or alter them. Why was she telling him this?

He straightened in his chair. "This is about Grateful?"
She nodded.

"And I thought it was me. Let me guess... You're happy for her, but there's an ache in your chest you just can't shake."

Polina stilled. "How could you know that?" She stared at her hands, her cheeks warming with embarrassment.

"Don't be ashamed. I understand more than you know."

She lifted her gaze to his.

"I mean, the pregnancy is just the icing on the cake," he began. "I think it's the intimacy that makes me want to take up smoking. I've never had that intimacy. You look at those two and you just know they stay up late every night sharing their deepest, darkest secrets. And now their perfect relationship has become the perfect family."

With one nod, she agreed.

"It's not jealousy, per se, the ache." He placed a hand on his chest and rubbed gently. "You don't want what she has. You want your own version of it. You want to create that..." He pressed his fingers together. "Connection with someone. The ache is the knowledge that maybe this type of thing won't ever be in the cards for you. Maybe people like you and me are simply not meant to fall in love."

"We're not worthy of love?"

"Worthy, yes. Lucky enough to find it? Not so much." He curled his nose. "Are you going to drink the rest of that?" He pointed a knuckle toward the vodka and tonic.

"No."

He drained the rest, the ice hitting his lips before falling back to the bottom of the glass.

The truth was an arrow that pierced Polina's heart and left the organ leaking emotions she hadn't felt in decades. He was right. And her truth went deeper than he could ever know. "I lost..." she began, placing a hand on her stomach.

The edges of Logan's mouth sank.

"I lost my chance at children when I became a witch," she said. "Despite what I said about your race, I was human once. When I was called into this role, I sacrificed my ability to reproduce."

"Oh," Logan said. "Do you regret that now?"

Her eyes drifted to the knotted fingers in her lap. "Do you think we ever move beyond the things we've lost?"

Logan's green eyes blazed and he leaned forward, placing one hand on hers. "Sometimes. Sometimes shit stays with you, but you just keep moving."

The strangest heat ignited where Logan's hand touched hers. The spot tingled like static electricity, spreading warmth through her body. She had a strong urge to place her hand over his, to stroke the soft curls of golden hair that covered his forearm. The muscle of that arm was lean and long, defined but not bulky, which seemed to describe how he was built in general. An unwanted image of what his chest must look like under his costume thrust to the forefront of her mind. For the first time in almost a century, a rush of attraction made her scalp tingle.

Her eyes lifted from his hand to find his face very close to hers. She cleared her throat. "I must be going." Hastily, she stood, adjusting her coconuts to make sure they hadn't been displaced.

"Are you sure? Would you like a slice of cake for the road? I'm not teasing. You can have one, on the house. Anytime you want. I was kidding before."

He was on his feet, moving toward her.

She shook her head, backed toward the door. "I'm not ready for cake," she whispered.

"You don't have to be ready for it. There's no prerequisite for cake."

With a smile, she said, "Thank you, Logan. I won't forget this. You are an asset to your race."

"I try," he said.

She curtsied, then reached into the slit of her skirt to retrieve a pinch of gold dust she kept in the leather satchel strapped to her thigh. Holding it above her head, she paused a moment to appreciate Logan's parted lips and hungry expression. She wasn't the only one with a pang of attraction.

It was inappropriate, of course, for both of them. It was a flame that had nowhere to burn. But, as she released the gold dust and came apart cell by cell, blending into the nearest metal to find her way home, she couldn't help but think how good it felt to be wanted.

Even by a human.

5

LOGAN

The fresh peas and mushrooms hit the hot olive oil with a pop and sizzle as Logan circled the frying pan over the flame. "Jonah, where are we on the mornay?" Logan yelled across the busy kitchen. He added the orecchiette and tossed to combine, hitting the mix with another shot of olive oil.

"Almost there." Sous-chef Jonah was new to Valentine's but was fast proving to be a valuable asset to the team. The guy could handle anything from a juicy burger to a delicate sole with equal precision.

Logan plated what was in his pan, and sure enough, by the time he had the pasta and vegetables arranged, Jonah was there with a perfect mornay sauce, silky smooth and smelling of parmesan and asiago. He dribbled it artistically in a winding river of white across Logan's creation and moved the dish to the warming window for the server.

"Order up. Table 5," Logan called. He turned his attention to the next ticket. "Jonah, you get the burger; I'll take the salmon."

"You got it." Jonah dropped a basket of French fries into

the fryer, pushing the sleeves of his black button-down uniform to the elbow.

Logan was about to pull a fillet from the cooler when his assistant manager, Dustin, shouldered open the swinging door to the kitchen.

"Logan, Silas is here to see you," he said.

Logan continued to yank the heavy cooler door open and grabbed what he needed, tossing the marinated fillet onto the grill. The salmon hissed against the hot grate. "Can you ask him to come back later? I'm swamped back here."

Dustin shook his head. "Sorry, man. He says he's here in an official capacity. Got his badge out for me and everything."

Pausing, Logan grimaced at Dustin with a look that could be described as shooting the messenger. Silas wouldn't use his detective title lightly, especially not at six o'clock on a Friday night. "Show him to my office. I'll be there in five."

Dustin disappeared through the swinging door.

"Silas Flynn? The detective from Carlton City PD?" Jonah asked.

"You know him?"

"Not really. Just of him. What do you think he wants?"

Logan flipped the fillet and wiped his hands on his apron. "No idea."

As soon as Logan had plated the salmon, he left the kitchen in Jonah's capable hands and rushed to his office. Silas was sitting with his back to the door, but turned when Logan entered, extending his hand.

Logan accepted the handshake. "I don't want to be an asshole, but can we do this another time? We're swamped."

"Sorry, buddy. Police business."

Logan took a seat behind his desk.

"What's going on?"

"Have you noticed anyone unusual passing through here? Maybe someone who seems like they've been on the run. Worn clothing. Not friendly."

Logan shook his head. "To be honest, with the hospital right across the street, we get strangers in here every day, and believe me, people who've been sleeping at the hospital with their loved ones do not exactly look sophisticated."

Silas sighed. "I thought as much. I need to warn you about something."

"Warn me about what?"

"Two years ago a member of a local werewolf pack murdered four prominent members of our high werewolf council, a group we call the Lycanthropic Society. He was apprehended and imprisoned before he could hurt anyone else and was incarcerated in the supernatural wing of the Menard Correctional Center in Illinois."

"There are supernatural wings in human prisons? I thought witches like Grateful sentenced evil supernatural creatures to their hellmouths."

"They do, if the supernatural threat is toward humans or another group of supers. This was wolf-on-wolf violence, and although we might have asked for her help, the packs prefer to handle these things themselves if at all possible."

"Okay, so bad dude went to prison."

"Bad dude has escaped from prison." Silas gave Logan a serious stare.

"Damn."

"And we have reason to believe he'll return to the area. This guy is mentally unstable. We think he's out for revenge."

Logan sighed. "What can I do to help?"

Silas reached into his messenger bag and retrieved a folder. He opened it and turned it toward Logan.

"You don't have a better picture than this?" The photo showed a bald man in a one-piece orange prison jumper, handcuffed and walking between two gorilla-sized guards.

"Unfortunately, no, and it wouldn't help you anyway. Werewolves can change the color of their eyes."

"No shit?"

Silas leaned across the desk. Logan jerked back as the detective's green eyes shifted to amber.

"Fuck."

"Yeah. So, a little hair dye and he can look like a new man. Try to focus on the bone structure, the nose. He can't change that.

Logan tried, but he wasn't sure he'd be able to pick the guy out of a lineup. "I'll try my best."

Silas nodded, folding up the file and putting it away. "Thanks, man. His last known alias was Mark Gray, but his name is as shifty as his appearance. You see anything suspicious, anything at all, call me."

"Will do."

"Thanks."

"Hey, how are things with Soleil? You work up the courage to ask her to marry you yet?"

Silas frowned. "Unfortunately, Soleil didn't like that plan. She broke up with me."

"Oh, fuck." Logan ran both hands through his hair. "I'm sorry if it's a sore spot. I had no idea."

Silas lifted a shoulder toward his ear, then let it drop abruptly. "Easy come. Easy go. Cross-species romances never last. Hey, speaking of cross-species romances, whatever happened with that little redheaded witch you were flirting with at Grateful's wedding?"

Logan leaned back in his chair and folded his arms. "You just said cross-species romances never work. What do you think happened?"

A crooked smile spread across the werewolf's face. "I thought you two had a spark."

"Witches don't like humans, Silas. You should know this. And to be honest, I've had enough of witches to last a lifetime." He didn't mention the hard-on she'd given him on his balcony or the way her hand had felt under his at his Halloween party. The soft, smooth length of her arm flashed in his mind, the waves of her red hair, her impossibly sapphire eyes. Suddenly, he was thankful to be sitting behind the large mahogany desk.

Silas snorted. "Hmm. I guess I called that one wrong." He scratched the stubble on his jaw. The guy was always sporting a five o'clock shadow, even at noon. "Have you ever thought about getting a dog?"

Logan laughed. "The last thing I need is a dog."

"Dogs are family, Logan. You need family. A dog would be there for you. You spend too much time alone."

Logan rolled his eyes. "I'm not always alone. I have friends and the restaurant. I go on dates."

"When? When was your last date?"

Logan shrugged. The last he could remember was Tabetha. Not something he wanted to get into.

"Thought so. Just promise me you'll think about the dog." Silas scratched behind his ear.

"I promise." Logan composed himself and stood. "I should get back. I'll show you out." He ushered his friend to the front door of the busy restaurant.

"We still on for the mission?" Silas asked.

Logan lowered his voice. "I never miss it." He hadn't

missed volunteering at the mission on Thanksgiving since the year after his mother died.

The werewolf waved two fingers before climbing into his unmarked. On his way back to the kitchen, Logan slapped the bar to get Dustin's attention. "Vodka and tonic."

"You drinking on the job, boss?" Dustin asked, double-handing the bar guns to mix the drink.

"I am tonight." Logan chugged the drink, the empty hitting the bar harder than necessary. He returned to the kitchen, his mind filled with memories of one little redheaded witch.

6

THE DATE

"Wow, so you own this place, huh?" The woman Logan ushered into his penthouse looked around with wide eyes. She dropped her purse on the sofa and walked to the wall of windows overlooking Carlton City. The view was spectacular this time of year. All Christmas lights and swags of evergreen. A sure bet to put her in the mood. Snow cut through the ambient light from the city beyond, adding to the effect.

His date was named Mindy, or maybe it was Mandy. He remembered an "M" name. The fact that they'd made it back to his place without him knowing for sure was a good indication of how the date was going. Oh, they'd talked, or rather she had, about movies and her nails, and the great state of California where she was originally from. He'd tuned most of it out.

"Yeah. I've lived here almost six years now," Logan said.

"Fuck. Valentine's must be doing well. This place is the bomb."

Logan cringed. It was the fourth or fifth time she'd made a comment about his assumed wealth. Did she want a bank statement? "I've got no complaints. What do you do?" He didn't actually care and really hoped she hadn't already told him.

"Didn't my cousin tell you?" Her cousin was Dustin, Logan's assistant manager and the orchestrator of this date. Dustin had mentioned little about Mandy aside from saying she was new in town and had large breasts. Strange thing to say about a cousin, but Logan had to admit it was her most noteworthy feature. Along with her jet-black hair and gigantic mascaraed brown eyes, it was probably the way he'd describe her to someone who asked.

"He said you were new in town."

"That's right. I've already got a job though. I'm working at Teasers."

"The strip club?" Logan tried to sound neutral, but even he could hear the disdain in his voice.

She laughed. "It's not what you think." She brushed her hair back from her shoulder. "I'm not a stripper or anything. I'm a bartender."

Logan nodded. "Must be doing well," he quipped, echoing her earlier comment.

The smile faded from her face, and her eyes shifted to the side. "Sometimes." She shrugged one shoulder.

"Would you like a drink?"

"Sure. What do you have?"

Logan walked to the kitchen and opened the wine fridge. "Just about anything. What are you in the mood for?"

"Tequila?"

He closed the fridge, laughing under his breath.

"What's so funny?" Mandy asked.

"Nothing." He reached above his head to the cabinet where he kept the hard liquor. "You're just so human."

"What else would I be? Is human a bad thing?"

He retrieved two shot glasses and turned to face her. "Nah. It's a very good thing."

She batted her eyelashes and leaned across the granite island. "Oh."

He poured the tequila. "Salt and lime?"

"Don't bother." She popped the shot glass off the counter, tossed the contents to the back of her throat, and swallowed. She might as well have been drinking Kool-Aid.

Not just a bartender, a drinker. The thought wasn't flattering. Logan raised his own shot, gave her a mock salute, and drank it down. By the time he lowered the glass, she'd rounded the island and pressed in close, very close.

"I love tequila," she said. "You can feel the heat travel straight to your toes... and other places."

Her nipples were hard and she pressed them into his chest. Her full, red lips hovered next to his. Instead of touching her, he rested his hands on the counter behind him. She had to straddle his legs to move closer. Her hands gripped the sides of his shirt and pulled. Their lips met. His stayed closed. When she pulled back, she seemed confused.

"What's wrong?" she asked. "You don't have to worry. I'm on the pill." She pulled his shirt out of his pants and reached for his belt.

There was a time when younger Logan would have enjoyed a girl like Mandy. She was a walking fuck-me doll, ready and willing. But her hair, nails, the way she dressed... high-maintenance. No long-term potential. At thirty-three years old, he didn't want an easy fling anymore. He wanted something real. As her hand slipped into his fly, he decided she wasn't it.

"Mandy," he said.

She froze, pulled back. "Who's Mandy?"

Heat crept up Logan's neck to his ears. "Mindy?" He turned one palm upward.

Slap. Her hand connected with his cheek. "It's Jade, you asshole!"

He frowned and rubbed his face.

Jade. Huh. Seemed like he'd remember that one. "Um, sorry. I, uh, I'll walk you out." He crossed to the sofa and held out her purse to her.

Tipping her head to the side, she pouted. "I can tell it was an honest mistake. We can still have sex if you want."

He stared at her tight leather skirt, stiletto heels, and scoop-neck shirt. She was ready and willing, and he couldn't have cared less. "No... thank you?" The words came out like a question, as if he was asking her permission not to have sex with her. The awkwardness twisted his lip up and raised his eyebrow.

"Fucking bastard." She ripped her purse out of his hands and stormed out the door.

He followed her, feeling oddly as if he should apologize for not using her like she wanted him to be used. He watched through his door as she got onto the elevator. She flipped him the finger.

"Good night, Mandy," he yelled. The doors closed on her curse.

ALONE IN BED, LOGAN STARED AT THE CEILING AND wondered why he couldn't get Polina out of his head. His latest dating disaster with Dustin's cousin was just one more example. The last woman he'd been with had been the wicked witch Tabetha. She'd traumatized him seven ways 'till Sunday, and what did he do? Nurse a crush on another witch. What the hell was he thinking?

That's what it was. The trauma. People often displaced strong emotions. His revulsion of Tabetha was turning into attraction to Polina. Nothing a therapist or some self-help books couldn't cure. He'd had unresolved crushes before. This was no different. He closed his eyes, determined to fall asleep, and forced his brain to go blank. Eventually, it worked; sleep swept over him.

"Are you looking for me?" Polina's face appeared above his, her red waves cascading over her shoulder and tickling his cheek. The sun shone behind her head like a halo.

He'd been transported to the rocky shores of an Oregon beach. *Crap.* He was dreaming about her again. His gaze drifted down her body. Coconut bra and a mermaid tail. Definitely dreaming.

"The Little Mermaid again?" He propped himself on his elbows.

She wiggled the emerald-green flukes that jutted out where her feet should be. "Don't ask me, sicko. This is your party. I am literally a figment of your imagination."

He grunted. "I'm not a sicko. Obviously this is my subconscious's way of working out my ridiculous attraction to you. You are wearing the last outfit I saw you in, at my Halloween party, and this is the beach where I washed up after the water witch tried to kill me. We were underwater, in her lair. You defended me against her, and when she flooded the cavern we were in, you wrapped your body around me to protect me. Your magic brought us to the surface and you revived me, right here on this beach."

"No way was I letting that bitch keep you as her human pet."

"Why would you save me? You've said time and again

that humans are the inferior species. Why not just let me die?"

Polina's long, tapered fingers traced his collarbone. "We've been over this. I can't tell you why. You don't know why, and I am the creation of your brain—Dream Polina. I can remind you, though, that you've come up with three possibilities for my actions. First, I might have saved you to spite Kendra, the water witch. Second, my purpose might have been to preserve your powers as a medium to help my friend Grateful, and third, I might be attracted to you."

Logan met her sapphire blue eyes, took pleasure in the bright contrast to her deep red hair. "I want to believe number three," he whispered. His hand moved to the back of her neck, pulling her head down to meet his lips.

Soft, warm, she accepted his kiss eagerly, thrusting her tongue into his mouth. He realized this was just a dream. A very good dream. But he didn't want to wake up. Polina's kiss trailed to his ear, down his throat, across his naked chest, over his belly button.

"Why am I naked?" he asked.

She tipped her face up from the place she was kissing and licked her lips. "It's your party, remember?"

He rested his head in his meshed fingers and closed his eyes, enjoying the feel of her mouth on his skin. She was still moving south, coming close to the physical evidence of his desire for her. Dream or no dream, he was going to enjoy this.

"If I had a chance with a woman like you, I'd change your mind about humans. I'd be the best you ever had," he said.

"What happened to not trusting witches?" Silas said.

Logan blinked rapidly, finding Dream Silas standing on the beach wearing swim trunks. Logan flinched to cover himself only to find he was fully dressed and Dream Polina was gone. "You, my friend, are a cockblocker."

Silas grinned. "I'm in your head. There must be a reason. Part of you must want me here."

"Whatever part wants you here needs to shut the fuck up and bring Polina back." He watched the ocean waves roll in, purple caps hugging a tangerine sky.

"You respect her too much to use her, even in your dreams."

He sat up on the rocks and buried his face in his hands. "Fuck, how sad is that? Why do I respect her? She doesn't respect me."

"Because she's smart and strong—strong enough to save your ass. And she's ridiculously beautiful," Dream Silas said.

"There's more to it than that. I just met her. Sure, we spent some time together helping Grateful out, but not enough to explain this. Why her? Why now? And why the hell can't I force myself to let go of this fantasy?" Logan groaned.

Dream Silas raised his bushy eyebrows. "Maybe because this time it matters."

Frustrated, Logan stood, shaking his head. "I barely know her. This can't matter."

"If you say so." Dream Silas melted into the sand leaving Logan on an empty beach.

"It matters because you almost died, twice." Logan spun on his heel to find a lanky woman with a brunette bob standing near the woods next to his beach.

"Mom?" Ever since Grateful had used her witchy powers to put his soul back into his body, he'd had the power to channel his mother, even when he was awake. Being a medium had come in handy a time or two. Was this particular visit part of his dream or an actual journey into the beyond?

"Follow me, my son, and I'll show you why it matters." Turning, his mother blended into the woods.

Puzzled, he followed her into the dense forest. Brunette hair and pale skin flashed between the trunks of the trees. He broke into a run. "Mom?" She didn't slow her pace. A fast left and a sprint through a kaleidoscope of evergreen and light, and the forest opened.

Logan spilled out of the woods onto the shoulder of a highway. Mom was gone, but something about this spot was familiar. A deep dread bloomed behind his breastbone. When was he here before?

The low rumble of a motorcycle approached from a distance. The rider topped the hill to his left, a silhouette against the bright blue September sky. As the motorcycle approached, Logan got a good look. His stomach sank. The custom paint on the Harley-Davidson softail was his doing and that matching helmet was his too, complete with the Valentine's logo on the side.

"No... No!" He waved his hands and stepped out into the road. He had to warn himself. He had to stop the dream, to change history. But it was no use. The semi truck came out of nowhere, concealed by the line of trees along the access road. The driver never even looked in his direction. Logan reacted, braking hard. No longer was he a bystander observing from the side of the road. He'd flashed into the body of his former self, just in time to slam on the brakes. The seat rose underneath him, and the bike slid sideways, laying down patches of rubber on the pavement as roughly seven hundred pounds of chrome and steel tipped over, sweeping him toward the blacktop.

The bike rotated, sliding off the road, and pounding his

helmet into the asphalt. His leather pants and jacket shredded with the skid. Bones snapped. Blood sprayed. Pain rendered him unable to breathe or think. A tree arose, both a blessing and a curse. It stopped his momentum but only after one hell of an impact. He landed under the bike, the back of his head hitting the grass.

Head, not helmet. The protective gear had cracked off during impact. As he sipped the air through tiny gasps of breath, he thought it was strange that his hip jutted straight up even though he thought he was lying flat. Something silver and sharp protruded from his abdomen. There was blood. So much blood.

The blue sky above called to him. He stopped sipping air. No one survived this. No one.

As his lungs ached for oxygen, the heavens opened up and an angel appeared, her hooded sapphire cloak billowing behind her. On slippered feet, she approached and paused by his side, a snowy white owl landing on her shoulder.

"This won't do, Hildegard. As soon as the sun sets, the scent of blood will attract mountain trolls."

The bird hooted and chirped near her ear.

"Absolutely not. He's too young. I can't bear it. Listen, even now his heart battles death. This one wants to live."

The owl flapped her wings and chattered indignantly.

"Don't tell me you've become so callous over the years that life means nothing to you, even a human's? Fine. Go home. I'll take care of this."

The owl took flight out of Logan's field of vision. Willowy hands reached up to lower the hood. Deep red hair. Piercing sapphire eyes. Polina.

The witch reached into the neck of her cloak and retrieved a wand from above her left breast. If he hadn't been dying, the sight of creamy flesh as she moved the cloth aside would have driven him to distraction, but as it was, black dots circled in his vision ruining the effect.

"Uh-oh." She squatted by his side. "Stay with me. I'll try to help you."

With a wave of her wand, the silver protrusion melted from his abdomen and he rolled onto his back, grunting from the pain. Blood gushed and a wave of feverish heat made him break a sweat. She pressed the crystal of her wand against his wound and muttered, "*Reinchide velecluse moribidatae vialanium.*" The bleeding slowed.

"I've never been good at healing spells," she said, a sad smile gracing her rose-colored lips. "Water witches are better at this. The human body is mostly water, after all. I think I can close you up, but I can't give you more blood." She lifted his head onto her lap and caressed his face with her hand. "Breathe. You can do it."

He tried, he really did. He opened his mouth and forced his lungs to contract but barely a trickle of air passed between his lips.

A tear broke from the corner of her eye and coursed to her chin. "How brave you are to fight. Such short, fragile lives you humans have and you fight for every moment of it, celebrate every struggle. I wish I could do more. I'm sorry. I'm not that kind of witch."

The black spots were bigger now, limiting his vision, but his ears still worked and they picked up a siren over the hill. "Help *is* coming." She smiled down at him, and damn it if his heart didn't beat just to see it. "Maybe there is one more thing I can do," she said tentatively, her wand raised between them. She kissed his forehead, then pressed the wand between his eyes. "All you need is more time. I can give you that." The wand glowed brighter. "You never saw me. *Memoriam exudate.*"

Light flashed between them, and then he plunged into total darkness.

Logan's body jacked off the bed, heart pounding, hands gripping his chest. He was back in his room. He patted his head, his arms, his hips. He was whole again. "Just a dream," he murmured, eyeing the predawn light through his window.

He flopped onto the mattress, still panting. "What the hell?" He rubbed the spot on his forehead where Polina's lips had touched his skin. The spot still burned. Polina had been there. She'd witnessed his accident and been with him on the side of the road. Was she the reason his soul ended up in Grateful's attic? Had she been responsible for his coma? Why did she keep it from him? He needed to talk to her. He needed to know. The only problem was, after everything... he was afraid to ask.

7

WINTER WOLVES

Polina couldn't sleep. It was late, or early depending on your perspective, and Hildegard's soft snore came from her perch in the corner of the bedroom. She'd done her rounds and her realm was safe for another night, but sleep eluded her. A certain human chef was to blame.

Why had Logan been so kind to her at his Halloween party? She hadn't welcomed his attentions, had she? Physical attraction to a human was idiotic, an invitation to heartbreak. Humans had short, brittle lives and questionable motivations. Men often confused their desire for wealth or power for their love of a witch. She'd known human males who'd treated their witch girlfriends like genies, calling on them only when they needed something. Not that Logan was that type of man. No, she suspected his attraction to her was the result of residual magic, although she'd rather not admit his attention wasn't warranted for other, more personal reasons.

The best course of action was to forget about Logan Valentine. The problem was, it had been months since she'd seen the man, and he still haunted her thoughts and her dreams. Like now, when she crossed and uncrossed her legs to try to alleviate the weight of need that had formed between them.

Slapping her hands down on the mattress, she exhaled. What she needed was fresh air. Icy cold fresh air. She swung her legs over the side of the bed and quietly, as not to wake Hildegard, tiptoed to the front door. It was snowing again, but she didn't bother with a coat. Barefoot, she stepped into the two-foot accumulation of white powder, her thin nightgown clinging to her body in the blowing flakes.

"Do you need assistance, mistress?" A metal-on-metal clang preceded a flash of green-stained copper slicing through the storm. One of her three gargoyles, Nicodemus, coasted on metal wings to her side. His small horns and pushed-in face were typical of his kind, although his animation was anything but. Nicodemus was the result of an enchantment powered by the dead buried behind Aurorean House. He came to life every sunset to help her guard her realm.

"No. I'm fine. Needed some air." Her flesh had taken on a reflective quality, the cold seeping to her bones and lifting her metal magic to her skin. She might as well have been made of steel. In this state, the cold didn't bother her at all.

"I have news," Nicodemus said. "Skogal and Rohilda reported visitors at Renegade Caverns tonight." Skogal and Rohilda were the other two gargoyles, although they'd never developed the ability to speak in a way humans could understand. Skogal, in particular, struggled to fly straight and had difficulty completing basic tasks. Along with an elongated tongue that lolled from the side of his demon-like face, he had an overtly unintelligent quality that made her wary of trusting his observations. Still, Rohilda, although mute, was a highly intelligent female gargoyle. Polina perked to attention.

"What kind of visitors?"

"Three men. One smells of the werewolf who passed through in the fall. He's back, and he's brought a pack."

She raised her eyebrows in surprise. "How many?"

"Three."

"Any problems with the trolls or fae in the area accepting the werewolves?"

"Skogal and Rohilda just discovered the pack tonight. We will continue to monitor them if you wish."

"Yes, please. I'll pay them a visit as well. As always, you are an asset to the realm, Nicodemus."

"You flatter me, my lady." He bowed, his horns sweeping the ground before he dismissed himself, his shiny webbed wings carrying him to his place on the eastern gable of Aurorean House.

Polina glided into the forest, her red hair transforming into strands of silver in the icy wind. She couldn't make herself invisible exactly, but she could become almost impossible to see. By reflecting the forest around her, she produced the illusion of transparency. Usually, that was all she needed to escape notice.

A mile trek east brought her to Renegade Caverns. Humans once used the openings in the mountainside for shelter while bootlegging goods across the Canadian border. The four caverns, which connected on the inside, provided sufficient shelter from the elements for even a human to survive a Vermont winter. And, they were conveniently vacant. Trolls, elves, or mountain fae already inhabited most of the caverns on the mountain. Not these. The relative nearness of the Renegade Caverns to the human camp made them a poor choice for most supernaturals.

In the clearing outside the caverns, three men had dug out a ring of snow and started a campfire. One was an older, heavyset male with a face full of gray stubble. He huddled inside his red plaid coat, eating steaming brown stew out of a metal pot. That was unusual for a wolf. Their core temperature ran hotter than most supernaturals. She wondered if he might be ill. Next to him was a man who looked to be in his mid-twenties, with wavy dark blond hair and a wool cap pulled low over his eyes. Polina was almost positive this was the man who had transformed into the red wolf, although she hadn't gotten a good look at him before he shifted. He wore jeans and a T-shirt but didn't seem the least bit cold. The third man was hardly a man at all. He looked to be in his teens, but judging by his light jacket, his werewolf gene had already switched itself on.

From Polina's limited experience with werewolves, she knew that the boy was born human and likely began showing signs of lycanthropy around puberty. But it wasn't rare for a werewolf to be sixteen or seventeen before shifting completely for the first time. This was a new pack member, still learning the ropes. So the red wolf had found a safe place to live and returned with a sick old man and a newbie werewolf. She ran a finger along her bottom lip.

Quietly, she backed away. An old man, a young boy, and a vagrant were no threat. No one was using the caverns. She'd leave them alone for now. If they kept to themselves, she'd allow them to stay.

Blending into the woods, she returned to Aurorean House as the horizon paled with the rising sun. She'd stayed up all night. Just as well. Even with the distraction of the werewolves, her brain kept wandering back to Logan: the feel of his hand on her arm, the way he'd looked at her. Sheer exhaustion was her only hope of getting any rest. That or acting on her feelings, which in her estimation was absolutely unacceptable.

8

THE CHRISTENING

Please join us for the baptism of
Lucas Matthew Knight
Noon, Sunday, July 21st
Monk's Hill Chapel
Reception immediately following at Valentine's restaurant

Polina arrived early to Monk's Hill Chapel. The only other soul in the place was an older man she didn't recognize praying near the front of the church. He didn't turn around when she came in. Just as well. She wanted to be alone.

The dress Polina chose to wear to Lucas's christening was a few centuries out of style. Ankle-length green linen, it boasted gold embroidery around the hem and a scooped neckline. A belt in the same Celtic pattern hung low on her hips. It was solid gold and matched the setting of her emerald necklace. She couldn't remember when or where she'd purchased the dress. It was similar to one she'd worn in the seventeenth century, but the fabric and stitching were in far too good of shape for it to be authentic. No. She supposed this was one of the many replicas she'd purchased over the years. Comfort clothing.

Shoed in saddle-colored leather flats, she shuffled across the stone floor and slid into a pew. The polished wood smelled of lemon oil. Homey.

"You look like a Disney princess," Logan said. He took a seat beside her, blocking her exit.

"I beg your pardon?"

"Your dress. It looks like you bought it at the Bippity Boopity boutique. This is the second time you've reminded me of a fairy-tale character. Do you always dress like you ride unicorns for a living, or is this just for special occasions?"

She narrowed her eyes at him, a flush warming her cheeks. "I prefer this clothing. It is comfortable to me. What's so special about this ensemble?" She motioned from his dress shirt to his shoes. "You look like Costco was having a sale."

He chuckled through a lopsided grin. "You've been to Costco?"

She rolled her eyes. "Of course I have."

"It's just... I'm having trouble picturing it. You, dressed like a medieval princess, buying ten-gallon vats of eye of newt?"

Her mouth twitched of its own accord, and she pretended to cough to hide her laugh. "Shows what you know. Witches buy eye of newt in bulk by the pound. Trouble is, they tend to roll off the scooper before you can get them into the baggie."

"Thank you for that. There will be rolling eyeballs in

my nightmares tonight." He leaned back in the pew, mouth twisting in distaste.

Polina chuckled. "Honestly, who started that rumor anyway about witches using eye of newt in everything? Do you know what a newt is? It's an amphibian. Looks like a lizard. Who has time to be plucking the eyes out of the little buggers? And why on earth would they have magical properties?"

"Not to mention, who fashions the canes for all the blind newts?"

She turned to face him, stifling a laugh, only to let it out when he pantomimed a newt using a guide cane for the blind. The man praying near the front of the chapel cast a harsh glance her way, and she covered her mouth with her fingers.

"Why are you here, Logan?" she asked, smoothing her dress.

"To see Lucas get baptized."

"Why are you here so early?"

"I like to be early. I'm a punctual person. Why are you here so early?"

She blinked at him. "Why would anyone purposefully be late?"

"I don't know." Their eyes met. Logan looked away first.

"Actually, I'm glad I ran into you. I need to ask you something."

"What could you possibly need to ask me?" She tipped her head and shook it gently.

"I'm going to let that obviously patronizing and offensive commentary pass and just come out with it. My dead mother says you did the hocus-pocus on me when I crashed my bike."

Polina frowned. "She just comes to you with these

things? Out of the blue? On any given Sunday? A spiritual tattletale?"

"Then it's true?"

Polina sighed and looked toward the front of the church. Another family had arrived and was taking a seat. "Yes. It is true. I found you on the side of the road in my territory. You were dying. I healed you as much as I could, then made it so your soul wouldn't pass over on its own. I gave your body extra time, so the humans could heal you the rest of the way."

Logan's mouth fell open. "What the hell, lady?"

"Shhh," Polina said, apologizing to the older man who'd turned to stare. "Keep it down."

"Do you know how close I came to haunting Grateful's attic for all eternity?"

She pursed her lips. "It was an honest mistake. I thought your soul would go to my room of reflection and that *I'd* be responsible for sorting you. How was I to know that they would take your body home and your soul would follow to that realm? Grateful's realm." She shrugged. "I honestly didn't know what happened to you. I assumed you'd died. Do you know, that first night I met you at Grateful's, I didn't realize who you were right away? You were terribly familiar, but I couldn't place it."

Rubbing his chin, Logan scrutinized her. "When did you realize who I was?"

"When I rescued you from the water witch. Once I saw you passed out on the beach, it came back to me."

He slapped his thighs, eliciting more intense glares from the gathering guests. "Why the hell didn't you say anything?" Logan whispered.

Polina spread her hands. "It didn't seem important.

Now that you know, if you'd like to say thank you, I'm all ears."

His face reddened and he rolled his eyes. "Thank you for almost causing my soul to wander the earth for eternity."

She straightened in her seat, ignoring his sarcasm. "You're welcome."

A piano began to play and Polina joined the other guests in standing as Rick and Grateful walked to the baptismal font with baby Lucas. Logan stood too, shuffling closer to make room for another couple who entered the pew. "It's not that I don't appreciate you saving my life," Logan whispered.

"Twice."

"Twice. It's just that I would think you'd be a little more empathetic about the unexpected results. It's also not something a person keeps from another person."

She turned to him as the minister began the ceremony. Neither of them were listening. "I am sorry that saving your life inconvenienced you and that I did not immediately inform you of the unselfish thing I did for you."

"Glad we got it out in the open," Logan said.

Polina turned back to the front and engaged in the ceremony. The babe was truly adorable in his white baptismal suit. He lay quietly in the crook of Grateful's arm as she and Rick answered questions for the minister. Polina had never been Christian, not even in her old human days, but she tried to follow along. There were prayers and promises and then the minister scooped water out of a basin and poured it over the child's forehead. Only, he missed. He tried again, and this time the water hit its mark.

"Did you see that?" Logan asked.

"Yes." Polina cleared her throat and narrowed her eyes. "The minister missed the babe's head."

Logan smirked. "Missed? It looked like the water curved out of the way."

She elbowed him in the side of the arm and shook her head. "Shhh."

"We are not done talking about my accident," he whispered in her ear.

With a sigh, she gave him a reluctant nod. So be it. It was best if he knew the truth anyway.

9

VALENTINE'S

"Does Lucas look sickly to you?" Grateful asked. They were in a dark wood booth at Valentine's, under swags of powder blue and silver cutouts of umbrellas and rubber duckies.

Polina leaned over the burrito-shaped bundle on the table. Lucas had a perfectly round head with saucer-sized blue eyes and a mouth perpetually shaped like an O. His chubby cheeks flushed bright red.

"I am not experienced with babies," Polina said, eyes darting to her friend. "But is it possible he's too hot?"

Grateful nervously unwrapped her son, who promptly shoved a fist into his mouth and kicked his feet joyfully. "Hmm. Thank you. I am no good at this. I never thought it would be this hard." She buried her face in her hands.

Polina touched Grateful's wrist. "What ails you, sister?"

"Oh, this?" She wiped tears from under her eyes and waved her wet fingers between them. "Let's see. He never sleeps, which means *we* rarely sleep. Even Rick is tired. Rick! He only needs to sleep one night a week. *I* feel like a zombie. Oh, and I'm obsessed with his comfort. Is he too hot, too cold? Hungry? Wet? And then there is the obvious worry."

Leaning forward, Polina shook her head. "Not obvious to me."

"Whether he's..." She rubbed circles over her temples and lowered her voice to a whisper. "Normal."

"Oh," Polina said, thinking back to the misaligned water. "Definitely not."

Grateful's face fell into a look of horror. Polina froze. Was it possible Grateful wanted her son to be human? What a bizarre thing to want for a child.

"You misunderstand," Polina backpedaled. "I simply mean he is obviously special. A special little boy. Not abnormal in any way."

Grateful let out a relieved breath. "So, you think he'll be human?"

Polina waved a hand in front of her face. "Pishposh. Most certainly. A special human child. Normal but certainly above average."

The reward for the lie was Grateful's smile. "I thought so," she said, scooping the baby back into her arms.

"Nothing to worry about," Polina reassured.

Grateful bounced the baby gently. "I saw you sitting with Logan at the ceremony. I thought you weren't interested in humans?"

"I'm not!" Polina said much too loudly. Too much. She internally chided herself for overreacting. After a composing breath, she added, "He wanted to ask me about his accident."

"What about his accident?"

Polina smoothed her dress. "I was there. I tried to heal him but wasn't strong enough to finish the job. I... I sent his soul to your attic in a final attempt to rescue him."

"What?" Grateful shook her head. "You never told me."

"I didn't remember at first. It was a long time ago, and in my defense, he was in bad shape when I found him. Hardly recognizable from the man he is today."

"How did Logan find out?"

"His mother." Polina raised her eyebrows.

Grateful snorted. "She has a way of showing up when you least expect it."

"It's creepy but fascinating."

With a sigh, Grateful studied a spot on the table. "You know I love you, Polina, but I saw the way you two were laughing together. He's attracted to you, and I think—"

Polina frowned and held up one hand. "Don't say it." She shook her head.

"It's the magic. Your magic touched his soul. It happened to me too. When he was in my attic, I thought I had feelings for him, but it turned out to be the metaphysical connection from being his soul sorter. You can't have a connection with someone's soul and escape a certain level of attraction."

Twirling her finger in a strand of her red hair, Polina nodded. "The connection isn't lost on me, although the effects are stronger than I expected. And distracting." She smoothed her dress again. "Well, I am happy with my solitary life. Do not worry yourself; your friend is safe from the likes of me."

"I didn't mean it that way. It's just—"

"Please." Polina held up two fingers. "You needn't say more."

"Thank you for taking this seriously. Logan has already been through so much." Grateful's gaze darted to Rick. "You know, the best cure for soul infatuation is true love. I know from experience." She fussed with the jacket of

Lucas's christening suit. "If it gets too bad or if you don't want to be alone anymore, you still have the positivity potion."

After a moment's consideration, Polina remembered. "The one you made for Tabetha that she wouldn't accept?"

"*The Book of Light* says it attracts your true love like a magnet. If you do get lonely, that's the spell to use. It'll break through anything temporary or artificial."

Polina was about to protest that she was fine on her own, when a dark-haired woman sauntered to the table. "Grateful, come see the cake Logan made you. It's in the shape of a raven."

"Thanks, Michelle." Grateful turned to Polina. "Would you mind holding Lucas for a second? I want to take a picture. Logan's cakes are to die for."

"I, uh..." Polina searched her brain for an appropriate excuse. She wasn't fast enough. The baby was thrust into her hands, and Grateful was gone before she could say no. Arms extended, Polina inspected the tiny person who dangled from her hands by the armpits. Lucas blinked his ridiculously large blue eyes at her. The boy looked like an animated Precious Moments doll.

"You are a cute one, aren't you?" Polina bounced him slightly, allowing his feet to press against the table. He kicked and smiled at her. "You're not difficult at all. Just small and underdeveloped." She crinkled her eyes as the babe made a face, pulling his knees to his chest and showing his toothless gums. "What? What are you doing now? Is this some kind of tiny warlock spell?"

Eh. Ehh. Bleeeck. A fountain of foul liquid spewed from the baby's mouth down the front of her emerald-green gown. Grateful appeared out of nowhere, scooping Lucas into her arms. "I'm so sorry. I thought he looked a little colicky. Let me get you a rag."

Polina blinked at her friend, lips pressed together against the onslaught of gastrointestinal emissions. "I don't think a rag will be sufficient. A little water and magic should do the trick."

Grateful babbled on about how sorry she was, bouncing Lucas on her hip. Polina reassured her that it was perfectly fine. Arms extended to her sides and dress dripping, she raced to the bathroom to clean up.

10

CAKE

Cleaning up after Lucas took longer than Polina anticipated. Magic wouldn't work on the stain. The reason why was as obvious as the day was long. The little bugger had more magic in him than his mother wanted to believe. Still, allowing the witch to come around on her own terms seemed like a good idea. Meanwhile, Polina set to work cleaning her dress the old-fashioned way.

She removed the gown and plunged the fabric under the cold water of the sink. It took a fair deal of scrubbing to rid it of the enchanted spit-up. Warlocks. She rolled her eyes. Once she finally had it clean, she tried to use the hand dryer to blow out the fabric only to find the machine was out of order. With any luck, now that she was dealing with water, magic would be effective again.

"*Dehydratium,*" she said with a flick of her wand. Water began to run from the hem of the dress, the wetness receding from the top of the garment and winding along the floor toward the drain. The process wasn't fast, but it was effective. Once dry, she ironed out the wrinkles with another pass of her wand.

With a turn of her shoulders, she checked her appearance in the mirror and emerged from the bathroom. Everyone was gone. The restaurant was empty, aside from Logan, who shoved paper plates into a black plastic bag. "Where is everyone?" she asked.

Logan jumped, gripping his chest. "Damn, Polina! I thought you left with everyone else. You scared the crap out of me."

"Everyone left?"

"Yeah. After cake, Lucas started acting up." He pointed toward the window. "Plus, storm's moving in. The weather service issued a flash flood warning. I guess everyone wanted to make it home before it hit."

Polina eyed the gray-green sky outside the window. It was early evening but the parking lot was dark as dusk. She sighed and approached the booth where she'd left her small purse.

The rustle of the garbage bag as Logan worked his way around the restaurant made it impossible for her to ignore the inexplicable pull she felt in his direction. Without thinking, she turned on her heel. "Would you like help with that?" Her voice sounded pinched.

He stopped, turning a surprised look in her direction. "I thought—" He cut himself off, shaking his head. "You know what? Thank you. I'd appreciate your help. I gave my staff the day off. Here, I'll get you a bag."

"No need," she said. Wand drawn, she circled the gem above her head. "*Dezinfectat uitaria.*" White fog rolled from the corners of the room, starting from behind her and working quickly over every chair and table.

Logan's mouth popped open. "What are you doing?"

Polina bobbed her wrist, concentrating. "Where do you want the clean glasses?"

"Cabinet left of the freezer."

She nodded. The fog thickened until she could no longer see the tables or chairs. One last circle above her head and the magic receded, leaving the tables and floor twinkling in its wake. Satisfied, she crossed her arms over her chest, and smiled in Logan's direction.

Flabbergasted, he turned the garbage bag in his hands upside down. It was empty. "Dare I ask what you did with the garbage?"

"Dumpster out back. What else would I do with it?"

He nodded, absently turning a circle. "Right. You are quick with that wand." His face fell.

"Say thank you, Logan."

He lifted his eyes to hers, seeming to contemplate what she was saying. "Thank you."

"Now," Polina holstered her wand and dusted off her hands, "I will take a slice of your famous chocolate cake. I missed the previous serving."

Logan frowned. "It's gone. Grateful took the leftovers home with her."

"Ah, well, another time." Polina leaned into the booth to grab her purse, just as heavy rain began to pelt the windows.

"We could make one," Logan added quickly.

There was an urgency in his tone, and when she turned from the booth, his body was only inches from her own. He smelled of baking and warm male. Goddess, his eyes were hauntingly green.

She licked her lips. "I'd like that," she answered without thinking.

A smile broke out across his face. "Good. Because you still need to explain about your involvement after my accident." He ran his fingers down the sleeve of her dress and took her hand in his before leading her into the well-appointed industrial kitchen.

"Witches as a species are stereotypically terrible cooks," Polina admitted.

A stainless steel bowl landed in front of her, the bottom circling on the counter with a hollow tinny sound. "I figured that out. Grateful couldn't make toast, and Tabetha..." Logan's voice trailed off, his eyes shifting away.

"Are you still having nightmares?" Polina asked, remembering his confession on the balcony some months back.

He swallowed hard. "Not as often."

"You said she used you."

He nodded. "I dated her for a few months, you know. Thought I loved her, or so I told other people. Turns out she'd poisoned me with mind control potion. She used me. Orchestrated everything to get to Grateful. When I'm awake, the entire relationship is a blur, aside from one thing."

"What's that?"

"She made me cook for her. A lot." Logan flurried around the kitchen, collecting eggs, butter, flour, cocoa.

Disturbed, Polina made a confession of her own. "She clubbed me from behind two years ago. She must have had help because I would have sensed another witch enter my realm. Regardless, when I came to, I was buried in her yard. She robbed me of my realm and my element for almost a year. The potion she fed you was made from fruit fertilized with my power. I was happy to help Grateful kill her."

"She had it coming," Logan said through his teeth.

Polina agreed.

A heavy weight settled over the room as they both remembered Tabetha. It was Logan who broke the awkward silence.

"You admit to murder quickly on a first date."

She chided, "This isn't a date."

Logan cracked three eggs into a small bowl and plunged in a whisk. "Of course not. You? Date a human?"

"Your voice holds bitterness," Polina said. "I don't understand. It seems you have the same prejudices against witches. You've made your disdain for me apparent."

Sugar, cocoa, salt. He whisked the ingredients together with expert precision. "Disdain is a strong word," Logan said. "It's not you, per se. I just don't trust magic. After Tabetha, I can't trust my emotions around you. Are you truly as gorgeous and bright as I think you are? Or have you hoodwinked my brain into believing in something that isn't real?"

Polina placed a hand on his arm, stopping his whisk. Her fingers caressed the soft tawny hair, registered the long lean muscle that worked to stir the bowl. A ripple of heat traveled from her fingertips to her crotch, a desire she hadn't felt in decades. "You think I'm beautiful?"

"Who wouldn't?" he murmured, meeting her gaze. Time stretched lazily between them. The air was sweet with cocoa and vanilla. She inhaled deeply.

He cleared his throat and pulled away, breaking the tar-pit attraction that threatened to pull her under. Moving toward the cooler at the back of the restaurant, he disappeared inside. Moments ticked by, enough time that Polina thought he might have gotten lost in the large steel box. "Do you need help?" she called

He emerged, shivering, and carrying a large plastic jug. "The secret ingredient to Valentine's chocolate cake resides in this tub." He added a heaping scoop of a creamy ivory substance to the batter.

"Aren't you going to tell me what it is?"

"I can't. It's classified. If I told you, I'd have to kill you." He cocked one eyebrow and pointed his whisk in her direction.

"I'm immortal," she said through a smile. "Give it your best shot."

"If I can't kill you, then I definitely can't tell you."

"Not under any circumstances?"

He stopped, raking his eyes over her from head to toe, before settling his gaze on her lips. The heat returned, her skin growing hot under his scrutiny. The bodice of her dress tightened with the swelling of her breasts. It had been a long time since a simple look from a man could make her combust from the inside out.

"Maybe one," he said. "But I would have to trust you absolutely."

She swallowed hard. "I see. Some secrets are worth keeping."

He nodded. "Exactly."

Abandoning the bowl, he stalked toward her, reaching for her waist. She inhaled sharply, anticipating his touch. It never happened. He reached past her.

"Excuse me." He turned a knob on the stove behind her. "Needs to preheat."

"Isn't it hot enough already?" Polina whispered under her breath.

"What's that?"

She tucked a strand of hair behind her ear. "I said, I am excited already."

His eyelids grew heavy and he stepped in close, face to face, breath to breath, meeting her eyes with an expression akin to longing. "The anticipation is half the fun," he drawled.

His lingering stare made her insides melt like butter. She narrowed her eyes. "Are you sure you're human?"

He laughed. "Last time I checked." He squeezed past her to get to the bowl. "Come here, I need your help."

She allowed him to pull her between himself and the bowl, his arms completely engulfing her, his lips aligning with her ear. He slid the handle of the whisk against her palm in a way that ignited her flesh. "You whisk. I'll measure." His voice sounded gritty and his breath brushed her cheek.

Focus, Polina. If she didn't concentrate, the damn whisk would melt between her fingers. The warm caress of his breath on her ear made her miss a beat as she stirred the concoction. Heat seemed to radiate from his body behind her. Did humans run hotter than witches? It seemed so. His presence was like a small sun, and she was a thing in his galaxy, stuck in his gravitational pull.

As his arm brushed past her waist to scoop in the flour, her attraction to Logan reached epic proportions. A vicious swarm of butterflies took up residence in her stomach and her breath became embarrassingly erratic. She pretended to lose her balance to press her backside into him. He grunted softly in appreciation.

"That's good." He removed the bowl from her hands. "Over-beating will make the cake dense."

"Wouldn't want that." Her voice cracked.

His hand drifted along the back of her thigh, up and over her hip, pulling her against him. She felt the length of him, hard and long against her lower back.

"Logan?" she croaked.

"Yes."

"Can I have some water?"

Slowly, he backed away, disappearing into the cooler

again for longer than necessary. When he emerged, he handed her a bottle of Evian. "I forget how hot it gets back here. Chefs like me get used to the heat. There's an old joke we're made of asbestos," he said softly.

She guzzled the water. Out of the corner of her eye, she watched his gaze linger on the place her lips met the bottle. He shook slightly, as if he'd gotten a chill, and squatted to remove a sheet pan from under the counter. He lifted the bowl and poured the batter.

"Grateful once told me you rarely leave your realm. How did you come across my accident? I was in Vermont, but I was not in Smuggler's Notch."

He motioned with his chin to a rubber spatula hanging from the pot rack. Polina grabbed the tool and scraped the sides of the bowl into the pan. "You were close. Not inside my realm but close enough for me to notice. I felt your impending death. Smelled the blood. Heard the crunch of metal."

"Why didn't you let me die?"

Polina balked at the unexpected question. Wouldn't most humans feel entitled to be saved? "You should have been dead already. Your injuries were extensive. But your heart called to me. It was a bass drum that said, *I want to live, I want to live*, with every beat. And the way you looked at me..."

"I thought you were an angel."

"I couldn't bear to disappoint you. I would have done more if I could. The audacity you showed, the will to live, the fact that you, with your singular life, would risk the ride to begin with, it all made me remember what it was like to be human."

Logan took a deep breath, perusing her features as if he were sifting through her words. After a moment, he snapped out of his trancelike state, tapped the cake pan on the counter to settle the batter, and swept the whole thing into the oven. "Convection oven. You are twenty minutes from heaven." He set the timer.

"I am sorry that the results weren't... optimal."

"I'm over it," he murmured, prowling toward her like a predator. "I believe you had the best of intentions."

A splotch of batter clung to the side of his thumb. She had the strongest desire to lick it off. *What are you doing, Polina? Grateful warned you the magic would lure you in. You're playing with fire.* Using all her willpower, she moved aside and took interest in Logan's inventory of knives.

If she were smart, she'd leave posthaste. She wasn't. Or else, it had been too long since she'd had male company, and she couldn't bring herself to leave.

"What made you want to become a chef?" she asked, hoping the story would redirect her energies from the part of her that wished to lick his fingers.

"I wanted a job working with food," he said softly. He washed his hands.

"Loved it from the beginning, did you?"

Arms crossing over his chest, he leaned against the counter, his eyes darting to hers before staring blankly at the stove. "Honestly, I was hungry all the time as a child and I swore if I had a choice, I wouldn't be hungry again. I thought if I worked with food, I'd be guaranteed meals."

Her jaw tensed and she moved to stand beside him, gripping the counter near her hips. Logan's aura had taken on a gray tinge. "Why were you hungry as a child?"

"I was homeless most of my childhood." He rubbed the back of his neck. "Sometimes we lived at the mission, but many times there just wasn't enough food. Don't get me wrong, my parents always made sure I had *something* to eat, even when they didn't. It just never seemed like enough. I was always hungry."

"Even while you're eating, all you can think about is where the next meal will come from," Polina said.

"You've been there?" Logan asked, surprised.

Polina nodded. "When I was human, my village was ravaged by illness. Plague. Many of the adults died, and children like me weren't as experienced with farming. There were too many lean years. I lived on turnip pottage for months. It was heaven when my suitor would catch a rabbit or down a deer."

"Your suitor?"

Polina spread her hands. "I was an only child. My parents were dead. As I was not yet married, the man who wanted me was my suitor and my only source of meat. I knew nothing of hunting and was too busy farming my land to learn."

Logan scratched the slight stubble of his jaw. "When was this Polina?"

She stiffened. "It's rude to ask a woman her age." She gave him a tight smile.

"I didn't ask your age, just around what year you were left orphaned."

"The 1530s."

Logan broke into a fit of coughing.

"Are you all right?"

He held up one hand as he stumbled to the refrigeration unit and retrieved another bottle of water. Twisting off the cap, he guzzled. Shook his head. When his chest stopped spasming, he stared at her, an impassive expression on his face.

"Hunger drives us to do things we never thought we'd do," she said absently under the weight of that stare.

The timer buzzed, rousing Logan from his thoughts. He jabbed his hand into an oven mitt and pulled out the pan, setting it down on the grate. "I usually let it cool, but since it's just us, I'll introduce you to the chef's way."

"Is it better warm?"

"The best." He used a spoon to gouge out a massive piece and tip it onto a plate. With a hop, he scooted onto the counter, dangling his legs and holding the cake in his lap. "Are you ready to regret every other cake you've ever eaten?"

She laughed and approached him. "I'm ready."

He spooned a bite of gooey, steaming chocolate and held it out to her. The smell alone was heavenly.

"No frosting?"

"Doesn't need it."

She reached up to take the utensil from him, but he jerked away. Did he intend to feed her like a child? With a wry half smile, he offered the spoon again, bringing it to her lips. His eyes were fixated on her face.

"Open," he said.

Goddess help her, she did, like a helpless baby bird. Logan spooned the cake into her mouth. Cocoa and butter rippled over her tongue. Moist but not dense. She closed her eyes, her tastebuds coming alive as the flavor permeated her mouth. Any sweetness bloomed as an afterthought to the fudgy chocolate that hit her palate first. Rich. Decadent. The velvety texture was as much a pleasure as the flavor. She swallowed, almost dizzy with delight.

A moan vibrated in her throat. Her eyes opened. "I was wrong," she said. "I can't handle it."

Logan's green eyes were hooded, his face so close. She opened her mouth again and he obliged, spooning in another bite. He set the dish down on the counter next to her hip.

"You are magic, Logan Valentine," she said. "You've ruined me for all other cakes."

She meant it as a joke, although every word was true. He didn't laugh. His hands reached out to cup her face. Inhaling deeply in surprise, her nostrils flared with the scent of warm male and chocolate.

And then he kissed her, pressed his lips against her mouth softly, as if tasting the cocoa on her breath. The kiss grew more urgent, his fingers threading into her hair, his hips pressing against hers, knocking her backside into the counter.

She wrapped her arms around his neck, relying on his him to hold her up because her head was spinning with pleasure. The room rippled with magic, her skin tingling, her lips burning. Chocolate and heat. Pleasure. Wanting.

There was something she was supposed to tell him. A warning. Several reasons this was a terrible idea. But when she parted her lips it was not to protest, but to invite him deeper inside.

11

THE KISS

Red flags and warning lights flashed in Logan's brain, but he found them easy to ignore. All his blood had rushed south, to the place where his hips circled against her belly. His first kiss was soft, a question. When Polina pulled him closer, he took that as his answer. He dug his hands into that bright red hair.

Hungry, he was so fucking hungry for her. He'd dreamed about kissing her a hundred times and hell if the real thing wasn't better than anything his sex-deprived brain had produced. Her lips were soft, full, eager against his. She followed his lead, adapting to his cues in a way that gave him the impression of inexperience, although her immortality meant that couldn't be the case.

She opened for him, took the kiss deeper, and he responded in kind, showing her with his mouth exactly what he'd like to do to the rest of her. He stoked her tongue with his, cupped the delicate bones of her neck in one hand. Her scent was enough to tip him over the edge, chrysanthemums and pumpkin spice. It mixed well with chocolate.

Intoxicating. Combusting. Damn, she practically melted in his arms.

His erection kicked. He wanted her, all of her. Tracing her ribs with his hands, he rounded her ass and scooped her up to set her on the counter. He slid between her thighs, the skirt of her dress bunching around her hips. In response, she arched into him, the full contact of her torso as much an invitation as her open and enticing mouth.

His hand coasted up her inner thigh. Smooth, milky-white. The tips of his feathered over the thin strip of cotton he found covering her core. He wanted to kiss her there, lick and touch until she screamed. He circled his thumb. She groaned.

But then his brain played a dirty trick on the rest of him. He pictured Dream Silas in his head saying, *You respect her too much to use her, even in your dreams.* He did respect her, despite the fact she was a witch who didn't normally care for humans. The way her lips moved, he suspected he'd changed her mind on the subject.

As painful as it was to stop, he retracted his hand and threaded his fingers behind her neck. Pulling back, he stroked her jawline with his thumbs. She looked at him with hooded bedroom eyes and swollen lips. The pulse in her neck throbbed against his palm. "Go out with me, Polina. A proper date. I want to know you better. I want to know everything about you. Before we do this."

She blinked three times quickly and straightened. She seemed to shake herself from a trance. "This was a mistake," she said.

"No. It's not a mistake. Just too soon." Logan groaned. "Is this about the human thing? Maybe if we got to know each other, you'd change your mind. I thought I'd never trust a witch again, but I'm willing to take a chance. I want you. I can't stop thinking about you."

Tears had formed in her eyes, causing them to glow sapphire. He almost gasped at the color, the contrast with her pale skin and deep red hair. Why was she crying? He wiped the tears from her cheeks with his thumbs. "What's wrong?"

"I can't." She swallowed. "This was a mistake. I'm sorry." She drew her wand.

"What are you doing?" Logan held his hands up, the wand's crystal tip glowing like a purple sun between them.

"It's for the best, Logan. If I wipe your memory, it will be easier for both of us." Her voice cracked.

A white-hot rage came over Logan. "Wipe my memory? Like I'm some kind of animal to use for your pleasure and then cast aside? Tell me, Polina, is this the first time we've made out or just the first time I remember?"

"It's the first time," she said. "And the last."

"It wouldn't surprise me if we'd had a torrid love affair and you'd simply struck it from my mind when things got tough. That would explain why I can't stop dreaming about you or thinking about you. Fuck, you're like a disease with no cure."

That made her take pause. "A disease?" she asked through her teeth.

"Yeah." He pointed a finger at her face. "You are a fucking flu that keeps on hanging on. You know something else, sweetheart? This is why I hate witches. You all think you're so goddamned superior. Rules don't apply to you. You take what you want, do want you want, and don't give a damn how it hurts people. If you wave that thing and wipe my memory, I will never forgive you, Polina. You will have proven to me you are no better than—"

"Don't say it. Don't you dare say it. I am nothing like her," she said, shaking. She lowered her wand. "You think I take what I want when I want? I can assure you I'm not doing so now. As much as it seems like I'm acting superior, if you had half a brain in your head you'd see this for what it is, taking responsibility. Relationships between witches and humans never work out—"

"Seemed to work okay for Grateful and Rick."

Polina tipped her chin up. "She was a reincarnated witch! You of all people should understand the complications."

"Complications? I kissed you and asked you on a date. It's not a marriage proposal. Why do we have to overthink it? Why can't you just go with it and see what happens?" He tossed up his hands in frustration.

"Can we agree to pretend tonight never happened?" she asked.

Logan planted his hands on his hips. "I only wish it hadn't."

She raised her wand again.

"Fine. It never happened."

She tucked her wand back into the neck of her dress, into the holster sewn into her bra strap—always next to her heart and within easy reach. "I wish I could 'go with it.' I wish I didn't know what happens. But I do. You might not believe this, but I think about you too. And, despite what you might believe, I don't feel superior, Logan. Especially not now. Not to you. But I am embarrassed, because I should know better." Wiping her eyes, she reached into her bag and grabbed a handful of gold dust.

"That doesn't make any sense. How can you say you know what happens? You can't possibly tell the future. Not for sure," Logan said.

She shook her head, looking as sad as Logan had ever seen her. "No one can see the future. Tomorrow isn't an absolute, aside from its coming and going. Witches like me don't see, we predict. And almost five centuries of living has made me quite good at noticing the patterns of things. I had a very nice time tonight. Can we leave it on a positive note? Remain friends?"

Logan could still smell her flesh, still feel her silky hair in his fist. He did not want to be friends. "Sure. Why the hell not?"

She nodded once and raised her fist over her head, then paused to snatch the pan of cake from the counter.

"Hey!" Logan said.

As she released the gold dust in her hand, it swirled around her, breaking her and the cake apart into floaty bits of metal that blew up the faucet of the stainless steel sink and out of his kitchen.

"I could have covered that for you," he yelled, wondering if the cake would arrive intact. He picked up the plate with the remains of the slice he'd fed her a moment ago. As he stared at it, the sense of being victimized stung in his chest.

"Best fucking cake I ever made." He hurled the plate into the sink, watched it shatter. And did nothing to pick up the pieces.

AUROREAN HOUSE

"Oh dear. Oh, oh, dear," Hildegard said worriedly from the bedpost.

"What? You've never seen a grown woman eat an entire chocolate cake?" Polina shoveled in another bite, avoiding her reflection in the mirror. As a metal witch, mirrors usually accentuated her power. But today, all they reflected was a wild-haired woman in pink flannel pajamas with a mouth covered in chocolate and a half-empty bottle of wine on her bedside table.

"What happened? You opened the Bordeaux. It must be serious."

"He kissed me, Hildie."

"Who kissed you?"

"Logan."

"The human?"

She picked up the pan from her lap. "He made me this cake." She dropped the pan and scooped another forkful of moist chocolate deliciousness.

"Looks tasty."

New tears streamed down Polina's face. She lifted the bottle of wine and sipped, wiping her mouth with the back of her hand as she returned it to her bedside table.

"That was rather unattractive," Hildie said.

"Who cares? Nobody here but us chickens. There's never anyone here but us." By the goddess, she was lonely and every fiber of her being wanted to fly straight back to Logan and dull the ache of it.

"This has really upset you. Was he unkind or inappropriate in some way?"

"No, he was sweet. Watch." Polina waved her hand in a wide arc toward the cheval mirror and said, "Reveal."

Logan's face appeared in the silver, even more handsome than she'd remembered. "Go out with me, Polina. On a proper date. I want to know you better. I want to know everything about you."

"A perfect gentleman. Why the tears?"

"It's the spell, Hildie. Even Grateful thought so. You can't touch someone's soul and not feel some attraction. It's not real, and even if it was, I know better than to get involved with a human again. It isn't worth the heartbreak."

"This is so much better?" Hildie cried. "Eating yourself sick on chocolate cake and wine while wearing granny jammies?"

"There are worse ways to pass the time." She raised another forkful to her lips, but Hildegard swooped down and snatched the utensil from her grip.

"Pull yourself together, my lady! We have trouble in the realm."

"What kind of trouble?"

"The werewolf pack staying in Renegade Caverns has grown to twelve, if I'm counting right. New wolves. Young men and women who look like they've never shifted before."

"Twelve? There were only three last time I checked."

"The gargoyles have kept an eye on them as you requested. These new additions are recent. But Nicodemus says he saw them stealing food and drink from the human campsite last night."

"Stealing? Interacting with humans? This is unacceptable. How long until the next full moon?" She sat up, wiping under her eyes.

"Three days. You need to talk with them. Get to know their leader and make sure he has a plan. The young ones will be hard to control."

"I know. I know." Bounding from bed, she carried the cake pan and wine to the kitchen. "Give me twenty minutes."

"Not a moment more. I'm worried about you." The owl landed on her perch, her head tipped in an almost maternal way.

With a deep, cleansing breath, Polina gave the owl a gentle hug. "Don't worry, Hildegard. I'm already over it." The owl bobbed her head and spread her wings, soaring out the open kitchen window.

Polina hated to lie to Hildegard. Her emotional state wasn't even on the same map as "over it." But she loved Hildie and didn't want her to worry. She would simply muscle through it.

She returned to her bedroom and dug in her closet for something to wear. An ankle-length black skirt, thin and flowing, would do the trick on this hot day. She paired it with a peasant blouse and red leather corset. When she reached into the shelving to retrieve a pair of black boots, a camo-green container caught on the toe and slid from the shelf. Only her superhuman reflexes saved it from hitting the floor.

"What's this?" She rotated the container in her palm. A *Duck Dynasty* thermos.

Polina dropped her clothes on the floor and clutched the thermos with both hands. This was the positivity potion Grateful had mentioned yesterday. The Monk's Hill witch had made it for Tabetha and then given it to Polina as a reward for helping her slay Salem's sorceress. A less-educated witch might call it a love potion, but Polina knew better. Positivity potion changed the drinker's chemistry to magically attract their perfect match. It didn't guarantee love. True love couldn't be created or destroyed with magic.

She unscrewed the lid and looked inside. The potion swirled within. Shades of ruby and scarlet, pale at the edges and deeper colored at the center, spiraled with a life of their own. As she peered through the mouth, a glittery purple heart formed and then morphed into an hourglass figure before dissolving into pinky red tones. The aroma emitted from the brew almost brought her to her knees, dark spices and leather—the scent of a man from a concoction evocative of a woman. She caught herself lifting it to her lips.

Clapping the lid back on, she shivered with the effort of denying herself. Could she take this? If she found her match, would the new attraction wipe Logan from her mind? Perhaps there was a warlock or fae male waiting for her on the other side of this potion. It could be her answer, the magic eraser to wipe her emotional slate clean of the human. She opened the container again and brought her face closer to the lip.

"Ten minutes," Hildegard called from the kitchen.

Polina returned the container to the shelf. With a firm shake of her head, she gathered her clothing and headed for the shower. She had more important things to worry about at the moment than falling in love. Besides, the potion she truly wanted was one to make the feelings go away rather than invite new ones. *Get a grip.* With a deep breath, she centered herself, and then she got back to work.

13

THE REAL SILAS

"Whoa!" Sous-chef Jonah grabbed the pan from Logan's hand and removed it from the flame, flipping the contents onto the plate he'd had ready. "Just because they call it sole doesn't mean it should be as tough as leather."

Logan scrubbed his face with his hands. "Fuck. Thanks. I didn't sleep well last night."

Jonah frowned. "Why not? The restaurant was closed for that private party, right? Should have been an early night."

Logan couldn't get into the Polina situation with his coworker. Nothing ruined a professional relationship like crying on someone's shoulder. "Right. Just couldn't sleep. No reason."

Jonah nodded slowly. "Well, if you want to take off, I can handle things back here. It's slow anyway."

"Thanks. Maybe I'll just take a moment." He left Jonah to finish the lunch shift and did a convincing *Walking Dead* impression toward his office. He had to pull himself together. No woman was worth this kind of anguish.

But when he opened his office door, Silas was sitting inside, a red folder squared on the desk in front of him.

"What the hell happened to you?" Logan asked. His friend looked like hell. Dark circles inhabited the space under his red-rimmed eyes and his face sagged. He hadn't shaved, and for a werewolf just days from the full moon, that made for a scruffy, bedraggled appearance.

"Sit down." Silas motioned toward the chair with his head.

Logan sat, suddenly worried. "Did something happen to my dad?"

"No. This isn't about you." Silas opened the file folder in front of him and removed a picture. He pushed it across the table. "Do you recognize this man?"

Logan inspected the image in front of him. It was a fuzzy picture. Physically fit man with short dark hair and light-colored eyes. "No. Why? Should I?"

"His body was found in a dumpster on the other end of your alley last night."

"What?"

"Do any other businesses share that dumpster with Valentine's?"

"Just the boutique across the alley—Scrub-a-lub-dub. They sell scrubs, shoes, stethoscopes—that sort of shit for the hospital workers across the street. But they were closed yesterday."

"You were closed too, for Grateful's party. Did you open the restaurant after we left?" Silas asked.

"No. Sunday nights are always slow anyway. It didn't make sense to open for just a couple hours business."

"I left just before four. When did you close up shop?"

Logan leaned back in his chair and groaned. "I'm not sure. Seven maybe."

"Seven? What were you doing here until seven?"

He rubbed the back of his neck and lifted one corner of his upper lip. "Uh, I had to clean up."

"After you cleaned up, did you throw anything away in the dumpster?"

"No... Yes. Yes, I did."

"Which is it?" Silas narrowed his eyes.

"I did."

"Did you do it yourself?"

Logan hesitated. "Who else would do it?"

The werewolf let that one slide, although he wrote himself some notes on his yellow legal pad. "What time would you say it was when you threw everything away?"

"A little after five."

"Did you notice anything in the dumpster?"

"No."

"What did you do after the dumpster? It didn't take you until seven to clean up."

"Work."

"What kind of work?"

Shit, was this the Inquisition? The last thing Logan wanted to do was tell anyone he'd had a romantic interlude with Polina. Not only had he promised her to pretend it never happened, he'd never hear the end of it from Silas. But this was murder. What if Silas thought he was a suspect? He focused his eyes on his desk calendar and tried to play it cool. "Business. End-of-month accounting."

The smile Silas gave wasn't the happy-happy-joy-joy sort. It was the gotcha kind. "You smell like you're lying."

Logan's eyes snapped to Silas's. "What exactly does a lie smell like?"

"How you smell right now. Like rancid bacon. Never lie to a werewolf just before the full moon."

"Well, fuck, Silas! Am I a suspect or what? You're giving me the third degree here."

"I am not giving you the third degree. A man's body was found in your dumpster. Normally, that would be enough evidence for me to take you downtown for questioning."

Running his hands through his hair, Logan swore and stood from his chair.

"Normally, Logan. Not this time. Sit down, okay? What is going on with you? I swear to god, if I didn't know you were innocent this shifty-ass crap would be a nail in your coffin."

He sat. "You know I'm innocent?"

Silas nodded.

"Then why are you here?"

"I need to know if you saw or spoke to anyone after Lucas's christening party. Did you? Yes or no."

He gritted his teeth. "Yes."

"Was this individual a supernatural being?"

Logan closed his eyes and pinched the bridge of his nose. "Yes."

With a deep breath, Silas adjusted in his chair. "Who was it, Logan? And don't try to lie, because I will know."

"I don't want to say."

A growl preceded Silas's face coming at him in 3-D. The guy's fist balled in Logan's collar. "You don't have a choice. I don't want to get rough with you, but so help me, if you don't cough up the name right now, I'll go wolf-shit on your ass."

"Polina," Logan spit out. "I was with Polina."

Silas's bushy eyebrows pinched together, and he slowly relaxed his fist. "Polina? The Smuggler's Notch witch?"

"The one and only."

"I thought you said she didn't like humans."

"She doesn't. I was teaching her how to make chocolate cake."

"Is that a euphemism for—"

"No. No, it is not." *Unfortunately*, he thought.

Silas scratched his head. "When did she leave?"

"Around eight. Just before I did. I watched her flush herself up my kitchen faucet. But she wasn't even in the alley, Silas. Neither of us were, to be honest."

The detective frowned. "Then how did you throw the garbage from the party away?"

"Polina did a little hocus-pocus and took care of it. She told me she sent it all back there, but she never left the building."

The detective straightened, then sank heavily into his chair. "Hmm." He scribbled something in his notes. "You were baking a cake for two hours?"

He shrugged. There was nothing left to do but tell the truth. The guy would know if he was lying, and as angry as he was with Polina for last night, she wasn't a murderer. "We talked. Baked. Ate. There was some, um, fooling around."

One bushy eyebrow shot toward the ceiling. "Fooling around, eh? So you two played hide the banana in the kitchen for three hours?"

"No! Nothing like that. We talked, and we ate. All kissing was fully clothed. I thought we had something. I asked her on a real date and she went batshit. Couldn't get away from me fast enough." Logan scowled just thinking about it.

"I feel ya, buddy. It's Soleil and me all over again. Inter-species dating is taboo among supernaturals. Some folks won't go there."

"It's prejudiced. Fuck, if anyone should be wary of

anyone, it should be me of her after what happened with Tabetha. Can you believe Polina had the nerve to threaten to wipe my memories?"

Silas stilled, his eyes narrowing. "Polina threatened to use magic to make you forget her? Why would she do that?"

Logan shrugged. "Guess she thought it would be easier if I couldn't remember the tonsil hockey we played on the counter."

"Or, she didn't want you to remember she was here at all," Silas said, taking notes.

"Hey now"—Logan shook his head—"Polina's a lot of things: complicated, mysterious, cold, wickedly beautiful. But she's not a murderer."

"I'm sure you're right." Silas scratched a few more notes on the pad.

"You said you knew I was innocent. How do you know? Can you smell guilt?"

Blinking, Silas tilted his head, assessing Logan. "We're friends, right?"

"Of course."

He nodded. "What I'm about to tell you is best kept secret. It's not exactly classified. People in the supernatural community know, but it won't do for a human to be mouthing off about it, understand?"

Logan mimed locking his lips with a key and throwing it over his shoulder.

"The man in the dumpster wasn't just a man."

"Duh. You wouldn't be on the case if he was," Logan said.

"He was a werewolf. One from the Fireborn Pack." Silas pushed the short sleeve of his dress shirt up over the top of his shoulder, revealing a tribal-style tattoo in the image of a phoenix. "He was from my pack."

Straightening, Logan leaned forward. "Fuck, Silas. You knew him well then."

"Yeah. I knew him and his family." Silas pulled his sleeve back down to cover the tat. "Anyway, I know it couldn't be you because the guy was ripped apart. A werewolf, days from the full moon, was ripped apart. Not cut up. Not sawed to pieces. Ripped. Apart. By hand. Only another supernatural could do that to a wolf. No way could a human."

"Who do you think did it?"

"The murdered wolf was a political decoy. We call the role a Zafka, a doppelgänger for our alpha."

Logan jerked, leaning forward across the desk. "You think it was another werewolf? The fugitive you told me about?"

Silas nodded. "I want to talk to Polina. Maybe she saw or heard something."

Logan nodded. "She's not going to like it. If it was up to her, no one would ever know what happened."

"No choice. This isn't just a crime to me, Logan. This is personal."

"I get it. He was a member of your pack. You gotta take care of your own."

"It's more than that. He was my family's responsibility."

Logan shook his head, not sure what his friend meant.

"My father is alpha of Fireborn pack. My siblings and I are pack royalty. The man killed was my father's Zafka. Something like this in our territory? It isn't just a crime. It's an act of war."

14

SMUGGLER'S NOTCH

Wand drawn, Polina approached Renegade Caverns. She'd expected the red wolf would stay after she saw him here with the old man and the boy. The magic that concealed this part of the park from humans added to the natural protection the mountain offered. A werewolf could run safely for miles in these woods. The caves provided shelter.

But as she approached the camp, she saw what Hildegard had seen. Whiskey bottles abandoned on the path. A fast-food bag flapping like a flag from a nearby bush. Napkins, wrappers, plastic silverware strewn about her woods. This couldn't continue. If the local wildlife ate any of it, the problems it could cause ranged from heartburn to death depending on the creature.

"Hello?" she called into the first cave. It was almost noon, but the distinct nasal rattle of snoring echoed out the opening. "Excuse me, is anyone here?"

"You don't want to do that," a man's voice said from the trees behind her. "Sam may be a werewolf, but he acts like a bear if you wake him up."

Polina turned to face the lithe young man she'd seen before, the one she assumed was the red wolf. Shirtless and golden brown from the sun, his wavy dark blond curls stuck out from under a Chicago Blackhawks cap. His khaki cargo shorts hung low on his hips, low enough that Polina decided to keep her gaze locked on his face. She flashed her friendliest smile. "I have no desire to wake a sleeping bear. Perhaps you can help me?"

"I'll try. Anything for a beautiful lady."

It sounded like a line, patronizing and insincere. She cleared her throat. "Are you the alpha of this pack?"

"I am." The man placed his hands on his hips.

"You are the one I allowed into this territory last fall?"

"That's me."

He was young to be an alpha. Then again, as she glanced around camp, the entire pack seemed to be either extremely young or old. The man in front of her was the only one who looked strong and experienced enough to lead. "I am Polina, Hecate of Smuggler's Notch."

"Hecate?"

"Sorceress of the dead, demigoddess, enforcer of the natural law in this realm."

"Sounds important," he said, adjusting the bill of his cap.

"Yes, well, you must be very young indeed to have not heard of my role."

He ran his tongue over his teeth. "Can I help you with something?"

"Yes. As I mentioned, this is my realm and as such there are rules. If you abide by the rules, we can live peacefully together. If you break the rules, it is my right and duty to sentence you to my hellmouth."

"Your hellmouth?"

"The opening to hell in the graveyard behind my home. It's a special place where supernaturals who don't follow the rules go to simmer down, and when I say simmer, I mean burn in everlasting flames." She was being snippy now, but she'd had about enough of his flippant attitude.

"M'kay." He shrugged.

Not a hint of worry flitted across his face. No inquiry crossed his lips as to what the rules were. Everything from his stance to the attitude seeping off him portrayed a man unimpressed by her credentials. "What is your name and pack?" she demanded.

He sighed. "Name's Alex. Bloodright pack." He pushed up his sleeve to reveal a tattoo of a harvest moon with three claw marks ripping through it. "Listen, lady, we're out here minding our own business. What's your beef?"

"The cardinal rule of the realm is no malevolent interaction with humans. As you know, there's a repellent and concealer charm on Silver Sparrow Mountain. It's meant to be a sanctuary for supernaturals in the area. Still, with humans camping less than four miles away, we must be careful not to garner their attention. It is possible for them to enter the sanctuary if they follow one of us here. I have been made aware of a few of your wolves stealing from humans, consorting with humans, and otherwise making a mess of the human camp. Not only is this unacceptable but familiarity with the human campsite could lead to an instinctual return by the younger wolves to the location when in their wolf form. The full moon is coming. I want your assurance that you have a plan to mitigate the risk."

Alex smiled a mouthful of straight white teeth. "Don't you worry your pretty little head about it."

"Excuse me?" Polina crossed her arms over her chest. Who did he think he was talking to?

Both of them were distracted by a human girl who emerged from the cave. She couldn't have been more than twenty with short-shorts that said Pink across the butt, a white T-shirt that left nothing to the imagination, and brown hair that curled to the middle of her back.

She sauntered toward Alex, tossed her arms around his neck, and kissed him. "Thanks for last night. You were an animal."

"You have no idea," he said.

Polina rolled her eyes.

"Do you mind waiting right over there while I finish my conversation?" Alex pointed at a boulder down the path from the caverns. "I'll walk you home."

"Sure." The girl practically skipped away.

Polina closed her gaping mouth. "A human? Here?"

He spread his hands. "You just told me about the rule today, Polina, and frankly, if it's malevolent contact you're worried about, last night was not it." He chuckled.

"Fine. What is your plan to protect that woman when your pack shifts in two nights? You'll have her scent. Your wolf will head straight for her door."

Alex adjusted his hat again. "Contrary to popular belief, we do have higher thought processes in our wolf forms. I'm their alpha. If I tell them to leave the humans alone, they must obey. You have my word that no werewolves from my pack will enter the human camp in wolf form."

"But—"

"I'll handle it. Thanks for the heads-up on the rules." He flashed her a patronizing thumbs up and turned on his heel to join the girl.

"How will you handle it?" Polina demanded.

The werewolf stopped and looked at her over his shoulder, his eyes settling on her breasts. "Pack business. Maybe you should get back to protecting your realm and let me worry about it."

"And if a human ends up dead?"

"Then I'm sure you will send the responsible party to your, uh, hellmouth." His eyes flicked down the length of her body and settled on her crotch.

She gasped. "And clean up your campsite!" she yelled toward his back. Polina tapped her wand against her palm in irritation. She had half a mind to hit the man in the back of the head with an itching pox. Rude. Hildegard swooped in and landed on her shoulder.

"He seemed less than receptive to your warning or your help," the owl said.

Polina marched toward Aurorean House, fuming. "Not receptive at all. A pack with a leader like that is in trouble. He didn't seem to give a rat's ass about the potential his pack might kill humans. What was it he said? 'If you can catch them.' As if it would be okay with him if his pack got away with murder."

"What are you going to do?" Hildie's white feathers bumped her ear.

"I can't sentence him or any of his pack if they haven't committed a crime against the goddess." She took a deep breath and blew it out slowly. "I'll have to use magic to create a barrier to keep the wolves inside. Something temporary that only works on their wolf forms."

"It will take strong magic and lots of it. Is it possible to make it in time? The enchantment to keep the humans out took weeks."

"I'm not sure. I'll have to do more research. If all else fails, I'll use the *lucubratus* to conjure a vision of the future and focus my efforts on the specific areas it shows me."

"Are you sure you're up to the task? I could ask Poe to see if Grateful could help."

"Of course I am up to the task! I don't need another witch or her familiar to help protect my realm."

"Don't sound so offended. The state I found you in this morning was anything but confidence producing. And last I checked there was chocolate cake left in the pan."

Polina brushed the bird from her shoulder and scowled. "I'm fine," she said. "Perfectly fine on my own."

15

THE POSITIVITY POTION

Polina was not fine. In fact she felt like she might crawl out of her skin. "Reveal!" she commanded, swiping her hand over the top of the table-sized stretch of silver. Her intention was to see the future, to tell what area of her realm might be prone to werewolf mischief. But something was wrong. The silver pooled like liquid mercury and then peaked into a mountainside covered in trees, but when she tried to focus in on Smuggler's Notch and the Bloodright pack, everything melted away. All the mirror reflected back at her was Logan.

He looks tired, she thought. His chin was covered in stubble and his eyes drooped. He wasn't sleeping well. Had she done that to him? Her mind shifted, and so did the image in the *lucubratus*. Her magic mirror went rogue. She'd asked it to show her the future but instead it flashed on the past. She saw herself kissing him in his kitchen, the taste of decadent chocolate filling her mouth. She ran her fingers along her lips. She could almost feel his hand coasting up her thigh.

"Again?" Hildegard said from her perch in the room of

reflection. "This isn't helping. We need a vision. How will we know where to place your enchantment if you keep getting distracted with this human?"

"I didn't do it on purpose," Polina said, wiping the tour-down-memory-lane from the mirror. "I can't get him out of my head. Every time I try to concentrate, he's all I see."

"You have feelings for him! You need to go see him and let nature take its course. Work the man out of your system."

She shook her head. "It's just residual magic. If I foster it, I'll make it worse for both of us."

Hildegard fluffed her feathers. "Then what shall we do? We have three days and only two nights for you to clear your head."

In a huff, Polina strode from the silver, passing through the maze of mirrors that led to the main part of the house. She saw herself reflected in a thousand fragmented ways in the silver. How appropriate. Logan had shattered her. She'd wanted him, needed him so much it almost hurt. The ache inside hadn't faded with her leaving him that night. It had blossomed into a blazing inferno that consumed her every thought. She had to douse the flames. She had to do something to free herself from this desire.

Passing through the cheval, she made a beeline to her closet. On tiptoe, she reached to the back of the shelf and hooked her hand on the *Duck Dynasty* thermos that held the positivity potion. She cradled it in front of her. Hildegard landed on the shelving near her head.

"What is that?" the owl asked.

"This is the key to finding my soulmate, the only man who can break the human's hold over me."

Hildegard pivoted her head entirely around her neck. "I believe all of those camouflaged men are already married."

Polina clucked her tongue. "Not the Robertson men, Hildegard. For the love of the goddess!"

"Then who?"

Polina unscrewed the lid. A shower of glitter sprayed into the air as if pressure had been building under the cap. The spicy scent of leather and musk filled the small space. The entire closet smelled of man.

Hildegard's already unusually large yellow eyes expanded. "That's a dangerous tincture you have there. Positivity potion."

"You know of it?" Polina scrutinized the bird.

"Rumor has it that Grace Kelly used it to capture the attentions of Prince Rainier."

"That seemed to work out quite well for the both of them and their three children."

"Rumor also has it that the potion is to blame for the romance of Anne Boleyn and King Henry VIII."

Polina tipped her head and rolled her eyes toward the ceiling. "Not such an auspicious union."

"The magic puts you in the path of someone you might have the perfect connection with, but it won't make them love you or you them. And if they are already married or otherwise inaccessible—"

"Inaccessible?"

"In prison, in a coma, homosexual, a child, a vampire... your match could be anyone, love, appropriate or not. The moment that potion touches your lips you open yourself up to heartbreak and disappointment."

"But also to curing myself of the pull Logan has over me."

"'Tis true."

"I'm going to do it. I have to. I can't work like this."

"The sun is setting."

"Let the gargoyles handle it."

"Are you sure about this?"

She closed her eyes and remembered the heat of Logan's body against hers, the rush of his tongue stroking her own, the way her nipples had hardened and her heart had pounded against her ribs like a caged beast. She couldn't take it anymore. She had to quench the fire, one way or another.

"I'm sure," she said.

She raised the thermos to her lips, inhaling deeply of masculine essence. This close, the smell not only reminded her of a man but of sex, although considering it had been almost a century since she'd engaged in that particular sport, she couldn't be sure.

"Ooooh," Hildegard worried.

The thick scarlet-and-purple liquid didn't pour into her mouth; it undulated, a thick and churning thing that fizzed when it hit her tongue. Like a too-thick shake, she had to scoop it into her mouth with her finger before she could swallow. Sweetness hit her palate first, followed by the tartness of under-ripe apricots and salted caramel. She licked her lips.

"It's good. Like a milkshake," Polina said. Her spine straightened. "Oh!" Her hips surged with a rush of warmth that coasted along her body. "I feel... I feel..." The thermos hit the floor.

"What's happening?" Hildegard cried.

Polina's head rolled on her neck and her limbs began to move of their own accord, swimming like snakes over her head and along her sides. The rest of her body joined in, belly dancing to some internal tune that only she could hear. A scarlet butterfly emerged from the thermos and fluttered just out of her reach.

"Who are you?" she asked, an unexpected intoxication taking hold. "Fluttery butterfly." She reached for it. It darted away. She stepped forward and reached for it again. "I think it wants me to follow it."

"What wants you to follow it?"

"The butterfly."

"Butterfly? I don't see any butterfly. Oh dear. Be careful, my lady."

The butterfly led Polina out of the closet, through the house, and to the front entrance. Throwing open the door, she hesitated at the sight waiting for her. It seemed the effects of the spell were far more than a glittering butterfly. Magic had come for her.

16

CONSEQUENCES

"Where did you come from?" Polina said to the white mare kneeling in her lawn. She floated down the stairs to the horse's side. The mare's white coat and mane carried hints of pink and purple, almost like it was reflecting a light that wasn't there.

"I don't like this," Hildegard said. "A strange horse shows up on the lawn. Who does it belong to? Are you supposed to ride it?"

"Why else would it be here?" The electric butterfly turned circles over the horse's back.

"Are you going to trust it? How do you know it's even a result of the potion? This could be anyone's old horse."

Polina climbed onto the mare's back, keeping her eye on the butterfly. "It's the potion," she said absently. It was all she could say. Her entire being was overcome with a sense of well-being and... focus, intense focus on reaching whoever lay ahead.

"Should I follow you?" Hildegard asked.

"Only if you can keep up," Polina called. The mare stood and she wrapped her hands in its mane. The horse took off, bounding into the forest at breakneck speed. This was no ordinary animal. Polina sensed magic in its blood, like it might be part unicorn or griffin. Its speed alone marked it as supernatural. Hildegard could not keep up.

The trees flew by until they blurred and the entire forest seemed to compress. Time and space folded in itself. How far had she traveled? It was impossible to tell. But when the horse stopped again, it disappeared from underneath her. She landed on her toes on a stretch of sidewalk in front of a vaguely familiar building built primarily of steel and glass.

"Can I help you, miss?" the doorman asked. White-haired and sour-faced, he stared at her over his bifocals. The scarlet butterfly flitted past his nose and into the building.

Polina smiled sweetly at the man. "I'm supposed to go inside."

"Who are you here to see?" He followed her, pausing in front of the security desk.

A glass-paneled interior door separated the foyer from the elevator. The scarlet butterfly passed through and hovered, waiting. "I don't know who," Polina said. She strode past him to the doors and found them locked.

"This is a private building, lady. I can't let you up there without permission from a homeowner." The doorman grabbed her by the elbow.

She paused, turning toward the man, eyes darting to his nametag. "Er, um, Fred, I know this is highly unusual, but I can't deal with you right now." Pulling her wand from the neck of her peasant blouse, she uttered a spell that left him staring at the wall, lips parted. She tugged her elbow free from his fingers. "Confusion spell. A weak one. You'll be yourself in a few minutes, minus the memory of me."

With new determination, she approached the doors. A

sprinkle of gold dust and her molecules blended with the metal frame, traveled along the electrical wires under the floor, and formed again inside the elevator. The butterfly indicated which button she should push. The compartment rose, each floor chiming in the display above her head. When she reached the top floor, the elevator opened. There was only one door on this floor, and the scarlet butterfly hovered in front of it.

"Here goes nothing." She approached, raised one hand, knocked twice.

Footsteps. Polina stopped breathing.

Arms spread wide to hold the door open, Logan stared at her from within. "Polina? What are you doing here?" he asked, jaw going slack.

Before she could answer, the scarlet butterfly flew straight into his open mouth.

17

CRASH INTO ME

W hat. The. Fuck.

The woman who'd haunted his thoughts for the last year stood right in front of him and all he could do was make unattractive hacking sounds in her direction. The look on her face! What was that? Disgust? Disappointment? He couldn't study her expression over his head bobbing with the spasms of his coughing lungs, but he could tell she wasn't happy.

When he finally cleared whatever had flown down his throat (was that a bug?), he straightened and looked her in the eye. She was crying and pale. Deathly pale. "Are you okay?"

As if in answer, her eyes rolled back in her head and she collapsed. He lunged over the threshold to catch her, scooping her up and holding her against his chest. Fuck, she smelled good. Cinnamon and clove with a hint of fresh-cut wildflowers. He lowered his face to her hair and inhaled. She weighed almost nothing in his arms, which was surprising because her curvy shape would suggest other-

123

wise. The mounds of her breasts peeked from under a thin white shirt held to her waist with a red leather corset. *Damn. Double damn.*

And now he had a hard-on. Great. She probably came here to talk about the murdered werewolf and he was ready to hump her in her sleep. As he moved to carry her inside, he paused. If he crossed the threshold with her in his arms, he'd be effectively inviting her in. That would render all of Grateful's enchantments ineffective against Polina. Did he trust her? She seemed so vulnerable in his arms, the exact opposite of the powerful sorceress he knew she was. With some effort, he conjured up thoughts of Tabetha. Could he ever trust a witch again?

With a low, throaty groan of protest against his own stupidity, he crossed the threshold and delivered her to his sofa.

"Are you hurt?" He ran his fingers through her hair, over her arms. A cursory inspection didn't suggest any blood or abrasions, only soft flowing tresses and graceful limbs. Her pulse was strong. She was breathing normally. "My god, you are beautiful."

He knelt by her head. "Polina?" He stroked her hair back from her temple. Her creamy skin seemed to glow against the deep red shine of her hair. Her full rose-colored lips taunted him. Totally kissable. He was impressed that she wore little makeup. Natural. Sexy as hell. One of his hands came to rest on the space between her bottom rib and where he guessed her belly button might be. The other continued to stroke her hair.

He tried to resist her. Really he did. But she was a drug, a temptation he couldn't deny. He licked his lips, swallowed, tried to push himself up off his knees. Anything to resist the temptation. He failed. Leaning in, he pressed his lips to hers.

Soft. Warm. He nibbled her bottom lip and inhaled deeply. Her closeness was intoxicating. Right here, hovering over her while she slept, he would have given her his soul had she asked. But she'd already held his soul, hadn't she? The day of his accident. The day she'd saved him. He pulled back and blinked.

A delicate hand dug into the back of his head. She opened her eyes. Bright blue and fixated on him. Didn't that make him feel like a king? What was it about her attention that made his chest swell? He had a sudden urge to hunt wild game with a spear. High-level thought had abandoned him. He was left with a headful of Neanderthal grunts and basal instincts. *Girl pretty. Kiss girl.*

Polina didn't say a word, but she pulled his face back down to hers. Lips brushed lips, and it was her turn to inhale. That small, needy sound sent his blood singing through his veins. He kissed her harder, repositioning his head for a better angle. Both her arms snaked around his neck.

Damn. The go light was flashing green. He slid his hand up, over her ribs to her breast, coaxing it from under the corset and flicking his thumb across the cotton-covered nipple. His erection kicked and he discreetly reached down to straighten himself. He took the opportunity to work his lips down her jaw to her neck, over her throat. She sighed encouragingly. He dipped lower, his breath gathering against her skin, warming his face. Lower. The tips of his fingers tugged her blouse down, revealing full breasts, perfect, creamy skin converging in beige taut nipples. His hand kneaded the flesh, and then his mouth took over.

She arched her back and moaned. Desire rolled up his body, a gathering electric cloud that sent hot current shooting to his extremities. The way she writhed under his torso, he guessed she felt the same way. If he had any doubt, it dissolved when her hand grabbed his from under her breast and slid it down her body, up and under her skirt. She tucked his fingers between her upper thighs.

Cotton. He stroked and rubbed through the material while her hips worked against his hand and her lips melded with his. Her nails scraped down the back of his head and sank into the muscles of his shoulders. She dug in, deep enough he was sure she'd draw blood. He didn't mind. He stroked the inside of her mouth with his tongue and moved aside her underwear. His fingers dipped inside.

God, she was wet. He entered her, thumb circling as he found a rhythm within her. She arched and bit his lip, her body bucking off the sofa, clinging to his neck as she rode out the aftershocks of the orgasm he'd given her. Fuck, she was an easy whistle to blow. It was almost like. Almost as if...

"Are you a virgin?" he asked into her mouth.

She pulled back, those haunting blue eyes searching his face. "Of course not," she said, voice husky. "I'm almost five hundred years old."

He smiled wickedly and returned his lips to hers. He planted a knee on the sofa between her legs, rubbing the length of his cock on one of her thighs. She was receptive and supple, but something was off. She didn't reach for his fly. She was eager but quiet. Unsure.

He paused, bracing his weight on his elbows so he could see her face.

"Why have you stopped?" she asked softly.

"When was the last time you had sex, Polina?" He made sure his voice was kind, matter of fact. He said it through a smile.

She swallowed and stared at his chin when she answered. "About ninety-five years ago."

18

LIKE A VIRGIN

"Ninety-five?" Logan squeaked. His throat had tightened, resulting in the high pitch. He pushed himself up to stand beside the sofa.

"Wha-what are you doing?"

He helped her up to a seated position and cupped her face in his hands. "You passed out at my door. Are you feeling okay?"

"I am fine. More than fine." She leaned in, her lips brushing his.

"Would you like something to drink? A hot beverage?"

The muscles in her jaw tightened. "Yes. I suppose that would be nice."

Logan planted a kiss on her forehead and wandered into the kitchen. As he pulled out milk, cocoa, sugar, and vanilla, all he could think was how sexually out of practice he was after two years. Polina had gone a lifetime without sex. He couldn't just lay her out on the couch and take advantage of her.

He lit the burner under his favorite cast-iron saucepan

and began warming the milk. The wooden spoon swirled at the same pace as the thoughts in his confused skull.

Polina's hands wrapped under his arms and pressed into his stomach and chest. "Why did you stop, Logan?" she whispered in his ear. "I am willing, and I can tell you are ready." Her lips pressed into his back.

Logan hesitated, flashing her a smile over his shoulder. He was more than ready. At the moment, his dick could cut glass. As much as he'd said he'd never date a witch again, he wanted her. The desire to bend her over the kitchen island was almost unbearable. But he needed more from her than ready and willing.

"When you left the other night, I didn't think I'd see you again." He added the cocoa powder and sugar.

She pressed her cheek against his back. "Honestly, I thought so too. But I can't stop thinking about you. I almost hurt myself eating every bite of the chocolate cake we made. I can't sleep. I can't work. I see your face, constantly. I had to see you or—"

"I'd lose my mind," he finished. "I've been dreaming about you too. Some nights, it's almost painful."

"It is painful. I ache for you, even now." She placed a kiss against the side of his neck.

He scraped some fresh vanilla bean into the pot. The perfect cup of cocoa was a lot like love; you had to be patient to brew the perfect cup. Too hot and the milk would scald. Too cool and the sugar and cocoa wouldn't thoroughly blend with the milk.

"Thing is, there's so much I don't know about you." He removed the cocoa from the burner and poured it evenly into two mugs. "If I'm going to be the first man you're with in ninety-five years, I want it to be perfect. I don't want us to rush it." He turned in the circle of her arms, a cocoa in each hand.

"But you're human."

"Yes. It seems like you won't ever let me forget that fact."

"Aren't you afraid you'll run out of time?"

He looked down into her eyes, her face close enough that an extension of his lips would touch hers. "I'd rather do it right once than do it wrong often."

"You're a gentleman."

He snorted. "No. Not really. Just with you. For some reason, it's more important to get it right with you."

Her face softened and her mouth bent into a smile. "I'm so glad it was you."

"Huh?"

Her eyes darted to the hot cocoa. "I... I'm happy it's you."

"Taste it." He brought his own to his lips and took a languorous sip. Perfect, if he did say so himself. Over his mug, he watched her bring the cup to her lips. This is what he lived for. The first taste.

Polina closed her eyes and tipped the cup. "Mmm. How do you do it?" She looked at him from under hooded eyes.

"The secret is the fresh vanilla."

"I don't mean the cocoa." The hint of a blush bloomed on her cheeks. "I mean, how you make me feel. You look at me like I'm the only thing in your universe."

"You are a goddess," he said, raising an eyebrow.

"Demigoddess," she corrected. "You could have a hundred different women. I pushed you away. And still you treat me like..."

"I want to know you, Polina. I'm not interested in

dousing the fire. I want to kindle it. I want to know every-thing about you. Again and again I've told myself to stay away. But I can't. And if we're going to do this, I want to do it right. I want you to be honest about what you want from me."

"What happened on the couch was exquisite." Polina licked her lips.

Logan gave a smug half grin. "You've never had an orgasm before?"

She stared into her cocoa. "Not like that."

Logan almost dropped his mug. For the love of all that was holy, he wanted to tear that skirt off her hips and show her all the different ways he could make her come. It took all his will power to take her hand and lead her to his glass dining room table. "Before this goes any further, I need you to tell me something. I want you to be honest."

"What?" she asked.

"Why tonight? What made you change your mind?"

19

MOST OF THE TRUTH

Polina couldn't tell Logan about the positivity potion. Nor could she tell him about the connection they shared from her sorting his soul. If there was one thing she knew about Logan, it was that he hated to be influenced or controlled by magic. If she told him, he'd accuse her of being just like Tabetha. He'd never talk to her again. She couldn't have that. Not now. Not when, thanks to the potion, he held her heart in his capable hands. Instead, she told him another truth, one she hadn't shared with anyone but Hildegard in centuries.

"I was married once," Polina murmured, taking a seat at the table.

Logan's jaw tightened and he lowered himself into the chair across from her. To his credit, he did a decent job of hiding his shock, taking a drink of his hot cocoa before saying, "Go on."

"In my village, people married younger than they do today. It wasn't unheard of for a girl to marry at fifteen or younger if the union was political in nature. I fell in love with Ronin around that age. He was an apprentice black-smith and I was the daughter of a laird."

"A Scottish landowner," Logan clarified.

"Yes. We owned our land, which was a blessing back then." She smoothed her skirt over her knees. "Ronin and I married in the year 1532. I was sixteen, and I was human. My father gifted us a small acreage of farmland and we built a home on it with the help of Ronin's clan and my father's laborers. It was a beautiful place with small stone rooms and warm fires. We were happy for a time."

"For a time."

"The plague came. In truth, it had been spreading for years, although our homes were rural enough to spare us direct contact with the early cases. My mother died and then my father. My brother fought valiantly but succumbed. His family. My sister. And then it came for Ronin."

"What did you do?"

"I took care of him. I expected to catch it. Everyone caught it. I didn't care. I cared for him through the bleeding and coughing, the aching bones, the diarrhea, the boils. I kept waiting for it all to happen to me. I pictured us dying together."

"But that didn't happen."

She shook her head. "Even before we become witches, potentials are rarely ill. The latent magic in our blood keeps us healthy. And I always had a knack for herbal remedies. I wouldn't have called what I gave Ronin a potion back then, but it worked almost as well as one. I did not die and neither did he. Unfortunately, the time he took to heal was a time our farm went poorly tended. I simply couldn't do it all myself. In 1532, you did not reap what you did not sow."

Raising her mug, she took another sip of the cocoa. Was

she scaring him away? Reminding him that her existence dwarfed his own? She pressed on. Logan must understand what she was, the good and the bad.

"We almost starved to death that winter," she continued. "We survived on pottage and only because we raided the homes of the dead and took their stores of oats and turnips. Very few people survived. At the time, I didn't understand why we had been the lucky ones." Her voice cracked with emotion. "Only later would I find out it was my nature as a potential witch that protected us."

Logan shook his head. "How did you become a witch?"

"I..." She paused. "Would you like to see? I can tell you, but I'd much rather show you."

Logan blinked, probably considering his tolerance to participate in additional magic. "Okay. Show me."

Polina crossed the room to the satchel that waited for her on the floor near the sofa and removed from it a small mirror, unframed and with a jagged edge. She returned to Logan's side and placed it on the table in front of him. She passed her hand over the silver in a long arc. "Reveal."

20

THE BECOMING

S *cotland* 1538

"Somethin's scarin' the sheep," Ronin said.

"Dinna worry 'bout it, love. Come by the fire. I've somethin' to tell ye." Polina smoothed her white shift over the mound of her lower belly and lowered herself into a chair near the hearth of their stone cottage.

The bleating grew louder, more urgent. Almost too much to bear. The animals sounded like they were screaming. "Not now, woman. I won' have the year's work end in the belly of a wolf."

"But Ronin—"

He held up one meaty finger. With his thick mass of red curls tied at the base of his skull, Polina had a clear view of the scar on the underside of his jaw where she'd lanced a particularly large black boil six years ago. She reminded herself that they'd been through worse than whatever was scaring the sheep.

"Ye reckon 'tis the wolves again?" she asked. They'd been wandering closer to the house lately, becoming braver with hunger.

"Aye." He selected a hickory bark torch from beside the door and moved to the fire to light it. "Only one way to ken for certain."

"Ronin, don't. I've a bad feelin' 'bout this." Polina clutched her stomach. "The spirits hound me tonight. My skin prickles."

"Weel then," he said through a smile, "I'll just have to face their magic. No one, ghost or wolf, is taking those sheep."

He slipped out the door into the night. Polina fretted, pacing before the fire. The sheep continued as loud as before, but it was the distant sound of Ronin's screams that spurred her into action. Taking up another torch, she gathered herself and charged out the door.

The night was dark but warm, a waxing moon providing a touch of light. In the distance, down the glade from her stone house, Polina saw a dark figure holding a torch near the sheep's pen. Ronin. She took off running, her slippers pounding the thick grass. But as she neared, she found it was a woman holding the torch, surrounded by seven deformed black dogs. At least, Polina assumed they were dogs. The closest thing she'd ever seen was a wolfhound. These were broader with fangs that protruded from their jowls. They circled the sheep, growling wicked and low.

"Who are ye?" Polina held the torch like a weapon between them.

The woman was tall as a man with long black hair that curled over the shoulders of her gossamer white gown. Her skin was visible through the body-skimming material. She may as well have been naked.

"I am the mother of night," the stranger said.

"Have ye seen me husband?"

The woman pointed toward the pen. Ronin was there, frozen as a statue, hand still held high as if holding a torch that wasn't there. The sheep ran to and fro in terror.

"Ronin!" Polina rushed toward him, scaling the fence to reach him. She shook his shoulder. "Husband. Wake, husband." But Ronin did not even blink, such was his stupor.

The woman curled her thin mouth into an expression that couldn't be confused with a smile. "He will not wake. He will remain thus until you've made your choice."

Polina pivoted to face the woman. "Choice?" She patted Ronin's cheeks and shook him again. His skin was cold, too cold. "What choice?"

"Six years heretofore, I answered your prayer and saved Ronin from death."

Polina shook her head. "I did not pray to thee."

"Not by my true name, but I could hardly hold your ignorance against you. Still, you called and I answered. Ronin lives because of my intervention."

"What do ye want? Payment? A sacrifice?"

The dogs circled faster. "Of sorts. You, Polina, have my blood in your veins. It is time for you to embrace what you are and become like me."

She shook her head violently. "What are ye? I know nothin' of you."

"Yes, you do. Look deep inside yourself. Like me, you are a sorceress of the dead, a witch, an immortal. Accept your duty and you will have the power to free your husband from my spell."

Polina's eyes filled with tears. The woman was obviously the evil spirit she'd feared. But what choice did she have? If she didn't succumb to the witch, Ronin would die.

"Tell me what I must do."

"Come here, child."

Polina dropped her torch in the mud where it extinguished itself. On trembling legs, she approached the woman, who met her halfway, passing through the pen's wooden barrier like a ghost. Polina wept with fear.

The spirit paused, her eyes focusing on Polina's abdomen. "This is unfortunate. An immortal being cannot carry a child."

Polina clutched her stomach protectively.

The woman tipped her dark head. "But this one will not live." She shook her head. "The babe is ill. She will not survive another month."

"A lass?" Polina asked, looking at her hands still gripping her abdomen.

"Yes, daughter. She is not meant to be born. Choose to join me and at least you will have your husband. Deny your rightful place and lose both."

"But I... I cannot." Tears rolled down her cheeks.

"Be wise, daughter. You know what you are. Your potions heal. You are never ill. Your presence can make a flower bloom. You are never cold. You are a witch, Polina, a Hecate. A daughter of the night. Accept it and take what is yours." She pointed at Ronin.

Polina raised her eyes to the woman whose glow rivaled the torch she'd dropped. Swallowing hard, she gave one curt nod.

The spirit smiled, looking genuinely pleased. She reached above her head, closed her fist, and pulled. There was a tearing sound. Confused, Polina focused on where her hand had been but saw only a distant star.

"Eat this," the spirit ordered, extending her fist and opening her hand. In the woman's palm was a piece of the night. Black. Foggy.

Polina grasped it with the tips of her fingers. It vibrated in her grip like a living thing, like a bee held by the wings. But as she brought it to her mouth, the strangest sensation flooded her. She was not afraid. The woman was right; deep inside, hidden somewhere out of sight, she had known she was something more. There was a reason she hadn't caught the plague. She was different.

She wrapped her lips around the slice of darkness in her fingers and swallowed. The texture was of cooked pear, but it tasted of rare wild game. When she pulled her fingers away from her lips, they were red with blood. "What's happening to me?" Polina asked, pitching forward from the pain that had blossomed in her innards.

"You're expanding," the woman said. "Don't fight it."

Fight it? Polina simply wanted to survive it. She fell to her knees, cradling her stomach and wishing for death. The night spun. The stars circled in her vision even with her eyes closed. The scent of wet foliage filled her nostrils. Another wave of pain brought cold. Her entire body plunged into a frozen loch without moving an inch. She couldn't move. She couldn't breathe. Her muscles tightened as tendrils of ice branched from her stomach and infected her limbs. But when she thought for sure that she would die, the pain stopped.

She raised her head. Had the sun risen? No. The moon was its same waxing self. Only, Polina could see in the dark. Every blade of grass, the hair on each of the hounds, the slither of a snake winding over the woman's feet—Polina could see it all. She breathed deeply and got to her feet. Everything around her was connected, held together by invisible string, all part of the same tapestry. The stuff she was made of didn't end at her skin. She continued on into eternity.

"Come, my daughter."

Polina staggered to the woman's side. "Ronin?" she asked.

"Face him, extend your hand, and call to him."

She did as the woman directed. Ronin's eyes fluttered. "Polina?" he said.

"I am here, my love. Come to me."

"What is wrong with your skin?"

She looked down at herself. Her skin was indeed glowing in the dark; the light shone through her clothing. "Nothing is wrong, Ronin. I have become. I am a witch. I am a sorceress of the dead."

Ronin stepped forward, pulling his dagger from his hip. "What have you done with my wife?"

"I am your wife," she pleaded.

He rushed her, thrusting his dagger into her stomach. "Where is my wife!" he yelled.

Her lips parted in a silent scream as she spread her arms and looked down at the dagger protruding from her stomach. Ronin backed away. Slowly, agonizingly, Polina wrapped her hands around the hilt and pulled the knife from her flesh. The pain abated as soon as it was free of her flesh. She handed it back to Ronin. "I am your wife."

He staggered then, shaking his head. She caught him before he could fall and started guiding him inside.

"Wait, daughter," the woman said. "I have a gift for you."

The earth under her feet began to quake, and to her horror, spit out a large book. The symbols on the front were unfamiliar but somehow she understood them. *Elemental Alchemy*.

"Practice. The knowledge will come to you in time."

Polina nodded. The woman disappeared.

Step by step, she dragged the massive man back inside as he mumbled, "My wife is not a witch."

THE PENTHOUSE

As the mirror finished its story, Logan turned toward Polina. "After all of that, after losing your..." He couldn't even say *baby*. The thought was too horrible. "Ronin didn't believe it was you. He tried to kill you."

"Yes," Polina said.

Logan was conflicted over what he saw. On the one hand, he'd wanted to jump into the mirror and shake Ronin, to force him to listen to reason. On the other hand, he wanted to kill the already dead Ronin. *Mine.* From the moment Polina had appeared at his door, he'd considered her *his*. It didn't matter that the man had lived over four hundred years ago. Just seeing him raised Logan's hackles.

"What happened next? Did he come around?" he asked.

"We needed each other to survive. In time, he accepted our circumstances, although he would never accept what I was. We lived out our lives as a brother and sister might. I loved him dearly. He tolerated me. Still, he would not accept a cure from me when he contracted smallpox in

1585. By then, he was old and I hadn't changed at all. He died in the fall, and I buried him on our land."

"Polina..." Logan's face betrayed his sympathy for her.

"Ronin made his choice. I could have cured him, but he refused me. Some part of him believed I was wicked to the very end. So, you see, when I left you in the kitchen that night, it was because I know what happens when a human and a witch fall in love. The human dies, and the witch is never the same."

"I understand why you left, but it doesn't have to be that way."

"It doesn't?" Polina scoffed. She leaned her elbows on the table. "What way can it be?"

Logan took her hands in his and kissed her fingers. "First difference is, I know what you are, and I don't think you're wicked."

"Do you think you could trust me after what happened with Tabetha?"

"I trusted you enough to invite you inside."

She laughed. "I'm not a vampire. It doesn't matter."

"No. After Tabetha, Grateful placed a protective enchantment around my apartment. Nothing supernatural can come in without an invitation. It's why I didn't invite you in the first night you came to my balcony. When I carried you through the door tonight, I was letting you in."

"Oh, Logan." She pressed her fingers into her lips. "Thank you."

"Trust is built over time. We'll never know if this is real unless we give it a chance. I'll take a chance on a witch if you take a chance on a human."

"Take it day by day and see where it leads?"

"Exactly."

She searched his face, the pull of the positivity potion

driving her toward him. "I don't think I have a choice. You asked me what changed, why I came here tonight. It's like someone has tethered me to you. The longer I'm away, the tighter the tether becomes until I can't stand the tension. I have to be near you. Can you feel it? This thing, drawing us together?"

He nodded, swallowed hard.

She rose from her chair and walked around the table to stand in front of him. Hiking her skirt up, she straddled his lap. Logan inhaled through his teeth with a hiss. He was instantly hard. If he made it through the evening without coming in his pants, it would be a miracle. She wrapped her arms around his neck, her breasts grazing his chest. He closed his eyes in an attempt to try to keep it together.

"Make love to me, Logan."

"We should wait," he murmured. "Shooting stars burn out fast." He couldn't risk it with her. He wasn't sure what was happening between them, but he had the sense it was gravely important. It would take will power, but in the long run it would pay off.

"You don't understand. I've got this hunger in me," she pleaded softly in his ear. "I won't be able to function unless it gets fed. I can hardly hold a thought. Please."

He lifted both hands to cup the sides of her face and searched her eyes for any hint of uncertainty. There was none. Fuck will power. Just this once, Logan was going to have dessert first.

FIRST TIME

Polina could feel the moment the wall came down between them. Logan had been holding back, fighting the attraction. She sensed he was afraid of it, afraid of her. The remnants of Tabetha's folly, she assumed. But she had almost a century of pent-up sexual need and after the appetizer she'd experienced on the sofa, she was ready for the meal.

Sure, what Logan said about shooting stars and taking things slow might be true. She didn't know. Frankly, she couldn't focus long enough to consider it. The fire deep within was blazing out of control and all her blood and thoughts had settled low, like a two-ton weight of need between her legs.

His kiss was harder this time, wanting. Her teeth tapped his as their tongues maneuvered for position. Fingers dug into her hair and tugged gently at the roots, the slight pain a counterpoint to the pleasure, salt against sweetness, a sharp edge, an intensity that made her pull him in tighter.

He stood then and guided her through the penthouse, into his bedroom. She had a moment to admire the upholstered headboard and pale gray comforter before he lowered her to her feet.

"Hold that thought," he said. Leaving her, he moved to a closet and pulled out three thick white candles, still in their plastic wrappers. "I keep these for emergencies. I'm designating your pleasure as one worthy of their use." He smiled and unwrapped them, arranging them on the nightstands and the dresser. "Matches," he said, opening and closing his drawers.

"*Incindia*," she whispered, and the three blazed to life.

He straightened, turned from the flame. "Handy."

She shrugged.

"Um, I just realized..." He pointed to his drawer.

She narrowed her eyes.

"It's been over a year." His cheeks blazed red. "Birth control."

A smile broke out across her face. "I'm immortal. I can't get pregnant or carry disease. But thank you for your concern."

He inhaled sharply. "I am the luckiest man alive."

She stepped in closer and reached for the drawstring on his athletic pants. With one tug, they fell from his hips. The bulge behind his briefs made her take pause before she shimmied out of her skirt.

"How do I do this?" He ran his fingers along the front of her corset. His voice broke.

"It ties in the back." She turned on her heel to give him access.

His breath quickened as he loosened the laces. She pulled the corset over her head, along with the peasant blouse. Her wand dropped from its holster and she leaned over to pick it up, teetering on her thigh-high boots. Logan grabbed her hips and pressed himself against her as she scooped it up and placed it on the dresser. And then he was kissing her back, between her shoulder blades, and down each individual vertebrae.

Her breath caught.

"These boots are sexy as hell," he whispered. He groaned, took the back of her cotton briefs in his teeth, and slid them from her body.

She stepped out of them and then turned to face him, wearing nothing but her tall boots. He looked up at her from his place kneeling on the floor, as if she were his whole world, his own personal goddess. And didn't that just make her wet? It had been a long time since anyone looked at her like that.

He grabbed her hips and pulled her forward. Worshipping one hip, then the other, his mouth moved lower. Would he dare kiss her there?

He did, licking up her center and sending her through the roof, the sensation so intense she thought she might pitch over the edge. He seemed to sense her pleasure. Shifting his torso, he hooked one of her legs over his shoulder. She braced herself, digging her fingers in his hair. His tongue picked up the pace. His mouth alternated between sucking and flicking her most delicate flesh. The warm, wet flutter tipped her over the edge, almost immediately. She fell forward, bracing herself on his shoulders, unable to support her own weight as the pleasure rocked her.

He laughed softly, scooping her up and laying her out on the bed. She watched him remove the rest of his clothing, his erection punching out from his body in a way that sent her flying again. He parted her knees with his hands and prowled to hover over her.

"Tell me if this hurts. I'll go slow," he whispered, pressing himself against her.

She wrapped her fingers around the base of his neck and pulled him to her. He kissed her as he entered her, and it did hurt, just a little. But the pain didn't come close to the pleasure. She raised her hips to meet his.

All she could think, through endless sensation, through ecstasy and skin on skin, was he fit. Logan fit her. Every part of her. They came together in one soul-shattering moment. She was still wearing her boots.

After a moment, he pulled back and helped her out of them.

When he tucked her into his bed and curled around her, nuzzling into her neck, she realized she'd vastly underestimated how this encounter would change her. As she slipped into sleep, it was clear the positivity potion had given her exactly what it had promised, and the thing she'd feared most of all.

She was falling in love with Logan.

BREAKFAST

Polina woke to the smell of bacon. She reached over to Logan's side of the bed, still rumpled and warm but empty. He must be making her breakfast. She pulled his pillow to her nose. His scent permeated the cotton. She couldn't help but smile.

Her body was blissfully sore, arms and legs aching from a late night of lovemaking. They'd done it more times than she could count, in ways she'd never imagined possible. She had no regrets. Logan turned out to be a careful and sensitive lover, unselfish, a man worthy of her affections. She hoped to the goddess that she was worthy of his.

In between lovemaking, they'd talked about everything: childhoods, education, hobbies. She'd spent the better part of an hour answering his questions about her time living in England and France, her trip to the New World on a pirate ship, and life among the colonial settlers. He'd told her about culinary school and motorcycles—he hadn't ridden one since he totaled his bike the day she'd saved him. She'd grilled him about the human concept of heaven and being a medium. And through it all, until the second sleep had overcome her, she unraveled Logan like a ball of twine and then rewrapped him carefully around her heart.

Climbing out of bed, she discovered that he'd left a T-shirt on the corner of the bed for her. The words "Imagine Dragons" scrolled in white letters across the chest. She pulled it over her head. In the process, she caught a glance at herself in the mirror above the dresser. Ruined makeup. Knotted hair. This would not do. Reaching for her wand, she focused and said, "*Renova.*" A swirl of sparkling pink energy started at her toes and spiraled up her body and over her head. When it dissipated, her red hair fell in perfectly formed curls to her shoulders. Her face held a hint of light makeup, perfectly applied. Her teeth were brushed, and she smelled slightly of lychee fruit, bright and sweet. She hurried from the room.

Logan was standing at the stove, wearing nothing but a pair of gray cotton shorts. His hair stuck up in the back and out one side, all sandy-blond sexiness. She'd mussed it with her fingers. For a moment, she held perfectly still, watching him crack eggs into a bowl of dry ingredients and whisk the concoction with a fork. Wires hung from his ears, and he sang something under his breath, dancing to the beat. He almost dropped the bowl when he noticed her out of the corner of his eye. He tugged an earbud from his ear.

"You look stunning. Did you find everything you needed?"

She lifted the corner of her mouth and held up her wand.

"Oh... great." He looked flustered. Polina frowned. She shouldn't have used magic. He'd made it clear it made him uncomfortable. She set her wand on the table and crossed into the kitchen in time to watch him pour batter into a pan.

"What are you making?"

"Berry crepes with crème fraîche."

"Mmm." She ran her hands around his waist and squeezed him from behind. "I can't remember the last time I had a crepe."

He turned his head and raised an eyebrow. "You've never had crepes until you've had mine."

Her lips parted. After an awkward pause, she laughed.

"Oh crap," he said, flipping the crepe. "You're going to make me burn breakfast. Damn, woman!"

She planted a kiss on his cheek but was distracted with a barrage of flapping from the balcony. Hildegard knocked her head and wings into the glass. "My familiar," she said. "Something must be wrong."

Polina jogged to the glass doors and popped the lock. "What is it Hildie?"

"Out all night! No message. No enchantment to ensure your well-being. That white mare from the positivity potion left me in its dust in Vermont! I had to go back home and try to conjure something in the mirror. Imagine my surprise." She lowered her voice. "There are some things you can't unsee!"

Polina darted a glance toward Logan, who was plating the crepes and bacon. Of course, he couldn't understand Hildegard. No one could, aside from her. Still, her face burned with embarrassment and a niggling guilt rooted in her gut. If Logan knew that last night was the result of magic, she wasn't sure what he'd do.

"Is everything okay in the ward?"

"Yes. The gargoyles managed. Nothing serious."

"Good."

"But the wolf pack is up to their tricks again. Partying all night with the humans. Calling attention to themselves."

"What?"

"A human police officer was called into camp. Of course, the cause of the complaint was concealed within the boundaries of Silver Sparrow by the time they arrived."

"Too close. We don't need that kind of attention."

"Aye. I don't trust them, my lady. The alpha didn't take you seriously enough yesterday. I'm afraid there'll be killings before he does. You must speak to the alpha again, before the full moon."

Polina nodded. "I'll meet you at home and see to it."

Hildegard took to the air through the glass doors and disappeared from sight.

"Sounds serious," Logan said, placing a plate of crepes and bacon in front of her on the table.

"It is." Pensive, she cut herself off a section and took a bite. The sweetness of the berries was perfectly balanced within the savory crepe. She moaned and closed her eyes. "Goddess, I could get used to this."

He grinned with pride. "I hope you will."

She took another bite.

"I can't understand your owl. Are you going to tell me what that was all about? Or is it top-secret witch stuff?"

"She came to tell me that the new pack of werewolves in my territory is causing trouble again. Their alpha isn't taking the impending full moon seriously."

"Werewolves?" Logan said. "Has Silas contacted you?"

"Who?"

"Silas Flynn, the detective I was with at Grateful's wedding. He's a werewolf."

"Oh... No, I haven't heard from him. Truly he'd have no way to reach me unless he went through Grateful. Why?"

Logan looked down at his plate for a moment. "The night after Lucas's baby shower, a werewolf from Silas's pack was found in the dumpster outside of Valentine's. He was murdered."

Polina inhaled sharply. "Oh no. Does Silas know who's responsible?"

Logan shook his head. "Not yet, but he suspects an escaped convict, a werewolf who has it in for his alpha. A new pack shows up and causes trouble in your ward around the same time a werewolf is murdered? Maybe it's not a coincidence."

"But in Vermont? I've been watching the pack since they moved in six months ago. They're mostly young wolves. A few old. A few sick. They like to drink and get into trouble, but it's hard for me to picture any of them being capable of coordinating a murder in another state. And the alpha is barely more than a kid himself. These wolves seem hardly able to care for themselves."

"Silas is working to find the killer. I told him you were with me that night. He said he might contact you, to see if you'd seen or heard anything."

"He hasn't yet, but I'll speak with him." Polina shoveled in the rest of her crepe in an extremely unladylike fashion and washed it down with the cup of coffee he'd provided. "I've got to go." She hugged him around the neck and kissed his cheek before reaching for her wand and satchel.

"When will I see you again?" he asked.

She ducked into his bedroom to gather last night's outfit. "Soon. The full moon starts tomorrow night and lasts three nights. I won't be able to leave my realm. Let me handle this thing with the werewolves and I'll be in touch."

"Can I call you?"

"I don't have a phone."

"How do I contact you?"

She reached into her bag and retrieved the small mirror,

the one she'd used to show him her past. "Use this mirror. If you need me, pass your hand across the top and call my name three times. I'll come to you as soon as I can."

"Will it work for me? I'm not magic."

"It will work for you." She stepped in closer, lowered her voice and cocked a brow. "And, I beg to differ. You are magic."

He kissed her then, a deep lingering kiss that tasted partly of crepes, coffee, and sleep. She didn't mind in the least.

"Well, it's not the size of the wand, but the magic you can make with it," Logan said with a laugh.

"Oh, I have no problem with the size. Your wand is quite adequate."

"We are talking about my penis, right?"

"Yes."

"I knew that. I just wanted to hear you say it."

She kissed him again, then released a handful of gold dust over her head. She came apart in a shower of gold that blew from his lips and melded into the metal frame of the building.

THE VERY GOOD DAY

Around three o'clock in the afternoon, Logan strutted into Valentine's with a spring in his step and a song on his lips—some hip-hop number from the radio. He whistled the melody as he passed Dustin to get to the kitchen. The guy didn't ask, but the look said it all. Logan never whistled.

After Polina left, he'd finished his crepes, then spent another hour milling around the house and thinking of her. For a good stretch of time, he laid in bed, reimagining every moment of their night together. He refused to wash her plate. At one point, he got to his knees to smell his goddamned couch.

As weird and obsessed as his actions were, his behavior was a sign of something else. Logan was happy. He couldn't remember the last time he felt like this. Totally content. Like he fit in his own skin for the first time ever. He'd never felt this way with Grateful or with any of his girlfriends before her. This thing with Polina, as complicated as it was, felt as natural and right as breathing.

"You're in a good mood," Jonah said.

"It's a good day. A very good day."

"Sounds like someone got lucky last night," Jonah said through a smile.

"You have no idea. I feel like the luckiest man alive."

Jonah plated the burger he'd been working on and slid it under the warmer. He'd handled the lunch rush with ease. The place was running like Logan never left for the night.

Logan tied on an apron and got to work. When it came to cooking, he was comfortable with almost anything. Valentine's served mainly American fare, with the occasional French cassoulet or German schnitzel, depending on the season. But it was the Italian side of the menu that lit his fire. His clam linguine was the best in the business, and his homemade meatballs were so delicious they were known to make grown women weep.

The hours passed like minutes. Not only was Logan doing his favorite thing, cooking, but he was still high from his night with Polina. Around eight, Dustin shouldered open the door. "Logan, someone wants to meet the chef. Table five."

"Got it." He washed up, hoping this was the good kind of meeting and not a complaint. But when he got to table five, it was Grateful and Rick, all dressed up. Lucas sat in his carrier on the table between them. Grateful had an empty plate in front of her with remnants of his clam linguine. The spot on the table in front of Rick was empty, like he hadn't eaten at all.

"What brings you three in tonight?" Logan asked, smiling and shaking Rick's hand.

"Dinner date. We tried your linguine special. It was fabulous, as usual," Grateful said.

Rick added, "Even I tried a bite. The best I've had in centuries." He gestured toward Grateful's plate.

"You didn't want your own?" Logan asked.

Rick shook his head, but it was Grateful who answered. "Rick doesn't need to eat like we do."

All at once, Logan remembered. Caretakers didn't gain nourishment from food. Their witch's blood and sex were their primary sustenance.

"Did you leave room for dessert?" he asked Grateful. "I have a special tiramisu that couples well with an espresso, or maybe a slice of chocolate cake?"

Grateful groaned and held her stomach. "Are you kidding? I couldn't eat another bite."

Rick grinned at her. "She'll regret passing it up at midnight. One tiramisu and one chocolate cake, boxed to go, please."

"You got it." Logan leaned across the table and lifted Lucas from his carrier. "And what about this guy? Did he get something to eat?" Lucas blinked saucer-sized blue eyes at Logan and smiled.

"He's just on rice cereal for now. He'll have to wait for chocolate cake," Grateful said.

Seemingly in response, Lucas began to fuss and then sneezed in Logan's arms. *Flash.* The lights blinked. Logan looked up and then at Lucas, who started laughing. Rick cleared his throat.

"You better check your fusebox, Logan," Grateful said.

Logan's gaze darted to Rick, who gave one curt shake of his head. Gently, he returned Lucas to his carrier. "Yeah. I'll do that. Okay. Two desserts, coming up. You know, Polina and I had our first date over chocolate cake."

He wasn't sure what made him say it. Maybe it was the awkward pause in conversation after the flashing lights. No. That wasn't it. He had to share because the joy he housed over his new relationship with Polina was ample enough to spill over the cup of his soul. He wanted to talk about Polina. He wanted everyone to know she was his. That's how he thought of her. His. He knew it was premature. Sex didn't mean commitment, but he couldn't help himself.

"You went on a date with Polina?" Grateful asked.

Logan nodded. "More than one." Technically they'd never been on a real date, but he considered the cake baking and last night as counting as dates for practical purposes. "I think things are getting serious." He laughed a little. There was more than a little wishful thinking in his statement.

"Hmm." Grateful's eyes shifted to Rick's. "Logan, can I speak to you alone for a moment? It's important."

He didn't like the sound of that or the timing. "Sure," he forced himself to say. "In my office."

He led the way, his stomach sinking. Grateful was a good friend. She'd saved his life more than once. He trusted her. So why was his intuition kicking like a rodeo bull? He took a seat behind his desk.

"What's going on?" he asked, pretending he didn't suspect this was about Polina.

Grateful bit her lip. "Polina told me that she helped you after your accident."

Logan nodded. "She found me on the side of the road and called the ambulance. I guess when she tried to heal me, she had to send my soul to your attic so that I wouldn't die."

Grateful nodded. "For lack of a better way to explain it, she moved your soul prematurely into the sorting queue, effectively putting your body into a coma. She wasn't sure what would happen. She hoped it would give you a few more minutes, time enough for the ambulance to reach you. She also thought you would go to her magical place, her room of reflection, but instead you came to my attic."

"She saved my life." Logan nodded. "That was why we seemed familiar to each other the first time we met."

"Right." Grateful chewed the corner of her lip again.

"You're killing me, Grateful. Just spit it out."

"Remember when you were in my attic, and we had feelings for each other?"

Logan furrowed his brow. "I remember."

"But those feelings weren't real."

"No. They weren't."

"We had those feelings because I was responsible for sorting your soul and a witch can't touch the soul of a human and not share a connection with that human. A strong connection that can be mistaken for love if those involved don't know any better."

Logan froze. A wave of nausea washed over him, and he raised a knuckle to his lips.

"It's just, Polina told me she had feelings for you at the christening party, and I warned her it could be the effects of the magic. I never thought she would act on those feelings."

"She knew?" Logan asked. "She knew that this could be an issue?"

Grateful winced. "We discussed it. She swore she'd stay away from you."

Logan felt dizzy. He held his head in his hands.

Grateful bound around the desk and hugged his shoulders. "Logan, I'm so sorry. I didn't know or I would have warned you earlier. I don't want to hurt you. I just felt like you had the right to know if she hadn't told you."

He nodded. "I should have known. The way it was... it was too perfect. Only magic could be responsible for a feeling like that." His voice cracked when he spoke.

"Oh... Fuck. You have it bad, huh?"

Logan nodded slowly. "You know what's the worst part?

She knew and didn't tell me. She used it to get what she wanted from me. She used me."

Grateful shook her head. "No, Logan. It's happening to her too. She likely thinks it's as real as you do."

"But you told her. You warned her."

"I did. But maybe she couldn't resist the temptation."

Logan balled his hands into fists and shook his head. "I made it clear to her that I detested being manipulated by magic. She had every chance to tell me the risks. No. This is inexcusable."

Grateful frowned. She backed to the other side of the desk.

"Thank you, Grateful. It couldn't have been easy for you to tell me this. I appreciate it."

Both of her palms hit the desk in front of him with a slap. "Not every relationship has to be *the* one. If Polina makes you happy, there's no harm in letting the relationship run its course. She's single. You're single. The magic will fade in time. It did between us."

Logan stared at her, eyes seeing right through her. "After Tabetha, I'd rather avoid prolonging the inevitable. Artificial feelings are no better than artificial ingredients. I don't use any when I cook. It's a lie, and in the end the customer gets cheated. I'd rather not cheat myself out of something real when it comes to love. Every moment living the illusion is a moment I'm not moving on to something better."

The corners of her mouth dipped. "I'm sorry I hurt you once again."

"Don't be. This was necessary."

Grateful stood and moved for the exit. "I better get back to Rick." She opened the door but paused. "Logan, can I ask you something?"

"Sure."

"Do you think Lucas is, um, normal?"

Red alert! As much as he owed Grateful the truth, this felt like a landmine.

"What do I know?" he said. "I couldn't tell you what a normal baby is like. Never had one." He shrugged his shoulders. It was an honest answer.

Grateful nodded. "Thanks."

She walked out the door, leaving Logan to pull himself together.

2 5

BLOODRIGHT PACK

Some days are magic. As Polina glided through the thickly treed forest of Silver Sparrow mountain, joy surrounded her in a visible golden aura. She felt physically stronger for having spent the night with Logan, like she lived in a world where nothing bad could ever happen.

It was a sunny day. A perfect, beautiful day.

And then the forest opened, and she saw what Hildegard had seen. The Bloodright pack. To her horror, the pack had grown again. No less than thirty werewolves milled around the caverns, some in tents, some huddled around small campfires. She scanned the crowd and found Alex talking to a waif of a girl who looked barely eighteen. She was nursing a nasty wound on her shoulder that was still bleeding.

Polina strode up to the alpha from behind and grabbed his upper arm.

He jerked from her grip and turned violently, baring his teeth. Alex advanced on her, human hands swiping at her head.

Polina dodged the attack and raised her wand. "Alex, we need to talk."

The werewolf took three big breaths before reining in his rage. He turned to the girl. "Give me a sec, Carla. I need to deal with this." *This* was Polina. Without another word, he led the witch to the edge of the wood, away from the rest of the pack.

"What do you want?" he asked through his teeth.

"What's going on here? I warned you about the risk of shifting so close to the new human campsite and instead of taking precautions, you tripled the size of your pack?"

Alex lifted his faded blue Cubs hat and scrubbed his head. "Pack business."

"Your pack is on my land. Now it's my business."

He puffed out his cheeks and blew a mouthful of air in her direction. "The timing isn't the best, I agree, but it couldn't be helped. See, my pack had to absorb another pack that lost its alpha family. They had nowhere to go. I gave them sanctuary here."

Polina frowned. "What happened to their alpha family?"

Alex shifted from foot to foot. "Murdered."

"Murdered!" After what Logan had told her about the werewolf found dead behind his restaurant, this couldn't be a coincidence. "Where was their home before this?"

"Catskills, New York."

"And they couldn't stay there? There was no one to take over leadership?"

Alex's expression morphed to something sinister, then recovered. The naive young man act snapped into place fast enough for her to question if she'd been mistaken. Was the darkness ever there at all?

"They were afraid and asked to join us. This place is safer."

"Because of me. Because of my spell."

"It's very possible that a human was responsible for the deaths of their pack royalty."

"Bullshit. No human could take out a family of werewolves."

"I'm not sure. Like I said, I was just trying to help. They've decided to be sworn into our pack today."

"Is that why the girl's shoulder is wounded? Was her pack symbol removed?"

"It's customary."

Customarily brutal, Polina thought.

"They'll be integrated. Every new member will have a sponsor. The men will form families."

"Families? Like they'll choose wives?"

He nodded. "Sometimes. Wolves mate for life, but until they're mated they can have up to five females they, uh, are domestic with. Others become like children. Everyone will be taken care of."

"How do you plan to keep them away from the humans when they shift tomorrow night? They look young. They'll have no fear, Alex. Twenty human families are camping down the mountain from you, some with children."

He rubbed the back of his neck. "You're the witch of the realm. Cast another spell to keep them safe."

"Cast another—" She balled her hands into fists and rested them on her hips. "You fail to understand where I'm coming from, Alpha. This is my ward. You are allowed to stay here under my good graces. If you don't bring your pack to heel... if we have another incident with the human police... not only will I send anyone involved to hell, but I will evict you."

The ground under his feet rumbled with her anger. There was a reason Polina made the Green Mountains her home. The mountain rock got its distinctive green color from minerals, minerals that held a high concentration of natural metal.

"You'll kick us off the mountain?" Alex chuckled under his breath, not at all flustered by the small earthquake going on below him. His eyes flicked up and down her body. "Okay, honey. I understand." His patronizing tone made her skin crawl.

"If you understand, then tell me what actions you will take to ensure the safety of those humans."

Lifting the corner of his mouth, he said, "In addition to giving them my alpha command, I'll walk the pack a few miles up the mountain before sunset and string up some chickens. Fresh meat, along with the natural quarry in that area, should keep our wolves more than busy."

She gave him a curt nod. "Do it. I will reinforce the border. Tell your pack that if one hair on a human's head is harmed, they will have to answer to me."

He raised two fingers to his forehead and saluted her, the gesture dripping with sarcasm. Turning, he wandered off toward his pack.

"Asshole," she said under her breath. She took one last look at the men and women gathered in front of the caverns. Something didn't add up. The new wolves were young, painfully thin. Surely this wasn't the entire Catskills wolf pack. But where were the rest of them? And more importantly, who was responsible for killing their alpha?

Moving toward Aurorean House, Polina made a decision. It was time for her to get better acquainted with werewolf society. And her first stop was detective Silas Flynn.

SILAS

Polina arrived at the Carlton City Police Department at a quarter till noon the next day. As she walked into the busy station house, a young woman in a blue uniform paused to assess Polina's appearance. Polina was wearing the same thing she'd worn when she went to see Alex, a sleeveless blue linen gown with silver buttons down the front—Roman denarius coins she'd found on a pirate ship in the 1700s. The dress had two slits, one for each leg, that came to mid-thigh and showed off tall boots.

The young woman assessing Polina wasn't human, although what she was remained a bit of a mystery. Her aura and the slightest point to her ears suggested elf, but her height and shape bespoke a human or two in her lineage.

"You want office 104A. It's back there." She pointed around the corner.

"How did you know?"

She tipped her head and lowered her voice. "Silas is the only supernatural detective that serves your kind on this force." She said it matter-of-factly, like there was no disputing Polina's status as a witch. Ah well, she'd never tried particularly hard to fit in. She nodded her head in lieu of thanking the girl and proceeded to Silas's office.

Silas hunched over his desk, staring into an ancient leather tome with yellowed pages. He was engrossed enough that he didn't seem to notice when Polina walked in his open door. His wolfish appearance was especially severe today, no doubt due to the forthcoming full moon. He already had a fully developed five o'clock shadow and his nose twitched in a canine sort of way.

"I'm not ignoring you, Polina. Have a seat. Give me two minutes." He scratched a series of notes on a yellow legal pad. Sitting brought Polina's face closer to the pages, and she noticed the book was in a different language, one she did not know. With a straight back, she folded her hands in her lap and waited patiently.

He scribbled a few more feverish notes, then sat back and placed the pen down. "What can I do for you?"

"Logan told me about the werewolf that was found murdered behind his restaurant. He said you wished to speak with me about it."

"I did, at first, until I realized you couldn't possibly know anything about the murder. The report came back from forensics. Time of death was twelve thirty that afternoon."

"That was—"

"During Lucas's baptism. I was sitting right behind you in the church."

"But then it happened in broad daylight."

"Strange, right? Very few supernaturals would be bold enough to attack during the day, and fewer still could tear apart a werewolf."

"Rules out vampires and ghouls. I'd be tempted to think it was a witch, although Grateful or I would likely have sensed the presence of another Hecate. An ordinary practitioner of witchcraft might escape our sight. Maybe a type of fae?"

Silas tapped his thumb on the back of his opposite hand. "It's unusual for someone to come to see me about a case when I haven't invited them here. Is there something you want to tell me?"

Polina nodded and shifted in her chair. "A pack of werewolves have taken up residence in my territory. They are a young group. Some of them look like they've rarely, if ever, shifted before."

"Not unusual. When werewolves are born, they look and act exactly like humans. Their parents teach them what will happen when they grow up. They tell them they'll shift. But it doesn't happen until puberty. Once the teenage hormones kick in, you get the combination of common teenage rebellion and wolfish rage. It leads to a high rate of runaways who tend to join up and support each other."

"Right. Although I haven't had many werewolves come through my woods over the centuries, I do know something about your kind. I presumed this was a young, inexperienced group as you suggest. Only, their pack is growing at an alarming rate."

Silas's eyebrows shot up, two fuzzy brown caterpillars arching toward his hairline. "Growing? From where? There aren't that many werewolf families in Vermont."

"First there were three, then twelve, and now thirty. Their alpha told me they absorbed the members of a pack from the Catskills who lost their alpha family."

The detective froze, his face paling. "He told you the alpha family of the Catskills is dead?"

Polina nodded. "Yes. He was very clear on that. And the young wolves he took in needed a home."

"Excuse me." Silas pulled out his phone and made a call. Polina could hear ringing. When no one picked up, Silas made another call and another, his face growing more and more grim with each unanswered ring. Finally, around call number eight, someone answered. Silas exchanged words in another language and hung up the phone. He covered his mouth as if he might vomit.

"The alpha family of the Catskills leads the Crescent Star pack." He pulled up his sleeve to reveal a phoenix tattoo. "Do the new wolves have a tattoo like this, only with a crescent moon?"

"The new wolves have wounds on their shoulders where their pack tattoos used to be."

"Fuck!"

"I'm guessing that's undesirable?" Polina frowned.

Silas tore off a piece of paper from his yellow pad and placed it in front of her with a pencil from his drawer. "The alpha who told you this, did he have a pack tattoo?"

"Yes."

"Can you draw it for me?"

She quickly sketched the harvest moon with the three claw marks ripping through it. She handed it to Silas. "He told me they call themselves the Bloodright pack."

Silas bolted out of his chair, digging his fingers into his hair. "Fuck. Fuck. Fuck no."

"What is it? What's wrong?"

Silas walked around Polina to stick his head into the hall, look both ways, and then close the door to his office. "The werewolf that was murdered and found in Logan's dumpster wasn't just a member of my pack. He held a position called Zafka. It's a security position. He was a decoy for … the alpha of my pack."

"What?" Polina's fingers gripped her wand tighter.

"The alpha family of the Catskills carry the last name of Maldivess. I know them well. They are werewolf royalty. There are seven members of that family. Seven extremely strong wolves. None of them answered their private lines. None of them have checked in with the werewolf council before the full moon. I've sent a member of my pack to their homes to check on them. The pack tattoo you just drew for me isn't a known pack. They have no representation on the council. "

"He said his name was Alex."

Silas snorted with anger. "Fucker is using his real name. Alex was cast out of the society three years ago after he killed his parents. He was imprisoned but last year he escaped. This whole time I've operated under the assumption that he was here, in the city." He shook his head. "I couldn't find him because he was hiding in your realm. I'm afraid for you, Polina. This guy could be the most dangerous werewolf that ever lived."

"You're telling me that a werewolf that other werewolves call the most dangerous of their kind is living in my realm?"

"I'm afraid so." Silas crossed his arms over his chest. "Alex isn't just a werewolf. You need to understand what you are up against."

"I'm listening."

"Five years ago, Alex was a member of the Lycanthropic Society—the high werewolf council. The Lycanthropic Society consists of representatives from the twelve alpha families."

"Twelve? There must be more packs than twelve in the world."

He nodded. "Of course there are, but all families are descended from the primary twelve. Unlike what you see in the movies, werewolves are born, not made. If I bit you in this form or my wolf form, there would be no consequence aside from the physical wounds of the bite itself. Werewolfism is a dominant gene. Over time, werewolves have mixed with other creatures and races, humans, other shifters, etcetera, but even a drop of werewolf blood in your heritage will make you a werewolf. It is said that all werewolves descended from twelve purebloods that originated at the beginning of time."

"That far back?"

He shrugged. "Are we here to talk origination stories or about the danger you are in?"

"Sorry. Twelve purebloods equal twelve alpha families."

"Exactly. Careful records have been kept to determine which families have the highest concentration of pure blood. My family is an alpha family. We are descendants of the Fireborn pack." He tapped the skin beneath his tattoo. "Alex was the son of an alpha family just like me."

"The Bloodright pack."

He shook his head. "The Nightstar pack."

Polina looked at him, confused.

Silas continued, "Alex was always a difficult child. Never knew where to draw the line, you know? Impulsive. Reckless."

"A bad dude. I get it."

"When he was of age, he met a dragon fae named Nickelova Rallinth, a princess of her people, while traveling in Siberia with his parents. She fell in love with him."

"Dragon fae? I didn't even know there were any left." Dragon fae channeled the magic of dragons. Since dragons had been hunted practically to extinction, dragon fae were likewise rare.

"Few, but a powerful few. He led her on, used her. He

convinced her that he would marry her if she provided him with a dowry, a token of her love. She made him an amulet from dragon's scale, a powerful magical object no one had possessed before. Once he had it, he left her. He broke her heart."

"I like this guy less and less each minute."

"You've heard the expression: *Hell hath no fury like a woman scorned?*"

"Of course."

"Well, a dragon fae scorned will make you beg for the fury of a woman. She did not go gentle into that good night. Nickelova contacted Mondo Ravien, Alex's father and alpha of Nightstar pack, and demanded the return of the amulet. Mondo apologized for his son and ordered Alex to return the magical item."

"Let me guess. He didn't."

Silas shook his head. "It isn't simply rebellious when the son of an alpha disobeys a direct order. It is impossible for a pack member to act against the alpha's wishes. But Alex was one of the rare exceptions. Because his father had mated with his purebred mother, Alex's blood was stronger than most, and being the oldest son of an alpha, he was next in line for the throne. He was able to resist the alpha bond and challenge his father for the role with the help of the amulet.

"He broke our oldest and most sacred law. No wolf of any pack can disobey a Lycanthropic Society alpha without punishment from the rest of the society. Alex did. He murdered his father, then used the power of the amulet to transport himself to a place or places unknown, and left the rest of his family to face the wrath of Nickelova."

"That doesn't sound good."

"It wasn't. With the amulet gone, Nickelova flew into a rage and accused the Nightstar pack of stealing it. She burned Alex's mother alive, along with his younger brother. His older sister survived only because she was away at college at the time and had stayed behind in the States."

"For the love of the goddess..."

With a deep sigh, Silas spread his hands on his desk and hunched his shoulders. "The sister mated a high-ranking male in Nightstar and saved the pack by providing an alpha family. She helped us find Alex. He was hiding near his family's home in a suburb of Chicago. But he'd already hidden the amulet by that point. We never found it. Alex was tried, found guilty, and sentenced to life. He was sent to the supernatural wing of a maximum security prison in Illinois."

"How did he escape?"

Silas shook his head. "We don't know."

Polina stiffened. "So he escaped without notice and is taking his revenge on society families?"

Silas scratched his cheek, his beard seeming to grow by the minute. "I think it's more than that." He reached for Polina's drawing of Alex's tattoo. Flipping through the tome in front of him, he found a page and turned the book to face her. "This is the symbol of the Nightstar pack."

The image in the book was of a simple harvest moon. "No claw marks."

"Alex is calling his pack Bloodright. He's wearing a symbol of a divided moon. I think he's trying to return to the society that rejected him. Only, the society as it stands would never allow him back. He's trying to change it. A few strategic murders and enough wolves behind him, and he might be able to force his way back into leadership."

"I'm guessing that would be bad."

"Terrible. Alex never liked the rules. He thought of

werewolves as the superior species. With him in charge, it would be chaos."

"Then I'll have to stop him. I'll sentence him to the hell-mouth immediately."

"No. You can't!" Silas held out his hands desperately. "If you leave the new pack without an alpha before the full moon, they'll lose their minds. I'm not speaking figuratively on this. Most, if not all, will go insane. You'll have a blood-bath on your hands. They'll tear apart anything they see."

Polina shifted nervously in her chair. "But the full moon is tonight. Surely you aren't asking me to babysit a killer and his pack. There are human families mere miles from their camp. I'm not sure any spell can hold back that many wolves. I've never done that type of magic before."

"That's exactly what I'm asking you. We need to know where he is so we can apprehend him. He'll have a Zafka, a decoy. All alphas have them. It is imperative that my people are able to find and apprehend the true Alex Ravien and successfully transition his pack to a new alpha."

"Oh hell," Polina cursed, rubbing her head. She rose and tapped her wand on her palm. "I'll do what you ask, but you better move on this, Silas Flynn. I can't control these wolves forever. I'll do my best, but if it's not handled by the second night of the full moon, all bets are off. I'll handle things my way, even if I have to send them all to the grave."

"I understand. But Polina?"

"Yes."

"There's something else."

"You're kidding."

"The amulet was never found. Alex picked your realm because no magical being can detect him there due to your enchantment. There's too much magical interference. He feels safe there. His guard will be down. But it's also likely that the thing that drew him to your realm in the first place was the amulet. He may be looking for it, and if he gets it, with the number of wolves you say he has in his pack, it would take a dragon to stop him."

"That doesn't make sense. If Alex hid it, wouldn't he know exactly where to find it? Wouldn't he have found it by now?"

"Not necessarily. The same enchantment keeping him safe could be interfering with him tracking the talisman. Even if he were working alone when he hid it—and we don't know that for sure—magic can be very disorienting."

Polina shook her head. "It's impossible. I would know if a magical object crossed the border of my realm."

Silas let out a deep breath. "He would have hidden it a little over two years ago."

Polina froze. "But that's when—"

"When you were buried under Tabetha's persigranate trees, and she was controlling your realm."

27

THE MISUNDERSTANDING

Polina left Silas's office feeling overwhelmed. She needed to get back to her realm and fast. It would take a stronger spell than she'd ever performed to keep the Bloodright pack where she wanted them. She had serious doubts there was enough time to execute it successfully, if at all. With a pinch of gold dust between her fingers, she prepared to sweep home and reference her grimoire about the task. There was too much at stake. She could not fail.

In a fog of spinning thoughts, she almost rammed into Grateful, who had turned a blind corner from the foyer.

"Oh!" she said. "Polina, what are you doing here?"

"Meeting with Silas," she said.

Grateful frowned. "Me too."

"I'll leave you to it." Normally, Polina might chat about the problem with Grateful, but the time pressure she was under meant she'd have to leave the explaining to Silas. She raised the gold dust above her head.

"Wait." Grateful caught her wrist. "I want to talk to you about Logan."

"Logan? Is he all right?" Polina forgot her rush and searched Grateful's face.

"Certainly not. He's in love with you! I warned you, Polina. You touched his soul. He couldn't help but be attracted to you. How dare you take advantage of him?"

Polina shook her head. "You think I used him? What, for sex?"

Grateful scoffed. "I don't know what you used him for, but you knew the attraction wasn't real and you acted on it. He's only human. You'll break his heart."

"I didn't."

"Of course you did! I saw him at Valentine's last night. Logan told me what happened between you."

Polina shook her head. "No. I mean, it wasn't what you think. I used the positivity potion and it led me right to his door."

Grateful stiffened. "No..."

With a nod of her head, Polina explained in quick, breathy spurts. "I couldn't stop thinking about him. I was obsessed. I used your spell, like you suggested. All I wanted was the endless yearning to cease. But when I drank the positivity potion, it led me straight back to him, Grateful. I love him. I never thought I could say that again, but goddess help me, I do. I'm so glad it was him." She grabbed her chest. "I wasn't using him. I just couldn't deny my feelings for him a moment more."

"Oh no." Grateful pressed her fingers into her lips.

"What did you do?"

"I told him."

"What?"

"I told him about the residual soul magic."

"How could you?" Polina yelled. "He'll never forgive me. He'll think I used him like Tabetha!"

"I didn't know! I thought you had."

"Was he very angry?"

Grateful's face screwed up. "I can fix this. I'll explain everything. Logan will listen to me."

Unbidden tears spilled over Polina's lower lids. "You don't understand. Logan will never love me if he thinks I used magic. *Any* magic. It's over. He'll never trust me again."

"I'll talk to him."

Polina raised the gold dust over her head. "I have to go. People's lives are at stake. But I'm not sure I can forgive you for this, Grateful." She sobbed, then caught her breath. "Strike that. Maybe I should thank you. We all know how it would end eventually. Maybe you've just accelerated the inevitable."

"Don't say that."

"Why not? It's true. Humans die. Humans leave. Maybe it's better it ends before it ever begins." She released the dust, Grateful's devastated expression dissolving as Polina blended into the pipes of the water fountain in the hall. It was more than her molecules that came apart. Her soul shattered with her body. Somehow, she had to find the strength and will to pull herself together. She didn't have time to grieve the loss. There was work to be done.

2 8

OVER

The weight in Logan's heart seemed to grow heavier by the minute, as did the fire in his blood. Twenty times today he'd picked up the mirror Polina had given him, intending to break up with her. She'd violated his trust, manipulated him like some sort of toy. The only thing that stopped him was he wanted to do it in person. He wanted to see her face when he told her he'd figured her out. He knew what she'd done. Would she deny it? Regret it?

A flash of blue almost knocked him out of his chair. "What's happening?" He positioned the silver squarely in front of him.

The mirror melted into a reflective pool of metal. Like a stone dropped in a puddle, concentric circles rippled from the center to the edges of his reflection. The movement blurred his image and then morphed into one with delicate features and full lips. When the reflection smoothed out again, he was looking at Polina.

"Logan, I just spoke to Grateful. I can explain—"

"You knew that the soul magic was the reason for our

attraction, and you didn't tell me," Logan snapped. "You used me."

"No. You don't understa—"

"I understand that you took advantage of a side effect of magic to get what you wanted from me. I understand that you are just like every other witch. You take what you want, when you want it, and don't worry about how you hurt anyone else in the process."

"No, Logan, I love you. I wouldn't hurt you."

"Stop lying to me!" A hot swell of anger balled Logan's hands into fists. He would not allow this to happen again. "My heart is not a toy for your entertainment. It's over, Polina."

"No! No, Logan. Listen to me!"

"I'm done. I warned you not to use magic on me. You used me and you lied."

"I didn't mean to—"

Logan slammed his fist on the table, sending a ripple through her reflection. "It's over!" He ground his teeth together. "You're no better than Tabetha."

Polina's reflection morphed from desperation to outright horror. He was almost convinced he'd hurt her, but then he remembered that a mere human could never hurt a witch.

In anger, he picked up the mirror and hurled it at the floor. It shattered, the pieces melting and seeping through the floorboards.

"Fuck. Good." He stood and paced his penthouse condo. "I am done with the lies. I am done with the supernatural mess. Fuck it all." He grabbed his keys off the counter and headed for the elevator, desperate for a fresh start.

29

SHATTERED

Polina's heart stopped as Logan's face disappeared from the *lucubratus*. The way the reflection had frozen, then cracked, she was sure he'd shattered the mirror and with it, her heart. He'd ended it. The worst part was he hadn't given her a chance to explain or apologize. He hadn't believed her feelings were real.

She staggered backward. The crushing realization that once again she'd been left, abandoned by a human, plowed through her. Her mind raced. The room of reflections, the seat of her power, returned everything she was sending out. A million visions of Logan came back to her in the diamond-like facets of the room: the way he looked at her the first time they'd met, their first kiss, the night they spent together.

A large fragment of mirror directly in front of her replayed the night she'd come to him on his balcony. He'd wanted so badly to prove to her that he was not a fragile human. As her tears turned to silver, carving trails down her cheeks and staining her shirt, no part of her thought of him as fragile. If anything, he was dangerous. He'd ruined her. She collapsed to her knees.

"My lady?" Hildegard soared into the room and landed on the floor in front of her. "Is there anything I can do?"

"No," Polina rasped. "Again. It happened again! They leave. They always leave." She spread her hands. "Five hundred years, Hildie. Am I not worthy of love? Will I never know what it is to be truly loved?"

The wise old owl hopped closer. "Of course you are worthy. And you are already loved. *I* love you. It's not the romantic type you were hoping for, but it is real and it is forever."

Polina let out a deep sob and cupped her familiar's feathery face. "I love you too, sweet bird."

Hildegard sighed. "You took a risk. You gave him your heart and it didn't work out."

Liquid metal spilled from Polina's stained cheeks. "Yes."

"But life goes on."

"Yes, it does," she whispered. "Mine goes on forever. And suddenly, forever seems longer than it did before."

"I am sorry, my lady. And I do hate to push, but the hour grows late. You must start the potion to protect the humans right away. There's no time."

Polina wiped her face, absorbing the liquid metal through her skin, and forced herself to stand. Her stomach churned, but she closed her eyes and centered herself. With a slow swipe of her wand, Logan's image disappeared from the mirrors around her. She cleared her throat.

"Let us begin. We have work to do."

30

DESPERATION

Logan strode into the Carlton City humane society with a singular purpose. He needed a pet, another living creature to focus on and occupy his time. With Jonah helping out at Valentine's, the restaurant would survive without him for a day or two while he licked his wounds. He was too depressed to cook. Silas had suggested a dog could be family. He needed that right now. He needed something, anything, to help fill the gaping hole in his chest.

"What type of pet are you considering?" The woman behind the counter's nametag read Carol. She wore a black polo and khaki pants but did not smile. Instead, she seemed size him up for pet ownership, more than willing to censure him and his plans if necessary.

"I've always considered myself a dog person."

"What kind of dog?"

"Labrador, golden retriever. You know, a bigger breed that likes to play."

"You got a fenced yard?"

"Uh, no. I live in a penthouse condominium."

She burst into laughter. "You will not be bringing home a large dog."

Logan rubbed the back of his neck. "What kind of dog do you recommend then?"

"For you? I don't recommend a dog. How about a guinea pig or a rabbit?" She opened the door to a room of cages containing small animals.

"Not what I had in mind," Logan said, staring at a pair of hamsters. "I just need something that's going to engage with me, you know? I don't want an animal that's in a cage all day."

"Rabbits can be litter trained."

Logan shook his head.

"Well, how about a cat? Certain cats have personalities similar to dogs. Some can even learn to play fetch."

Considering it, Logan gave her a small smile. "Yeah. I think a cat might be good."

"Come this way."

He followed Carol through a door labeled Cat Room. Every imaginable type of cat filled the four walls. A humungous orange tabby with a pushed-in face clawed at him from a carpeted stand.

"Don't mind Oscar. He's grumpy." She lifted a calico kitten from the floor. "This one here is just a couple of weeks old. Easily trainable. Good disposition."

Logan pulled the kitten into his arms and scratched it behind the ears. It leaned into his fingers and closed its eyes. It was an agreeable animal. Perfect in some ways. He was sure Carol was right; this cat could adapt to almost any environment. But as Logan looked at the tiny feline, he felt no connection with it. For some reason he didn't fully understand, it just didn't feel right. He bent over and put the kitten down.

Carol frowned. "Well then, let me see..." She pressed her pointer finger into her chin and looked around the room. Logan did too. As his eyes fell on cat after cat, he discounted each one. Too old. Too hairy. Too mean. Too sleepy. And then his gaze fell on something interesting.

Crouched low and ready to spring, a white shorthair prepared to jump to the next carpeted tower. A patch of brown fur over one eye made him look like a pirate. Logan noticed a thin hairless scar behind his left ear. When the cat leapt, it hit its head on the opposite post and fell to the floor, crying.

"Oh, Bonny girl, when will you learn?" Carol picked the cat off the floor and placed it on the platform it was targeting. It was a *her*, not a him. Hmm. Logan took a closer look. Where the cat's tail should have been was nothing but a stump, and to his surprise, she only had three legs. He hadn't noticed before because the good leg was facing him, hiding what was missing.

"What happened to that one?"

"Hit by a car. Barely survived, the poor girl. We named her Bonny after the pirate Anne Bonny because of her patch. Maybe we can get her a peg leg, huh?" Carol laughed.

"I'll take that one," Logan said.

Carol shook her head. "You don't want this cat. She's special needs. She loses her balance all the time. Cries incessantly because she can't do the things she wants to do. And she gets depressed. Sometimes she hardly eats. To be honest, I'm not sure how long she'll make it."

Logan stepped over to Bonny and scooped her up into his arms. She laid her head on his bicep as if she didn't have the energy for anything more and blinked up at Logan. He rubbed circles over the scar behind her ear. The purr she rewarded him with seemed too loud to come from such a small body. All he could think was that this cat was like him, a survivor. He could relate to this cat. "She's perfect. I'll take her."

Carol shrugged, eyeing Bonny in his arms. "Okay. Why the hell not? Come on up to the counter and I'll ring your adoption fee. She's on a few medications. I'll get you a list and instructions. Oh, and she needs a special litter box because she has trouble getting into the ones with the higher edge."

He grinned and kissed Bonny's head. "It's fine. Whatever she needs."

31

PREPARATIONS

"Hildegard, bring me the wolfsbane."

Polina huddled over the cauldron, stirring with two hands. She had to. The potion within was thick with molten silver and twenty-five other rare ingredients from her stores. The heavy mixture had taken her hours to create. Long hours she spent weeping over her work.

Logan was gone. The only good thing about her broken heart was it drove her to try harder, and it had paid off. This was the most potent wolf repellent she'd ever made. She'd surround the human campsite with it, then warn the campers of a wolf attack in the area. She'd tell them they shouldn't venture out at night. With any luck, the humans would stay on their side of the line, and the wolves would avoid the campsite altogether.

Hand to the back of her nose, Polina breathed through her mouth as the repellent neared completion. It smelled of a cross between raw sewage and a chemical treatment plant. Hildegard coasted over the pot and dropped a talonful of wolfsbane into the mix. Bubbles formed like a rich head on a freshly poured draught beer. Polina stopped stirring.

Copper-orange fumes rose from the potion. "It's ready." Polina pulled a glass decanter from a rack in her kitchen and ladled in the syrupy brew. She filled another and another.

"Not a moment too soon. The sun is setting," Hildegard said. "I am worried about you, crying all day over the human. Will you be strong enough to do this?"

"I'll have to be. What good is being immortal if you can't push the boundaries of existence every now and then?"

"Hmm." Hildegard flapped her wings disapprovingly.

"Let's get on with it. Help carry these out front." Polina grabbed her wand and charged out into the front yard. She cast her eyes up to the three gargoyles who guarded her home, perched on the Tudor's gables. The sun hadn't fully set yet. It would require magic to wake her three guardians early.

"*Excitae*," she commanded, raising her wand. The green-stained copper above her twitched and then the metal-on-metal sound of colliding swords rang out with the stretch of gargoyle wings. "Nicodemus, come."

With his great curled horns and demon-like face, Nicodemus was a frightening sight to behold but a loyal and faithful guardian. He soared down from the eastern gable and bowed to her. "What is your command, mistress?"

"Take your brethren and distribute this potion evenly around the human camp. There are twelve of these." She handed him the decanter. "Be discreet. It won't do to frighten the humans."

"Yes, my lady."

Skogal coasted from the center gable and landed on her left.

"Good evening, Skogal." The gargoyle's tongue lolled

from the corner of his mouth. "Follow Nicodemus and do as he does."

The gargoyle bowed low enough for his snout to touch the dirt. He grasped the decanter Hildegard brought from the house and focused on Nicodemus with the intensity of a trained dog.

Rohilda yawned as she landed and waited while Polina brought her another decanter.

"Do you understand what you must do?" Polina asked her.

The female gargoyle nodded her metal head, her keen eyes shifting toward the human camp.

"Very well. I will leave the rest here on the stoop for you. I will check your progress at sundown."

Polina watched as the three took to the air and glided south toward the campground. She ran into the house and grabbed the other containers, placing them outside her door.

Hildegard landed on her shoulder. "You'd better have the gargoyles keep watch on the border tonight."

"Oh, I plan to. But you and I are going to do better than that. We are going to spy on the wolves and go where they go."

The owl ruffled her feathers. "I don't like this. Wolves eat owls, you know. Couldn't we just use the mirror?"

"We'll be careful. I don't trust them, Hildie. My mirror will show us any acts of harm the wolves might attempt tonight, but I want to know more. I want to see the shift. It might hold a clue to the pack's intentions. If the alpha, Alex, is after the dragon fae amulet as Silas fears, following him will be our best chance to intercept it."

"As you wish," Hildegard said, her tone reluctant and longsuffering. "Don't listen to the wise old owl. Force us both to death's door."

Polina grimaced. "It's our responsibility. It's why we're here." Squaring her shoulders, she led the way into the woods.

Renegade Caverns came into view just as long purple clouds chased the sun from the sky like the fingers of a closing fist. Following Polina's command, Hildegard took to the trees as Polina morphed into the reflective metallic form that made her virtually invisible. She silently navigated her woods, stopping behind the broad trunk of a pine tree near the clearing to spy on the gathering wolves. Not that she was surprised, but Alex hadn't kept his promise about taking the pack farther up the mountain, and there was not a chicken carcass in sight.

Alex stood on a massive stump at the center of the pack, naked, as were all the other wolves. Polina supposed if your body would shift, it didn't make sense to rip your clothes. The stump serving as alpha's stage hadn't been there yesterday. Around the bottom, faces of wolves, claw marks, and harvest moons were carved into the wood. A totem pole of sorts... and a pulpit.

"Our time is coming," he said to them. "For some of you, this will be your first shift. It will be painful. Don't fight it. If you fight the change, chances are you'll lose your mind as well as your body. The pack needs your mind." Alex removed a square of fabric from his pocket and handed it to a man on his left. The man sniffed it and passed it to the woman next to him. "When the shift comes, I want you nine to head up the mountain." He pointed to a group of men and women beginning to stretch and groan in front of him. "You eight go east. You eight, west. And the rest of you, come with me."

Polina eyed Alex and the remaining four. There was only one direction left to go, toward the humans. What were his intentions? If Silas was right, they were looking for the amulet. She'd have to keep her eyes open and intervene if they found it. If she was capable of intervening. She was already exhausted, and her first priority was the humans at the border.

Above her, the darkness finally took hold, the full moon shining like a beacon from the night sky. Human screams mixed with beastly howls, a horrible din that made Polina want to cover her ears. The snap of breaking bones echoed around her. Her jaw clenched as Alex's ears extended up the sides of his head. He pitched forward, hands landing on the stump in front of his feet like a game of Twister gone wrong. Fluid oozed from the alpha's temples, glinting in the light of the moon, while his jaw popped and extended, teeth protruding past the lips, face lengthening. Claws ejected from his knuckles and hair sprouted along his spine.

By the time a dark red tail sprung from Alex's backside, she thought she might be sick. The shift wasn't quick and certainly wasn't painless. And then the unthinkable. Alex turned to face her. He sniffed the air, looked directly at her, and growled.

Could he see her? No. But he could *smell* her. The two leathery bellows of his wolf nose collapsed and expanded with his sniff. *Fuck.* Polina retreated into the woods as quietly as she could. It wasn't quiet enough. Alex, now in the form of the huge red wolf, stalked toward her, his golden eyes narrowing.

She broke into a run. So did he. And he was faster.

JUST TO CLARIFY

"This is what they told me to get, but it doesn't look very appetizing." Logan placed a dish of dry kibble on his dining room table in front of Bonny the pirate cat.

She sniffed the food and blinked up at him disapprovingly.

"I didn't think so." He removed the offending dish and rummaged through his cupboard. "I save this for when I'm in the mood for some East Coast fixings. I think you'll approve." He opened a can of lump crabmeat and tipped it over the dry kibble.

Bonny meowed and paced, sniffing the air as he approached. He was impressed at how well she got around with just the three legs and a missing tail. This was definitely his cat. Scarred. Damaged. Just like him.

As soon as he set the dish down on the placemat he'd put out for her, she dug in. Yes, he was going to let her eat on the table. Why not? It's not like anyone else would be eating across from him. Ever. He was finished with women. Heart officially crushed.

"Why couldn't it have been real, Bonny? You know,

when I found out Tabetha was messing with my emotions, I let it go pretty easily. She was an evil witch who did a wicked thing. You expect evil to be evil. But this, this is the worst. Thing is, I believe Polina was hoodwinked too. But she knew. She knew about the effects and she didn't warn me. She didn't ask me if it was okay if she toyed with my heart."

Bonny licked her chops and walked across the table to arch her back and stick her butt in his face. Obligingly, he gave her back a scratch from shoulders to stubby tail. The cat purred like a lawnmower.

"She felt it. I know she felt it too. But she also kept the truth from me, manipulated me. And it was perfect. Too perfect. Even now, I want to forgive her. I want to just go with it, real or not, and allow myself to be happy for a while. Maybe I should. Maybe I should pretend Grateful never told me about the soul magic. Does it matter, really, why I feel the way I do?"

He wished he could call her. Talk to her. Take a tiny sip of the intoxicating poison.

Brrrng. Brrrng. His phone vibrated in his back pocket. Weird. Who was calling tonight?

"Mr. Valentine?" It was the doorman.

"Yes, Fred."

"There's a Grateful Knight here to see you, sir."

"Send her up." Grateful? What did she want? To rub salt in his wounds? He knew that wasn't exactly fair. Her heart was in the right place. But it was hard not to resent the person who ruined you, even if she had good intentions.

Logan scooped Bonny into his arms, afraid she might try to jump down from the table and hurt herself. He plastered a smile on his face and opened the door just as Grateful was getting off the elevator.

"Grateful—"

"I need to talk to you." She was not smiling. In fact, she seemed downright disturbed.

"Where's Lucas?" Logan asked, sticking his head in the elevator.

Grateful smirked. "I didn't leave my infant son in there if that's what you're wondering."

He rolled his eyes. "I thought Rick might be with you."

"No. He's watching Lucas to give me a chance to talk to you." She sighed deeply.

"Well, come on in. Tea? Chocolate?"

"I'm not going to turn down your famous hot chocolate."

Logan placed Bonny on the floor and headed for the kitchen.

"Who's this?" Grateful asked, squatting down to scratch Bonny behind the ears. "And what happened to her?"

"Bonny. She was hit by a car. I adopted her today."

"She's sweet."

"Well, I needed something to distract me after our conversation last night." He stirred the milk in the pot, adding the other ingredients one by one. After a stretch of silence he mumbled, "I needed somewhere to put it all."

"Oh god, Logan. I made a mistake."

Logan stopped stirring and looked at her over his shoulder. "What kind of mistake?"

"I ran into Polina today." Logan dropped the spoon with a clang against the pot and spun on his heel.

"Where? When?"

"Outside Carlton City PD. Silas asked me to come by to talk about the werewolf murder that happened behind Valentine's. She was on her way out at the same time I was on my way in."

Logan started stirring again. "What were you mistaken about, Grateful?" The chocolate wasn't hot enough but he poured it into two mugs anyway, sliding one across the counter into her hands.

She licked her lips. "I told you your attraction to Polina was due to soul magic, and initially it was." She paused.

Logan made a gimme motion with his hand.

"Polina used a positivity potion to try to forget about you."

"What the fuck is a positivity potion?" Logan's body was a lit match. Emotion flared near his middle and fanned out, threatening to consume him.

"A positivity potion attracts you to the perfect match for you, like a magnet. It doesn't create love and it doesn't force the person to love you back, but it leads you to the person with whom you have the greatest potential for true love."

"And?"

"The potion led her here, Logan. I made that potion for her, but when I spoke to you before, I hadn't realized she used it. Her feelings for you are real. Your feelings are real. They may have been influenced at some point by the soul magic, but they are not anymore."

Logan's brows shot skyward. "Are you fucking with me, Grateful?"

"I would not fuck with you about this."

"The magic doesn't cause it?" He narrowed his eyes on her.

Grateful shook her head. "I've been a complete ass. I should have spoken to her before I talked with you. I'm so sorry, Logan."

He could hardly hear her. Blood pounded in his ears. Part of it was anger, but that part was swiftly overcome by an intense joy that worked its way through him.

"There's something else."

Inhaling sharply, he turned toward her. "What else could there be?"

"Do you remember that day at the Red Mound motel in Washington when you helped me by channeling your mother?"

"I remember that day. I don't remember what I channeled aside from what you told me."

"I remembered something she said to me right at the end. She said, 'Tell my son he'll soon be given a choice, and I...'"

"And I what?"

"She didn't finish. You woke up."

Logan smacked his forehead. "How is that helpful?"

"If you take just the words, it isn't, which is why I forgot about it and never told you."

"Why are you telling me now?"

"I had this feeling when she said it. I had a feeling that how it was supposed to end was 'he'll be given a choice and I'll love him no matter what.'"

Logan shook his head. "What choice? What choice am I supposed to make?"

"Maybe you're supposed to be with Polina. Maybe your mom was trying to tell you that after all of her warnings and all of the craziness and swearing off witches... Maybe she was trying to tell you it was okay to choose Polina."

There were only a few moments in Logan's life that he experienced with absolute clarity, from the light in the room to the smell on the air and everything in between. The day he learned his mother died was one. His first day working at his own restaurant was another. And now, this. The smell of chocolate hung in the air over Grateful's contrite expression across the counter. Bonny purred at his feet. The glow from the full moon spilled over the porch railing and through the window, blending with the light from the kitchen. And Logan admitted he loved Polina.

He checked that Bonny's food and water dishes were full and set them on the floor. "Can you let yourself out, Grateful? There's something I have to do." He grabbed his keys and was out the door before she had a chance to answer him.

33

THE SMUGGLER'S NOTCH WITCH

Sprinting as fast as she could, Polina screamed as the red wolf accelerated and attacked. His front claws sailed toward her head. Polina plunged her hand into her leather satchel and tossed a pinch of gold dust. She dissolved between his paws, sinking into the mountain and traveling through the layers of minerals below. She emerged on the edge of her realm, near the human campsite.

Nicodemus, Skogal, and Rohilda heard her unspoken call and landed close by. Nicodemus, the largest of the three, bowed and arched his wings. "The barrier is complete, mistress."

"Excellent."

Hildegard landed in a branch above their heads, panting hard. "By the goddess, that was close. Why didn't you strike him down?"

"Alex is wanted by the werewolf council. I promised Silas I would wait until they had a chance to bring him to justice. Taking out an alpha and leaving thirty pack members in chaos is counterproductive. Besides, he's trying to find a dangerous talisman on my mountain, and I need to stop him."

"What now? Wait for them to get here?"

"I'll take the border with Nicodemus. Hildie, you follow the northward wolves. Skogal, go east. Rohilda, west. Don't interfere unless a human life is at stake. Be prepared to report back to me everything you see. If the wolves find a magical object of any kind, I want to know."

Hildegard twisted her body toward the north but kept her head facing Polina. "Take care. An agreement with the werewolf council is far less important than remaining a whole and functioning witch."

Polina nodded her head and smiled. "Do not concern yourself. You'll have your witch at sunrise."

Hildegard took to the air without another word.

The rustle of branches from deep inside the woods indicated the wolves were close. Polina motioned for Nicodemus to take to the sky. With a flick and a muttered incantation, she masked herself from view, and this time, she did not forget to mask her smell, although the stink of wolf repellent potion was probably enough to do it without magic.

The beast or beasts barreled closer, the sound of panting breath causing her heart to flutter. Aside from the sheer size of a werewolf, their durability made them difficult to incapacitate without finishing the job in the form of killing them or sending them to the hellmouth. Her best bet was to avoid engaging at all if possible.

The beast broke from the woods. This one had a thick white coat and slightly smaller frame than Alex's wolf. Perhaps a female? She thought back to the group of four outside the clearing and remembered the woman. She hoped she wouldn't have to hurt her.

The white wolf stopped short, sniffing the air in front of Polina's face. The wolf's teeth, long and sharp, hovered close to her cheek. Polina held her breath. With a snort, the wolf pawed at her snout and shook her head. The potion was working.

Come on. Come on, Polina thought. *Turn around.*

Finally, the wolf's giant body pivoted and jogged deeper into the woods. "It worked," Polina whispered. "The potion is working."

Nicodemus made a grunt of approval from his hiding place in the tree above.

"Come on," she whispered, following the wolf. "Let's hope she leads us to what we're looking for." *And doesn't kill us first.*

34

RESISTANCE

Smuggler's Notch was a two-hour drive from Carlton City, but Logan made it in just over an hour. He sped toward Polina's realm like the ass of his car was on fire. He had to see her. He had to talk to her about the positivity potion, why she'd kept it a secret. The only way this relationship was going to work was if he cleared the air between them, got everything out in the open.

He pulled into Smuggler's Notch State Park and drove as deep into the forest as he could before he parked. A short trail led to the campground she'd mentioned a few times. The place was pretty quiet, but then it was late, past midnight.

"What you doin' out here this time a night?" a man said to him. Logan hadn't noticed him sitting quietly outside his tent in the dark.

"Out for a walk," Logan said. "Couldn't sleep."

"You stayin' in camp? Thought I'd met everyone here."

"I arrived late." Logan moved toward the woods. Logic suggested that Polina's home would be up the mountain a ways. There'd have to be a path, wouldn't there?

"Don't wanna go that way," the man warned. "Ranger says there was a wolf attack in these woods. A girl's leg was damned near bit off. We've all been told never to venture in that direction. I'm not always one to follow the rules, but even at high noon that part of the forest gives me the heebie-jeebies." The man pointed down the mountain to a sign at the head of a well-worn trail. "There's some terrific hiking trails back there. Completely safe."

"Thank you." Logan turned as if to head to the trail then paused. Of course Polina would protect her home and privacy by keeping the humans away. If he wanted to find her, he needed to head in the direction that humans weren't supposed to go. He made a one-eighty and headed back up the mountain.

"Hey! Did you hear me, boy? Don't go that way!" the man called.

Logan ignored him and pressed on. The man had been right about the foreboding nature of the woods. Everything about the situation told him to hightail it back to his car. It was dark, dreary, and an evil fog seemed to linger over the ferns and plants of the forest floor. His stomach twisted with unease. His heart pounded thinking about what might attack him from the darkness. But worst of all was the smell. The pungent odor reminded him of a mix of outhouse and burned plastic. He covered his nose and breathed through his mouth. It was all an effort to keep him away, along with the other humans, but Logan had enough experience with witches to know he was headed in the right direction.

He forced his steps forward, foot over foot, deeper into the forest. At one point, the desire to run was so great, he became ill all over a birch tree, but he didn't turn back. No way. He pointed his body in the direction where he felt the most resistance and kept moving. Finally, as if he'd passed some invisible barrier, the woods changed. The fog dissipated, and a path, although not well worn, appeared before him. He set foot to it and began to climb the mountain, trusting his gut to guide the way.

The dense woods were dark despite the full moon, and Logan pulled out his phone to use his flashlight app. The beam of light bobbed in the foliage as he progressed, revealing flashes of fallen logs, odd-shaped mushrooms, and the trunks of lichen-covered trees. A rustle came from his left and he twisted to see what it was. His light fell on an opossum that hissed and arched its back at Logan's interruption.

"Holy shit, you scared—" Logan was cut off by a set of too-large-to-be-real gray jaws that clamped around the hissing opossum, choked it to the back of its throat, and swallowed it whole. A wolf. A fucking huge wolf, the size of a bear. "Holy shit!"

Logan sprinted. The thing barreled after him, shouldering through trees and underbrush like a living bulldozer. Hot breath hit his neck. A paw shredded the lower leg of his blue jeans, slicing open his calf. He howled in pain, leaping over a fallen log to escape the wolf's bite as blood pooled in his shoe.

He had the sense that the wolf was toying with him. Judging by its sheer size and speed, it might have taken him out moments ago. And then a horrific thought crossed his mind. Maybe this was a werewolf. He'd never seen Silas as a wolf. Could it be him? A member of his pack? *Fuck.* He didn't know anything about werewolves. Now that he'd been scratched, would he turn into a wolf?

The wolf was on him. No way could he outrun this

thing. He had to try something else. Dodging behind a tree, he ventured off the path and then stopped abruptly. At first the wolf's momentum carried it past him, further down the path, but then the beast turned, spotted Logan, and lowered its head. The growl emanating from its throat was threatening and completely unnatural.

"Easy, big fella." Logan held out his hands. "Who are you? I have a friend who's a wolf. His name is Silas. Believe me, I realize you're having a bad night, but you don't want to eat me. You'll feel terrible tomorrow if you do."

The wolf stepped closer, stalking Logan with crouched limbs and peeled-back lips.

"Whoever you are, you're better than this. Go on. There's a forest full of snack-sized rodents up there." He gestured one shaking hand toward the mountain peak.

The wolf flashed amber eyes.

"Please."

No dice. Teeth and fur pounced. Hundreds of pounds of wolf flattened Logan to the forest floor. Jaws snapped and Logan curled to keep his head out of the bite, but it didn't help much. The wolf's razor-sharp teeth sank into his shoulder, impaling his chest and back.

Logan cried out. The overwhelming feeling that this was the end coursed through him, but as the blood sprayed across his face and his bones snapped, all he could think was that he was unfinished. This was wrong. It was too early. There was more he had to do. He fought and pushed and kicked and even bit the thick fur of the beast. It was no use.

And then there was a flash of light so bright it drowned out the surrounding woods. Logan saw a tunnel, and at the end of it was Polina. Heaven. This must be heaven. The wolf dissolved off him. The pain faded. And then she was gathering him into her outstretched arms. Her lips moved, but he couldn't hear what she said. All he could do was smile at his Polina and in her arms go happily to his eternal rest.

35

HEALING GRACE

"No. No. No." Polina gathered Logan into her arms. His blood smeared the front of her dress. A sickening crunch told her his shoulder was seriously injured. His left arm dangled as if the bones were shattered. Logan was a tall man, muscular, and heavy as a slab of stone, but she needed to get him home and treat his wounds before he bled to death.

"Don't you die, you bastard."

She dug in her satchel for a pinch of gold dust. There was hardly any left after her escape from Alex. Just enough to carry them both, she hoped. She sprinkled it over her head and focused on Aurorean House. They came apart. He was human and she was exhausted. The process was sluggish and jerky. His composition fought the elemental change, and she begged the goddess that she hadn't made a serious mistake trying to move him by gold dust in his condition. Ultimately, the dust gave out in her front yard.

With supernatural effort, she carried him inside, into her room of reflections, her most personal and sacred magical space. The mirrors repositioned themselves to make

215

room for her, and a soft bed was first reflected in them and then physically appeared in front of her. She laid him down, tried to make him comfortable.

His breath came in tiny sips and his complexion was a frightening shade of gray. It reminded her too much of his condition the first time she'd found him on the side of the road. Fisting his shirt, she tore it from the ugly wound with a resounding rip. Half his chest was a gaping, bloody hole. Shoulder crushed. Lung punctured.

Healing spells were slow and draining. She was not an accomplished healer. Neither her life, nor her element, had afforded her much opportunity for practice in the art. But by the goddess, she intended to become one if it would heal this man. At the shoulder, the site of the most damage, she pressed the crystal of her wand to his chest and repeated, "*Reinchide velecluse moribidatae vialanium.*" The chant had no English translation, but in the old language it was a plea for the goddess to rebuild his body from the inside out. She'd used it once before to keep Logan alive. Could she do it again?

She felt his soul rise to the surface. He was dying, on the cusp of giving up the ghost. "Don't you dare!" she yelled through tears. With one hand she pressed his spirit back into his body and held it there.

The bleeding stopped. Unfortunately, as she continued her healing spell, his face took on a worrisome shade of red. He was burning up. Sweat beaded across his forehead.

Swaying on her feet, she repeated the spell. Bones snapped into place and his shoulder filled from within. Panting, she retracted her wand. She didn't have much power left, even here with the mirrors focusing her energy. Something was wrong. If anything, he seemed worse. His red face had gone as white as the sheets and his fever had turned to shivering. She took a step back, supporting herself with her hands on her knees. Her eyes scanned Logan's body from head to foot.

Fresh blood. His calf was shredded. Gathering herself, she rolled the bleeding leg slightly and parted the shredded jeans. "By the goddess, it's a miracle you're still alive." She touched her wand to the shredded flesh and repeated her incantation. The bleeding stopped. She hoped it was enough. She wouldn't let him die. She couldn't.

Up until then, she'd told herself she could live without him. She was prepared to walk away if that's what he wanted. But the fact that he came here, at night, when he knew the risks, must mean he still cared. And she couldn't let him go without knowing how he felt. Without knowing why he'd come.

She stumbled toward one of the mirrors with a singular purpose. The reflection of the box appeared in front of her and then manifested in the space before her. She flipped open the small square to reveal the balm inside and carried it to the bed with shaking hands.

The caretaker spell was a three-step process. First came the mark, the spell was cast on the host. Second, the trigger, the spell was activated. Third, an element was given, binding the two souls. Polina told herself she would not complete the spell, but compulsively she dipped her finger in the balm, scooped out a generous dose and smeared it over his heart in the shape of a scythe. The spell would bind him to her life force if it came to that. She hoped it wouldn't. He might never forgive her if it did.

Exhausted, she stepped back and surveyed her patient. He didn't seem to be bleeding anymore, but she wasn't taking any chances. She rolled him on his side and checked his back, ran her hands down each leg. She found no further wounds.

What was he doing here?

Thankfully, he was breathing more evenly now, although his skin was still frighteningly pale. Too exhausted to use magic, she removed his bloody clothing by hand. She stumbled, catching herself on the bed. Immortal or not, she was drained.

She collapsed on the bed next to him and everything went black.

REFLECTIONS

Logan woke to a thousand faces staring in his direction. No, a thousand versions of the same face. It took him a minute to realize the swollen, sweaty reflection was his. He tried to sit up but failed miserably. Pain shot through his torso. His head pounded. His mouth went dry as a stone. What the hell was this place?

He didn't know where he was, but he knew who he was with—Polina. As perfect as she looked nestled in the puffy white bedspread, her usual princess-like demeanor was gone, replaced with obvious exhaustion. He let her rest. He was too sore to move to wake her up, anyway.

Aside from the bed, everything in the room was made of mirrors. The floor, the walls, the ceiling. Blue light came from some indistinguishable place and bounced around the room, giving him the distinct impression of being encased inside a diamond. And encased he was. He could see no door, no way out. Of course the layers and facets of the walls tricked the eye into feeling turned around and upside down. He closed his eyes, head throbbing from the effort of taking it all in.

He should be dead. The wolf's jaws had clamped down on him and an angel had come to carry him away. The angel was Polina. She'd saved him. Again.

"Are you awake?" He opened his eyes to find Polina leaning over him.

"Sorry I woke you," he croaked through his parched throat.

She frowned. "You need something to drink. You are dehydrated."

He tried to smile but his face hurt too much. His eyes darted to the mirror behind her. She was not reflected in it. The only face staring back at him was his own. It was as if she wasn't even there.

"Are you real?" he rasped.

"I'm afraid so." She followed his gaze. "Oh, you mean because the mirrors swallow my reflection. It's part of the magic of this place. It protects me, which means it hides me. Here. I'll, make it easier for you." She blinked her eyes and her reflection returned.

"What is this place?"

"My magical hearth. Um, the equivalent of Grateful's attic. This is where I keep my grimoire most of the time and where I have the most power. And the place I sort lost souls occasionally."

"Am I dead?"

"No!" Polina clarified. "I was able to heal you." She helped him into a seated position, which was more painful than he expected. She propped him up in a nest of pillows.

"My head is killing me."

"You've lost too much blood." With a groan she crawled out of the bed and hobbled toward one of the mirrors as if her entire body hurt. "You need tea," she said. "Ginger and horehound. It will help heal you."

"You don't have to—" But she was already gone. The silver swallowed her, the sway of her back receding in the reflection although she was no longer in the same room.

"Mindfuck if I ever saw one." He closed his eyes and rubbed his head. He must've fallen asleep because when he opened them again, Polina was standing beside him with a tray. She rested the goods on a bedside table and poured him a cup of herbal tea.

"Here, drink this." She brought the delicate floral teacup to his lips. He took a long sip and then another. The stuff tasted awful, like herbal shampoo in a cup, but he was thirsty enough to drain the cup dry. "Very good. It's a potion, not a beverage. Tastes horrible but it will help, trust me. Now a scone." She broke off a piece and held it to his lips.

He took a bite, chewed, and swallowed. The confection was tasty and did a good job of chasing the bitter tea from his palate. "Thank you," he muttered, leaning his head back.

"Well, I can't take credit for these. They came from Costco." She grinned. "Right next to the—"

"Eye of newt," he finished, laughing painfully.

Her smile faded and she lowered herself onto the side of the bed. "Coming here, especially in the middle of the night, was extremely stupid," she chided. "What were you thinking? You couldn't wait until tomorrow to berate me for using magic on you?"

"I didn't come to berate you," Logan said softly. "I came to apologize."

Her eyebrows lifted and her chin dropped. "Apologize?"

"Grateful told me about the positivity potion."

She shrugged. "Why should that matter? More magic. More reason for you not to trust me."

He swallowed hard. "She said the positivity potion only attracts two people to each other if they have the potential to be soul mates."

"Potential. That's the keyword. It doesn't make you fall in love." She started to cry then, tears winding in rivers down her cheeks. Pink with embarrassment, she looked away, her red waves sweeping forward to conceal her face. Logan's heart ached.

"But sometimes you do," he said softly.

"Yes." She swallowed and wiped her face with the bell sleeves of her dress. "I did. I fell in love with you, Logan. I couldn't help it. I tried to stop myself, but it just happened. And I couldn't tell you how or why because I knew when you found out that magic brought me to your door, you'd hate me."

He propped himself up, feeling stronger, as a result of the tea or the rest or the adrenaline pumping through his veins, he wasn't sure. Seeing her cry brought out protective instincts he didn't know he had. "Polina, look at me. Look. At. Me."

She blinked long dark lashes at him.

"Do you love me? Genuinely, without the aid of magic?"

She wrapped her long red hair around her hand. "You can't bring about real love by magic. I love you, Logan. I know you don't love me back. It happens sometimes. I knew the risks when I used the potion. A witch doesn't cast her heart outside her body without knowing it might never come back. You must believe me. I never meant to hurt you."

"Did you use the potion to try to control me? To use me?"

"Use you?" Polina shook her head. "Can't you see? I've

given you my soul. You own me, Logan. I'm yours. I'd do anything for you."

"Anything?"

Her eyebrows pulled in and up. She nodded once.

"Put your hands on your head."

"Logan..."

He raised his eyebrows.

She put her hands on her head.

"Get on your knees."

She climbed off the bed and knelt on the mirrored floor, her red hair wild around her shoulders, her hands still on her head. With a grunt, he pushed himself up and crawled from the bed. He shuffled forward and gathered her hair in his hand, tugging her head back so she was looking up at him with wet eyes. Part of him hated to do this to her, to overpower her like this by force of will. But another part, an insistent voice at the back of his brain, had to do it. There was a difference between saying a thing and doing it, living it. He had to be sure what she said wasn't just words.

"Will you tell me the truth about what magic you use on me?"

She swallowed. "Yes. I need to tell you... I..."

"You what?"

"I prepared you for the caretaker spell," she blurted. "Just in case. I wasn't going to use it without your permission. I was afraid you might die. I wanted to be able to save you if I had to."

"The caretaker spell. You'd make me like Rick? Give me your immortality?" A chill climbed his vertebrae.

"Yes."

"But you didn't finish it."

"No. It's a three-step spell. I only did the first part."

Logan blew out a deep breath in relief. "Why didn't you finish it?"

"You survived on your own. Besides, I didn't want to do it without your permission. I couldn't bind you to me for eternity without it."

"And you won't use magic on me without my permission in the future?"

She shook her head.

He released her hair.

"Please, Logan, I swear to you, I'm not like Tabetha. Can't you see that? I'm kneeling in front of you. I'm yours." She gripped his hips, eyes pleading with him.

He grabbed her wrist. "I came here tonight to tell you something, and you're going to listen to me." He shook her gently. "I love you."

Her lips parted, and she searched his face.

"I've loved you since the first night we spent together, maybe longer. I loved you the day I told myself I didn't, even when I thought you'd manipulated the emotion out of me. I couldn't help myself. I loved you when I left my condo to come here tonight, and even though I almost died because your life is a royally fucked-up trap for a human like me, I love you now."

Her tears flowed freely, and goddamn it if he wasn't a little shaken up too.

"Is this happening?" she asked.

He nodded. "It is. I think it's time we both gave ourselves permission to take a chance on each other. We deserve a shot. Can't we try to make it happen?"

Polina leaned forward and pressed her lips to his lower abdomen. He pulled her up off her knees and kissed her properly. "Polina?" he said into her mouth.

"Yes, Logan."

"I know this isn't romantic, but my face hurts. In fact, everything hurts. I think I need a hospital."

"I'm sorry. It's too dangerous. My forest is crawling with werewolves, and I'm too weak from healing you to carry you using gold dust. But if it is any consolation, I can tell you are not going to die tonight. Your soul is firmly entrenched in your body."

He nodded. "That's good news." He looked around the room at the cold glass reflecting his swollen body from every angle.

"Can we get out of this room?"

She smiled. "Absolutely." She threaded her fingers into his and led him toward one of the walls. Before he knew what was happening, he was walking through the silver, stepping into a normal-looking bedroom with warmer, homey accouterments. She guided him to pale gray sheets and climbed in beside him.

Pain or no pain, he welcomed her head on his chest. He wrapped his arms around her and pressed his lips to her hair. As her breath evened out, he wondered at how easily she slipped into sleep. The night had not been easy for her either.

"God help me, but it wouldn't be the worst thing to be bound to you for eternity," he whispered. He tucked a strand of her hair behind her ear, blinked twice, and fell back asleep.

37

MORNING

P olina awoke tucked into Logan's side, her palm resting on his chest. The steady rhythm of his heart was reassuring. He was stronger, healthier. The swelling had gone down, although one side of his face was still bruised. Now that she was rested, she'd complete the healing spell. He'd be as good as new by the time she sent him home. And she would send him home. It wasn't safe for him to be here.

Alex and his pack were going to pay for this. She planned to contact Silas and confirm the Bloodright pack was searching for the dragon fae amulet. With any luck, the werewolf council would find a way to collect him presently. She pushed herself up and reached for her wand.

"What do you plan to do with that?" Logan asked, his green eyes burning into her.

She trailed her fingers through his hair. "I was going to take care of that nasty bruise on your cheek."

He pushed himself up on his elbows. "Were you going to ask my permission or simply shove your wand against my person?"

She balked. "It's just a healing spell. The same one I used to save you last night. Nothing new. Completely innocuous."

He sat up the rest of the way, pushing back the comforter. "Don't you get it, Polina? It's not that I'm not grateful that you saved me from the brink of death, and I do love you and trust you, but I want you to treat me as an equal. If you truly love me, you'll respect that I have a choice and ask my permission before pulling the ol' hocus-pocus. Even with the simple stuff, okay?"

She frowned. He was right. Even now, she had the strongest desire to treat him like a child, heal him, force him to eat a healthy breakfast, then wrap him in a protective spell and usher him to his car. But Logan wasn't a child. Although his human state made him fragile, that didn't give her the right to take away his free will. He wasn't a pet or a slave. She'd promised him as much, and she'd meant it.

"Fine," she said forcefully. "Logan, would you like to heal naturally, or will you accept my help to hasten the process?"

Logan blinked at her, eyes flashing over the nightgown she'd changed into while he was sleeping. It was a thigh-length cream-colored silk with spaghetti straps, comfortable but revealing now that she thought about it. He swallowed and licked his lips.

"I'll take the magic," he said.

She smiled. "Thank the goddess." She slid to his side of the bed and wrapped her arms and legs around him from behind. He leaned back against her, the back of his head tucking in next to her cheek. Pressing her wand to his chest, she uttered the spell. Energy seeped from her skin, the magic wrapping around him, filling him. The side of his face changed from red-tinged purple to flesh colored. The remaining wound in his chest filled and faded, and an inconspicuous tightness in his torso softened. He sagged into her.

She removed her wand and slumped against the headboard.

"Are you all right?" Logan asked.

"I'm good." She yawned. "The healing drains me. A witch draws on her own life force to heal. Just give me a minute." She closed her eyes.

Logan shifted. His hand stroked through her hair and his lips pressed into her cheek. "Thank you."

She opened one eye. "You're welcome. I was hoping I wouldn't have to watch you suffer for... I don't know, how long would it have taken for you to heal?"

"Three weeks, maybe?"

"Hmm." She closed her eyes again.

"How about I make us some breakfast?" he asked.

She roused herself and sat up. "Unfortunately, the scones you ate last night were the extent of what was in my cupboard."

"Do you have staples? Eggs, flour?"

She shook her head. "I'll go to the market once I handle this werewolf situation."

"There's more of a situation than what I saw last night?"

She nodded. "The pack in my realm is responsible for the murder of the werewolf they found behind your restaurant."

"What?"

"The pack leader is the escaped convict Silas has been looking for. He's dangerous, and the pack itself is growing larger than normal. Silas thinks the leader's planning some kind of coup. I've agreed to keep them here until Silas can take down the alpha and assimilate the pack."

"Fuck that!" Logan yelled.

"Excuse me?"

"Silas knows that you have a murderous escaped convict outside your back door and he thinks it's appropriate to leave him here until he can get his act together? No fucking way. I don't want you near that guy."

Polina stared at Logan's finger, pointed at her chest. "Are you concerned for my safety?"

"Yes! Aren't you? Did you see that thing that almost ate me last night?"

"I did. And I sent him to hell. I'm immortal. You don't have to worry about me." Polina smiled sweetly, heart warmed by the idea he would worry about her.

"Tabetha was immortal and you and Grateful killed her."

"True. I can be... dismantled, but it would take an extremely powerful magical creature to do it. Not a werewolf. Believe me, I have this under control. They can't hurt me." She stood and ran her hands down his outer arms.

"I don't like it. I—"

Polina placed a hand on either side of his face. "Let me see if I can find a way to comfort you." She kissed him long and slow until she could hear his heart pound within his chest. His hands smoothed over the line of her spine, cupped her thigh, and pulled her on top of him.

"You're distracting me from my point."

She ground against the hard length of him beneath her. "I think I found your point."

He moaned.

"I have a suggestion," she said. "How about a shower and then breakfast at the diner in Stowe?"

"Mhmm," he said, roiling his hips and pressing himself into her.

Now that Logan was healed and hers, there were a few more distractions Polina had in mind.

3 8

A NEW DAY

Logan followed Polina into her bathroom but halted inside the archway that served as a door. The room gave new meaning to the term *open concept*. Floor-to-ceiling windows offered a clear view into the forest beyond where a grazing doe twitched her ears and stared at him inquisitively.

"Don't mind her," Polina said. "She's after the blackberries."

"This is... exposing."

"The forest directly around Aurorean House is enchanted. No one can enter without my invitation, other than the natural wildlife."

Aside from the wall of windows, the floor was stone as were the other three walls. A partition provided a natural separation to the room. He stepped deeper into the space and discovered the rest of the fixtures behind it. "So you shower and, uh, everything else, right here in the open, huh?"

She smirked. "Does that bother you?"

In fact, it did give him a mild case of the heebie-jeebies,

but looking at her, the silk of her nightgown straining against her nipples, he wasn't about to complain. He shook his head.

"Good," she said with a smile. She approached the wall and placed her hand on a stainless steel pad. The shower turned on, water raining from a metal square in the ceiling. The spray misted across the ivory silk, revealing the petal-pink areolas at the tips of her pert breasts. His gaze drifted from her creamy shoulder to her elbow, the curve of her waist, the round and full mound of her hip, and the dark triangle of her sex barely visible through the fabric.

Everything inside Logan became singularly focused. *Mine.* His mind blanked and his legs carried him across the room to her of their own accord. Fingers digging into her hair, he cradled her neck. The kiss he gave her was hard, pressing, even invasive—a flag of ownership planted in the territory of her mouth. It wasn't gentle, and he did not ask permission. She would be justified if she pushed him away.

But she didn't. She melted into the kiss, sagging against his chest in surrender. Polina was a warrior. An immortal. She could crush him with a flick of her little finger. But all the signals she was tossing his way were the exact opposite of her nature. She made him feel like a king.

The thought made him desperate to be inside her, as if he could prove to her through physical prowess that he was man enough to be her mate. Unlike their first night together, when he'd been gentle with her, knowing it was her first time in almost a century, today he wanted to make her believe that, human or not, he was all the man she needed.

Warm mist from the waterfall wet his back. He moved his kiss to the corner of her mouth, around to her ear, and pulled her earlobe between his teeth. "I want to be inside you, in every way."

She groaned. Her nails trailed over the outsides of his shoulders, scraping down his back. He hooked his thumbs in the waistband of his briefs and worked them off, over his erection. He was hard as a rock, ready for her. He bent over her petite frame to move his kiss to her shoulder.

She sank to the floor in front of him. "You said you wanted me on my knees," she said.

He stared at her with hooded eyes. Before he could say another word, she took him in her mouth, opened her throat, and pulled him in deep.

Logan closed his eyes to keep from going over the edge.

"Fuck, what you do to me," he said, the words laden with awe, worship in every syllable. Her warm tongue worked against his shaft until he thought he'd lose his mind as well as his resolve. "Not yet. Stop." He tugged her to her feet.

She complied, her lids heavy with need. He lifted her nightgown over her head and cast it in the direction of his briefs. Hot damn. No underwear.

Dragging a knuckle down her abdomen, he stopped at the place where her thighs met and curled two fingers along her most sensitive flesh. She was wet and ready. A moan escaped her lips as his fingers entered her and began to stroke. Her head fell back and he caught her around the waist, her knees going soft.

She arched over his flexed arm, providing convenient access to her breasts. He flicked his tongue over her nipple as his fingers picked up the pace. He sucked harder on her breast, biting the nipple gently.

"Logan, mmm." Her nails dug into his hair. He could feel the muscles inside her draw him in, her abdomen tense with pleasure as she worked herself into his hand. She was close. He wanted to watch her orgasm, see her shatter in his arms, but he needed to mark her as his own.

He removed his hand, smiling at her tiny whimpers at the absence of his touch. Hooking his hands under her ass, he bent his knees and lifted, spreading her legs and wrapping her thighs around his hips.

One step and her back was against the wall, his length sliding into her slick, wet velvet. Once fully inside, he paused, heart pounding and body enjoying the tight squeeze of her. He examined her face—hooded blue eyes, full, slightly parted lips, a hint of a smile tightening her cheeks.

"Tell me," he whispered.

She opened her eyes a bit wider. She knew what he wanted. "I love you."

He gripped her thighs, slid halfway out, and thrust back in. She gasped, squeezing her arms around his neck. "Whose are you?" His voice was breathy with restraint.

"I'm yours. I'm all yours."

"I love to hear that." He pumped into her again, slow out and sharp in, finding a rhythm and gaining speed. Her moans grew louder, echoing against the stone of the room, until finally he felt her clench around him. There was no holding back. He went over the edge, her sex milking his erection, clench and release, clench and release.

Only when she was completely spent, the last aftershock flowing from her body, did he lower her to her feet and pull her into the spray. The warm shower hit his sensitive skin, prolonging the intensity.

He reached for the bottle of shampoo on the ledge and motioned for her to turn around. As he took her wet hair into his hands and started working up a lather, he caught the eyes of the doe through the window. She was definitely watching.

"Berries, my ass," Logan murmured.

"Huh?" Polina asked, eyes closed.

"Nothing." He kissed her on the cheek and went back to lathering her red tresses. She eased into his touch. *His.* She was *his.*

And he didn't take the responsibility lightly.

HOME AGAIN

"I don't like leaving you alone to deal with these werewolves. I know I'm only human, but give me a shotgun and some silver ammo and I can make a hell of a sidekick." Logan sat across the breakfast table at the Stowe Diner dressed in his clothes from the night before. Polina had cleaned and repaired them for him, a spell she'd made him ask for twice.

She smiled and lowered her voice. "After this morning, I'm having trouble thinking of you as only human. In fact, I'd venture to say you've enchanted this witch."

Logan's chest visibly swelled, and he pointed his fork at her. "Please tell me you're not just saying that."

Blushing, she shook her head.

Logan tipped his face toward the ceiling. "Alleluia!"

The other restaurant patrons turned heads to look his way. A man with a long gray beard and leather vest pumped his arm and yelled, "Amen, brother!"

Polina snickered.

"So, you'll let me stay and help you tonight?"

She shook her head. "Let me do my job, Logan. You have the restaurant."

"I have a sous-chef. He can handle it."

"You're not one of those men who think women are helpless, are you?" she asked sternly.

"Of course not."

"Then thank you very much. I appreciate your offer, but I will be managing my realm on my own. I promise I will call for you should I need help."

"Call for me? How? The mirror you gave me is... gone."

"I'll make you another."

"Wouldn't a cell phone be more efficient?"

With a smug grin, she shoveled in a bite of hash browns. "The magic of the mountain interferes with cell service. You will become acquainted with the ways of magic over time. These things were strange to me at first, as well."

"Believe me, between you, Grateful, Tabetha, and the water witch of Astoria—"

"Kendra."

"Right, Kendra. Between the four of you, I think I've become adequately acquainted with the ways of magic."

"I just mean..." She paused. "I should have introduced you to my gargoyles."

Logan, who was about to take a sip of coffee, almost poured it in his lap. "Gargoyles?"

"Nicodemus, Skogal, and Rohilda. They live on the roof of Aurorean House. I would have introduced you, but it slipped my mind. Has anyone ever told you how distracting you are?"

He pressed the tips of his fingers together. "Not in a long time."

"But once?"

He nodded slowly. "I was engaged once."

She straightened. "You were?"

"Yeah."

"What ended it?"

"She did. I found her in bed with someone else."

Polina crossed her arms and leaned on the table. "*She* cheated?"

"Yep." He laughed. "I guess nothing in life is permanent."

"But why? You are a coveted human suitor. Why would she risk your alienation for pleasure?"

"I don't think she shared your opinion of me. I worked too much. I wasn't sensitive to her needs. She thought she deserved better."

Polina furrowed her brow. "You seem adequate to me."

Logan grinned. "Things are looking up. I've advanced from worthless to an adequate human."

A slight blush crept from her neck to her cheeks. "You've changed my perspective. You've changed me," she said softly.

"I try."

Straightening, Polina asked, "Can I come to see you again, tomorrow when I've managed things here?"

Logan flashed a wry grin. "And the day after, and the one after that, until you are sick of me and send me away."

"You may never go home."

"Home." Logan dropped his fork. "Shit! I am very sorry Polina, but I need to go. I have to feed my cat."

"You have a cat?"

"I do now."

He kissed her long and hard. "Tomorrow. Will you come to me, or should I come to you?"

"I'll come to you," she said, her eyes twinkling with what Logan hoped was anticipation. God, she was beautiful. He'd take her again right now if they weren't in a crowded restaurant.

He paid the check, watching her walk out the door wearing a purple dress that would look at home in any Renaissance fair.

"Your change," the cashier said. Logan turned to accept the money. When he turned back a moment later, Polina was gone.

40

MISSING PIECES

Polina arrived at Aurorean House more concerned about her realm than when she left. She'd been so caught up in Logan that she hadn't even considered what Hildegard and the gargoyles had seen the night before, or the fate of the camp of humans. It did not escape her notice that her feelings for Logan were all consuming and dangerously distracting. She could still feel him moving inside her, filling her. It wasn't just physical. His love was a warm blanket of affection that wrapped her in an encompassing embrace. He seeped through her skin, taking up residency in her heart. Even now, she felt swollen with it, blissfully heavy with wanting.

"There you are," Hildegard said from an oak branch above her. "From the reek of man in the house, I take it you kept company last night while the rest of us were protecting the realm."

Hand moving to her hip, Polina pursed her lips at the snowy-white barn owl. "The human was injured inside my realm. It was my duty to heal him. I saw him off, just a moment ago."

Hildegard laughed. "It was Logan Valentine I smelled in the room of reflection when I went looking for you, and unless I'm mistaken, the type of healing going on extended beyond blood and bone."

A giggle escaped Polina's lips. "I never could swing anything by you, old girl. It was Logan Valentine, and I'm afraid this witch's heart is all tangled up with his at the moment. Would you ever believe in all your years that I would love another human?"

"Nay, lady. I thought your heart had closed itself off to the possibility centuries ago. You've spent a long time alone." Hildegard's mirth-filled voice became soft and serious. "I'm glad to see the change. You look like an opening flower this morn."

"Thank you, Hildie."

"Don't thank me yet. I have a fair bit of bad news to share with ye."

Polina frowned. "What sort of bad news?"

Hildegard rotated her head on her neck. "This is a conversation better suited for the indoors."

It wasn't like Hildie to be needlessly cautious. Polina nodded her agreement and they passed into the house, under the gargoyles asleep for the day on the gables. Polina made her way to the big leather chair in her library. Hildegard soared past her to land on her carved perch near the window.

"What did you and the gargoyles see?"

"The gargoyles saw nothing. The wolves they followed hunted the local wildlife. Nothing unusual. Nicodemus confirmed that none of the wolves crossed the border into the human camp. He was concerned about you but he did his duty and guarded the human campsite until dawn."

"Good. And you?"

"I did as you asked and followed the northward group. They made it almost to the peak of Silver Sparrow. After Alex's red wolf tried to kill you, he circled around and joined the northerners, and let me tell you, he was on a mission. That wolf scoured the mountain with his nose to the ground."

"What did they find, Hildegard?"

"I thought they'd run out of time. The sun had begun to rise and the lot of them risked shifting back and standing knee deep and naked in the mountain snow. But Alex sniffed and searched far past the time the rest of his pack abandoned him for lower altitudes. He found a cave. I dared not follow him inside, but there was a glow, my lady, an intense red glow that poured out the mouth of that cavern and lit up the night like a torch. I heard laughing, the wicked and twisted sort that makes your feathers stand on end. It was still dark, but Alex walked out of that cave on two legs with a dragon scale amulet hanging around his neck."

"Naked? In the snow?"

"The cold didn't seem to bother him any, and even if it did, he didn't suffer from it long. He disappeared right in front of my owl eyes. You know, dear witch, my sight in the darkness is better than most any creature, but I'm telling you, he blinked out of existence like... like..."

"Dragon fae. He found the amulet." Polina stood and paced the floor. "Silas was right; he must have hidden it here while I was buried in Tabetha's garden. Hmm." Polina stroked her chin. "Damn it. I need to tell Silas. We must find a way to neutralize this madman and his pack of orphans. That amulet will make him as powerful as any witch. Maybe more. No wonder he laughed at my threat to kick him off the mountain. He knew that in a matter of hours, he'd have what he needed to make sure I couldn't."

"If you plan to speak to the detective, may I suggest you do it sooner rather than later? I fear the clock. Alex is gaining power with every moment we hesitate."

"You're absolutely right. We'll go now." Polina grabbed her wand and headed for the kitchen where she kept her extra stores of gold dust. She'd be in Carlton City in seconds.

But the sight outside her kitchen window chilled her to the bone.

The doe that'd wandered her yard feasting on her blackberries hung limply, neck at an odd angle, over the arm of a man glowing with power. He stood where he should not be able to stand, over the protective enchantment around Aurorean House.

Polina reached for her gold dust but was seized by an invisible fist that held her to the spot.

"Oh no, Hecate," Alex said. "You're not going anywhere."

41

RETRIBUTION

"A member of my pack, a wolf named Sam, has gone missing," Alex said. "You wouldn't know anything about that, would you?"

The pendant around his neck held a carving of a twisting dragon with a red stone eye. The dragon's body looked to be made of pewter, but Polina knew better. It was dragon's scale, rare and powerful. The amulet throbbed with energy. Polina could feel its presence through the window like the warmth from a small sun.

Snap out of it, she ordered herself. Drawing power from the metal bones of her house and the dead beneath it, she mustered enough strength to break Alex's hold on her and muttered a defensive spell.

"Where is my wolf?" he demanded.

"Your wolf almost killed a human last night. I sentenced him to the hellmouth." Polina raised her wand.

"He attacked your human lover, inside the bounds of your territory. The man was where he shouldn't have been. Hardly fair to blame Sam for that. Bring him back. Show me you're on my side. If we work together, Polina, we could rule the entire northeast, and soon beyond."

"I'm good with ruling my own realm, thank you. I've never been much of a megalomaniac. I see we differ in that respect."

"Careful," Hildegard said in that special language only Polina could understand. "The power coming off that thing is practically making me molt."

Alex took a step closer and Polina reached for her gold dust again. The leaded glass between them was working to her advantage but Polina knew she had to get out of there. Silas wasn't kidding about the strength of the amulet. With it on, Alex was as powerful as any witch.

"We're not done talking."

Polina released the dust over her head. But something went wrong. The dust didn't fall. She tilted her chin up to see it hanging in the air. Alex stared at her, eyes pinning her like a butterfly to a display board. A step closer and a crack formed in the leaded glass. Another step and she couldn't move.

"Hildie, fly!" Polina ordered, focusing all her energy on freeing the bird. The owl left her shoulder just as the glass shattered, blowing through the kitchen in sharp, fragmented waves. She screamed as it sliced her flesh and tore her wand from her hand. The wounds healed almost immediately, but the assault stung. Her body tumbled through the glass toward Alex, caught in the grip of his power.

"I hope you don't mind, I detained your owl as well. I can't have her interfering," he said, as Polina struggled against the invisible vise compressing her arms to her sides.

"What do you want with me, Alex?"

"It's not you. It's never been about you, Hecate. It's your realm. The enchantment you have around this mountain has done an excellent job of concealing and protecting my pack. It's funny, when I hid the amulet here years ago, I had no idea it would be so difficult to find it again. But the magic of this place..." He shook his head. "It wasn't the same under Tabetha's rule. I had to find it the old-fashioned way, by smell. It takes a long time to smell an entire mountain."

"So now you have it. Just go."

"See, that's the problem. Tabetha promised me this land in exchange for my help in your abduction."

"Tabetha?"

"Have you ever wondered how the witch of Salem was able to get the best of you? You, the recluse of Smuggler's Notch, who never left the security of her realm. *I* sniffed you out. *I* used the amulet to abduct you from your own realm before I hid it here. I upheld my end of the bargain with Tabetha, only she did not. You didn't stay buried."

"She didn't have the right—"

"This is my home, and I can't have you threatening to evict me or my pack every time we kill someone. And we *need* to kill someone, Hecate. Tonight."

"Kill someone? Who?" Polina asked.

"Silas Flynn."

"Silas? Why do you need to kill Silas?"

Alex laughed and rolled his eyes. "He never told you? Is he still propagating that story about his father being the true alpha?" Alex snorted. "Silas is the alpha of Fireborn pack and has been since the day I slaughtered his parents. He is the leader of the largest pack of wolves in North America. If I take him out, with the numbers I already have answering to me, I'll not only restore my birthright, I'll take control of the entire Lycanthropic Society. They will answer to me, or die. Silas would already be dead if not for his decoy. I killed his Zafka."

"The werewolf you murdered behind Valentine's was Silas's double?"

Alex nodded."

A haunting tension spread across Polina's body. This man was dangerous. Not just a murderer, a gangster. "And what do you intend to do with me?"

"You're immortal. I can't kill you. But thanks to this"—he pointed to the dragon talisman around his neck—"I can incapacitate you, permanently. One thing Tabetha taught me is that a captured witch is better than a dead witch. No replacement. No weakening of your protective enchantments. I plan to keep you safe and sound for all eternity, a prisoner in your own realm."

She glanced to the gargoyles on her roof but in full sun and without her wand, they were useless.

"Come, Hecate. Let me show you to your new room."

42
VALENTINE'S

"Good kitty," Logan said, scooping Bonny up in his arms. "You used the litter box. Nothing chewed. What a good, good kitty." He made kissing noises as he scratched behind Bonny's ears. Digging into his pocket, he flipped a can of Yummy Vittles Chicken Flavor in the air and caught it. "Look what I picked up for you on the way home."

He carried Bonny to the kitchen where he dug out a can opener and, setting the cat down, twisted the crank to cut the food open. He tipped it onto a small plate. Bonny meowed and paced the granite island with her trademark irregular gate. Logan slid the plate toward the cat, who dug in without pause, then he retrieved the water dish from the floor.

"So, what did you do all night while I was gone?" Logan scratched along the cat's back starting at her shoulders. Bonny rounded her back as she ate, pressing her soft fur against Logan's fingertips.

"You'll never guess what I did," Logan said. "Spent the night at Polina's. Yeah, it was weird. She's definitely not human. But strangely, I don't care. She's not like anyone. I trust her. I even love her." He folded his arms into a pillow and laid his head down on the counter. "How's that for a surprise? I never thought I'd love a witch again."

Bonny finished her breakfast and proceeded to lick her front paws, purring like a lawn mower.

"You like this stuff, eh? I'll have to get more." Logan looked at the can. "Huh. It says here I was only supposed to give you half the can. I guess this is your lucky day."

"Logan." His mother's voice made him jump. She stood in the great room, glowing like a lantern, her dark brown hair curled to her shoulders. The sleeves of her pale pink cardigan were pushed to her elbows.

"Mom?" He hadn't seen her in months. Not since the dream where she'd told him about how Polina had rescued him.

"Polina needs you, Logan. She's in trouble." Her voice reverberated in the open space.

He shook his head. "I just left her."

"Find Silas. You'll need him."

"Silas? Does this have to do with the werewolves? The sun hasn't even set."

His mother's translucent head turned toward his front door. "Trouble."

One knock, then two. "Logan?" a man's voice called through the door. "It's Jonah. I need to talk to you about Valentine's." His voice was firm, matter of fact.

"Do not go with him, my son. They've come for you. Do not take the bait."

Logan crept to the peephole and peered out into the foyer. Jonah waited. He wasn't dressed for work, but the restaurant didn't open for another three hours. The man raised his fist and knocked again. "Logan! It's important, my man. You in there?"

Maybe it was important. As much as he trusted his ghostly mother, he couldn't abandon his restaurant.

"Don't," his mother said again, shaking her translucent head.

"I can smell you in there, Logan," Jonah said.

An odd thing for a human to say. Logan's eyes narrowed. Jonah's wavy dark blond hair was wilder than normal and the stubble on his face was almost long enough to be called a beard.

He looked at his mother's ghost again. She unraveled from the inside out and disappeared. Logan cracked the door. "You can smell me? I'll have to change my cologne."

"Thank the goddess. You've got to come with me. There's something I have to show you."

"What? Tell me."

Jonah balked. "It's hard to explain. It'll be better if you see for yourself."

"Try." Logan's gaze flicked to his threshold, hoping that Grateful's enchantment was all it was cracked up to be.

Jonah's face fell. His hand shot out toward Logan in an attempt to push through the door, but his knuckles hit the invisible barrier between them, the magic rippling faintly purple.

"What the fuck?" Jonah asked.

Logan's eyes drifted to Jonah's shoulder, to a tattoo of a harvest moon with three claw marks ripping through it. The placement was high on his shoulder. Had the man been wearing his uniform, he would have never seen it under the sleeves. It was an odd tattoo, and he'd only seen something like it one time before.

"You can't come in because you're a werewolf. Why are

you here, Jonah? Full moon tonight. Don't you have something better to do with your time?"

Jonah's smile melted into a sneer. "Don't fight me on this one. You're a nice enough human but there are bigger forces at work here."

"What kind of forces?"

Jonah shook his head and took a step back from the door. "You made friends with the wrong werewolf, bro. It's not you we're after. You're just the bait. Cooperate, and I'm sure the alpha will release you when it's all said and done."

Logan remembered what Silas had said about the leadership of his pack. This was obviously some sort of pack war. Which reminded him of the dead man in his alley. "Who killed that werewolf they found in my dumpster?"

"A simple case of mistaken identity. I thought he was Silas. That was his job, you know. He was a decoy."

Logan didn't understand. Silas had said the man was a decoy for the alpha. "I'm not coming with you."

"I can wait here all day, brother, and if I'm still here when I shift tonight? Well then, we are going to find out what a three-hundred-pound wolf can do to your foyer."

"Wait, you shifted last night. Who managed the restaurant?"

"Closed it down before sunset. You've got some angry customers."

"You bastard." Logan slammed the door and locked it for good measure.

"What do I need to do?" he asked the empty space next to his coffee table.

His mom appeared again. "Find Silas. Show him how to get to Polina. Trust your heart. The time has come for you to make a choice. You have my blessing either way, my son." She faded away. Bonny meowed at the fade-to-black routine, and continued to stare at the space where his mom had been.

Was it too much to ask for his mother to provide him a few details? Maybe explain how he was supposed to get out of his own apartment with a werewolf watching the front door. But no. An explanation was not forthcoming.

Not sure how much Jonah could hear standing in the hall, Logan texted Silas.

Where are you?

Just woke up. Recovering from last night.

Trouble. Meet me in your office in twenty?

What kind of trouble?

The kind my dead mother thinks is important.

Oh fuck. See you in twenty. Be careful.

Logan bolted into his room and changed into mountain gear: jeans, steel-toed work boots, a T-shirt, and jacket. He packed some necessities in a backpack, then rushed to the window in his spare bedroom. There was a fire escape, although the thing hadn't been used in decades. Logan didn't even think it was technically operational. It was more the type of thing that had remained due to the building's historical significance.

Praying the rusty hinges would hold, he unlocked and pried the window open, then stepped out on the rickety piece of metal. At eighteen stories up, the narrow stairway to the alley below seemed indefinite. But nothing was going to keep him from helping Polina. Leaving the safety of his condominium, he gritted his teeth and started down.

43
AWAY

At the top of Silver Sparrow mountain, where the snow never melted and the air was thin from the altitude, Alex forced Polina and Hildegard into a dark cavern. Polina had never encountered power like the amulet's. It wrapped around her, holding her fast, and caused a worrisome red glow around Hildegard. Alex dropped her and her owl in the back of the cavern. Finally free, Polina called on the metal of the mountain below her for help, but she couldn't connect.

"Don't bother," Alex said.

There was no door or walls, but Polina discovered she was locked within a six-foot cube of energy. She could feel the magical force buzzing around her. It made her skin prickle. She banged on the invisible wall with her hands. "Let me out! Alex, you must know you can't get away with this. Other witches will come. They'll find me."

"Like they did before? They may come, but they won't find you. Not here. Ironically, the same enchantment that masked my amulet will mask you. You know, when you refused to return Sam from your hellmouth, I knew what you deserved. This is your own personal hellmouth. Enjoy your eternal prison. Goodbye, Polina."

His footsteps receded with the light he'd carried. A bend in the cavern and they were plunged into total darkness. All went quiet aside from the howl of the wind outside the entrance to the cavern.

"Can you free us?" Hildegard's small voice asked in the darkness.

Polina flattened her hands against the force that walled them in and shook her head in the darkness. "Not an ounce of metal in this enchantment. I can't even make contact with the other side."

"I can't see," Hildegard confessed. "An owl can see in the dark, even with a new moon. In order to blind me, this place must have no light. None at all."

Polina backed away from the wall. "He means to bury us alive."

"Aye," Hildegard said.

Polina's heart started to pound. The memory of the year she spent as a prisoner under Tabetha's tree came back to her, and then being buried alive with Grateful in Washington. The walls closed in. There wasn't enough air. She pounded her fists against the inside of the container. Screamed and then screamed again. Sprinting, she threw her weight against the wall. It didn't budge.

She jumped and punched the roof to no effect. Shoulders, feet, head, and hands were fruitlessly ineffectual. All she managed to accomplish was to bruise herself to the point of pain. Defeated, she slid down the side of the prison, buried her head in her hands, and cried. There was a flutter of wings, and then Hildegard's feathers pressed into her side.

"Don't worry yourself, my lady. When Poe notices I'm missing, he'll tell his witch. Grateful will come."

"Do you think she'll be able to find us?"

There was a long pause. "I don't know."

A horrifying realization had Polina grabbing her stomach. "Logan expects to hear from me. What if he comes looking for me? What if they hurt him?"

"He knows better," Hildegard scoffed.

"He most certainly does not," Polina said. "I could hardly get him to leave this morning. For someone with only one life, the man is foolishly brave."

"You love him."

"Yes."

"A foul time to be buried alive."

"Yes, it is." She stroked Hildegard's wing. As she pulled her hand away, a clump of feathers fell off into her fingers. "What's happening, Hildie? You're molting."

Hildegard coughed. "I'm not sure. I feel strange. I feel..."

Polina's familiar toppled onto her side, her body suddenly rigid. Polina gathered her into her arms. "Hildie? Hildegard? What's happening?"

But Polina knew what was happening. Hildegard was dying. She could feel the life force drain from the tiny body in her arms. There was more than one way to torture and kill someone, even a witch who couldn't physically die. It wasn't enough for Alex to bury her alive. He'd ensured the loss of the one thing she had left, the living creature she'd shared the bulk of her existence with. He'd cursed the familiar she loved.

44

SILVER SPARROW

"How long until sunset?" Logan asked, staring up at the sky above Smuggler's Notch.

"Four hours." Silas had his gun drawn and was following Logan away from the marked path. "Are you sure this is the right way?"

"Positive." Logan plowed into the thick fog.

"The smell is... indescribable." Silas covered his nose with his sleeve and breathed through his mouth.

"You called Grateful, right?" Logan asked.

"Yeah, but she didn't answer her phone. I had to leave a message."

"Fuck."

"I have backup on the way from the supernatural police force and the Lycanthropic Society."

"Should we wait? It sounds like this guy wants you dead," Logan said.

"No. We've waited long enough. Alex is dangerous. We're going to find Polina and then we're going to take him down."

Logan nodded. "Man, I wish just this once my mother

was wrong and Polina is okay."

"Hmm."

Logan navigated between the trees. This was the way. As long as he kept heading uphill, he should run into Polina's place, Aurorean House, eventually.

"So, you and Polina, eh?" Silas asked. Unlike Logan, who had to watch every step, Silas navigated the woods like he was born to be there. As a werewolf, maybe he was.

"Yeah," Logan said. "I think she could be the one. I know it's crazy, but I've never felt this way before. It feels, I don't know, destined somehow."

Silas laughed. "Or it could be the sex."

Logan paused and looked back at his friend. "Excuse me? I'm over thirty years old. I think I can tell the difference between love and lust." He hooked a hand around a birch tree and pulled himself up a steep incline.

"Yeah, but that was human sex. This is magic vagina. Magic vagina can tame the wildest of beasts. Take Soleil and me. I thought we were forever, then she dumped me like a hot rock."

"Love isn't always forever. I get it. But I intend to enjoy it while it lasts." Logan ran a hand through his hair and continued up the mountain.

It took almost an hour for them to reach the front yard of Aurorean House and ten seconds to notice the blown-out front window. "Whoa. What happened here?" Silas drew his gun again.

Logan sprinted over the lawn and through the door that hung open on its hinges. "Polina? Polina?" He yelled her name and scoured the house. "Fuck. She's not here. There's glass all over the kitchen. He has her. I know it."

A preternatural growl came from the front yard, followed by two gunshots. "Silas!" Logan rushed to the door. A man had Silas pinned to the ground and was kneeling on his arms.

"What the hell?" Logan charged at the attacker only to be stopped in his tracks by an invisible force.

The man turned to face him. He looked a hell of a lot like Jonah, enough that Logan did a double take. There was a slight difference in the length of his hair and he was dressed differently than his sous-chef had been just hours ago. Two gunshot wounds gaped in his chest. As Logan watched, the holes filled themselves in.

"Run!" Silas yelled.

Logan couldn't move from the neck down.

"You must be Logan," the man said with a wicked smile. "I'm Alex, alpha of the Bloodright pack. I believe you've already met my Zafka, Jonah. You're in my territory."

"Why can't I move?" Logan asked.

"Oh, that. You should know, I'm not like other werewolves. I've evolved." He lifted the dragon amulet that hung around his neck. Logan had seen a similar talisman around Tabetha's neck once, a scarab beetle that accentuated her power.

"Yeah? Who gave you that pretty necklace?" Logan asked, voice thick with ridicule.

Alex's smile morphed into a sneer. "I should thank you for leading Silas here. See, I recently marked this realm as my own, and when an alpha assaults another alpha, like me, inside their territory, werewolf law says I have the right to take his life."

"Silas isn't an alpha," Logan said.

Now a genuine smile slid across Alex's face. "Is that what he told you? He's always so careful to protect his position. Let me educate you. Silas Flynn has not only been the alpha of Fireborn pack since the day I murdered his parents, he's also head of the Lycanthropic Society. And now, I have the legal right to kill him and usurp his position in his pack. Oh, and with the size of the pack that will give me, the Lycanthropic Society will have no choice but to install me as their new leader."

Logan looked at Silas, who had calmed beneath Alex, eyes dulling and staring right through Logan. At once he knew it was true. Silas was the alpha. A deep well of guilt rose within him, and his mind filled with questions. Why had Silas lied? Why had his mother told him to bring Silas when she must have known the truth? And worst of all, what had Alex done to Polina to mark her realm as his own?

"I'm sure you two can come to some arrangement," Logan said. "Maybe, if we all sat down and took a deep breath, we could work something out without anyone getting hurt."

"You're thinking like a human. That's not how werewolf culture works. Here's what's going to happen. I am going to take Silas here to my pack's camp. As custom dictates, I'm going to chain him to the sacred totem of my people. Tonight, when the pack shifts, they'll eat him alive. It's how it's always been done, and it's how it will be."

Logan's eyes shifted toward the human camp.

"I hope you're not counting on the other alphas to come to his rescue. They can't. He gave up all rights to their protection when he crossed into my territory. Of course, he probably couldn't smell my marking over Polina's enchantment. That witch is the gift that keeps on giving."

Bile rose in Logan's throat. "What have you done with her?"

"You'll find out soon enough."

A sharp pain exploded at the back of Logan's skull and then everything went black.

45

A LIGHT IN THE DARKNESS

It must have been a terrible nightmare. As Logan slowly came awake, he was aware that the room was all too dark but that Polina's fingers were stroking his face. He could smell her too, that spicy sweet scent that was distinctly her own. Only, the pain at the back of his head was real, and whatever he was laying on was terribly uncomfortable.

"Logan? Logan, wake up," Polina said, her voice raw and broken.

Logan blinked in the darkness, then pushed himself up. "Where are we?"

She hesitated. "We're prisoners inside a cavern on my mountain. Alex took my wand." She spread her hands. "Witches manipulate the elements. The only thing here is air, and that isn't my element."

"Do all supernaturals underestimate humans?"

"I hardly think this is the time for barbs or trick questions."

Logan exhaled. "I just mean, he left my backpack on." He pulled the pack from his shoulders, felt his way to unzip the zipper, and retrieved his flashlight. *Click.* The bulb blazed to life.

Polina's face was a mask of pain, pale and streaked with mascara. Her arms were covered in bruises and her hair was a tangled mess. Logan didn't say a word; he pulled her into his arms as a fresh burst of sobs bubbled up her throat.

"Shhh. Shhh," Logan cooed in her ear. "This is bad, but we can figure it out. I have more things in my bag. Maybe there's something we can use." He'd never seen her like this. Distraught and beaten down. If he hadn't known better, he'd think she'd lost weight. She felt like a skeleton in his arms, all poking joints and frail bones. But that was impossible. He'd been with her only hours ago.

With a long, rattling inhale, she steadied herself. "Hildegard." The word was hardly audible but the sense of dread she communicated with it came across clearly.

Logan moved his flashlight along the floor of their cell. The light caught on a tiny, naked body. He could only tell it was once the snowy owl by the talons on its feet and the tufts of feathers still clinging erratically to its hide.

"What happened to her?"

Polina shook her head. "Some kind of magic or poison. The amulet Alex is wearing is very powerful. He means for this to be my torture. He hurt her to hurt me."

Pressing two fingers against Hildegard's chest, Logan felt a faint heartbeat. "She's still alive," he said.

"She can't die as long as she's bound to my life force."

Logan looked back at Polina. "You're keeping her alive?" he asked, eyebrows pinching above his nose. He hadn't been mistaken. She was definitely thinner, her complexion sallow.

"I have for hours. But I have no elements to draw on here, so I can only feed her on myself... the magic that makes up my body. Alex knows I will eventually run out of power. Once I'm drained, our connection will fade. She'll be cut off and I'll be forced to watch her die. He put you here so that I'd have to watch you die too. And then I'll spend eternity in this box with both of your decaying corpses."

Logan's mouth dropped open. "Fuck. That. This asshole does not get to win. I'm going to get us out of here, and you are going to find a way to save Hildegard."

Polina's eyes flicked to the floor.

"Do you think I'm weak?" Logan asked.

"No," she whispered.

"Helpless?"

"No."

"When I say I'm going to get you out of here, I mean it. Tell me you believe in me."

She nodded weakly in the light of his flashlight.

Logan dumped out the contents of his backpack. The water bottle was empty. "Plastic," he said disappointedly. "I should have switched to aluminum." He put on the hooded jacket. "Aha!" Out of the pocket, he pulled a small Swiss army knife, holding it out to her in his outstretched palm like it was a great prize.

She took the knife, weighing it in her palm. "Let me see the flashlight."

He handed it over.

"Almost nothing. The batteries might help but not enough to make a difference. Not worth losing the light." She stood with the knife and limped closer to him, touching the zipper of his coat. At once, the metal teeth and slider melted from the cloth and soaked into her hand. Logan might have been mistaken, but he thought he saw some color come back to her cheeks. "Anything else in there?"

"Money, bandages."

She shook her head. "The zipper on the bag?"

He held it up to her. She made short work of it, then turned toward the wall of the container. "Shine the light over here."

He pointed the flashlight in the direction of her voice. "The magic sealed itself once he moved you inside, but maybe, if I can find a crack or seam, I can get us out of here."

She ran her hands along the wall, twirling the pocketknife between her fingers. The metal morphed into a living thing and inched its way along with her. A small river of liquid silver.

"Well?" he asked as she arrived at the place she'd begun.

"There's no seam," she murmured. "Not even an area of weakness, as far as I can tell."

Logan balanced the flashlight on its end to evenly spread light across the small area. He stood up and started running his hands along the invisible barrier. He was six feet two inches tall and could easily reach the ceiling. The box they were in was barely longer than it was tall. In minutes they had searched every square inch.

"It's sealed," Polina said. She turned toward Logan, the upward-facing light giving her face a ghoulish appearance. The blob of metal re-formed into his pocketknife and she handed it back to him.

"What else can we try? If you absorb this, can you blast us out of here?"

She shook her head. "I couldn't blast us out of here when I was at my strongest."

Logan slid down the wall, digging in the empty pockets of the backpack and flipping the bottle and knife over in his hands. He refused to accept that there was no way out.

"They're going to kill Silas," Logan said.

"Alex has him?" Polina asked.

Logan nodded.

"Then perhaps it's best we die in here. If Alex takes control of all werewolf packs and has the dragon fae amulet, no witch or supernatural being, short of Hecate herself, will rival his power. And humans..." She shook her head.

"Grateful and Rick will come. Silas called them for help."

"Silas spoke with Grateful Knight?"

"Well, no, he left her a message."

Polina licked her lips and paced the cell. "Poe will notice Hildegard is missing. They'll come, but it will be too late for Silas. If they have him, he's probably already dead."

"No. Alex said there was some ritual. He had to wait for the pack to shift and then they would... eat Silas."

"I'd forgotten about that ritual."

Logan shrugged. "When is sunset? Alex did not leave me my phone, and I don't have a watch."

"We have less than an hour," she murmured. "I can feel the coming of night, even in here." She folded her hands against her heart and stared at the wall.

Panic rose in Logan's chest. The sight of Hildegard dying on the floor, Polina wasting away before his eyes, and the thought that he would die in here, in this box, was so unfair. For the first time in his life, he loved someone and felt loved in return and before he could even enjoy it, it was over. Everything was over.

He rubbed his chest, his heart beating so hard it ached. His mind wandered to Rick, to that scar on his chest, and to Polina, kneeling on the floor in the room of reflections, admitting that she'd prepped him to become her caretaker, just in case, in order to save his life if she'd had to.

A chill calm came over Logan. Flashes of suffering and

scenes of elation coursed through his brain, the faces of friends, past lovers, people he knew through the restaurant. Everything he was, had been, would be, washed into him all at once. The tide had come in on the edge of a storm. In the eye of the hurricane, in the center of the swirl of emotions as he considered the end of his life, all he could see was Polina. All he could feel was dread at the thought that he would die but she would go on and on, an eternity of suffering. He couldn't have it. He wouldn't.

"Change me," he said.

"What?" Polina asked, turning from the wall, her eyes wide in the dim light.

"Make me your caretaker."

6

CHANGES

"You don't mean that," Polina said. She wasn't sure what she feared more, that he might be serious or that he wasn't.

"I do mean it. I've seen what Rick becomes, and he could bust out of this place just by shifting. You'll change me, I'll shift, and we'll be free."

"You don't know what you're asking. This isn't like a marriage, Logan. It's not till death do us part. We will be bound for eternity. Mountains will fall and rivers will turn to dust and still we will be bound."

"I'm willing."

"But you're not ready. How could you be? I've lived almost five hundred years and I've only begun to wrap my head around what forever means. It's as much a curse as a blessing."

"I choose this. I have the right to choose."

"You're a chef, Logan. You won't want to eat anymore. Food will give you little joy. You don't know what you're saying."

That gave him pause. Food was his livelihood, his passion. After a moment, Logan stood to approach her. "But I do know what I'm saying. When I met you, I thought the last thing I needed was another witch in my life. I wanted a normal relationship. A house, two kids, a dog in the yard. But you know what? I recently had a chance to adopt a dog and I found out I'm a cat person."

"What does any of this have to do with you adopting a cat?" Polina asked in frustration.

"A three-legged cat with no tail. See, I didn't know what I wanted until it was right there in front of me. If you had asked me if I'd wanted a three-legged cat before I met her, I would've said no. But I knew the moment I saw her. See, I'm damaged—"

"You are not damaged."

"I am damaged. I've been dead. Do you think any human woman is ever going to understand and accept that not only do I live with my mother, she happens to be dead and visits me occasionally with warnings about the future? No. They're going to run from me like I'm Norman Bates. I've been a ghost, Polina. I've slipped under someone's skin and seen them from the inside out. I'm not normal. I'll never survive a normal life."

"You could. It is possible."

"It's not possible, because I love *you*. I risked my life to come here tonight to save you. That plan went completely and totally wrong, as wrong as it could go, actually. But I knew the risks, and even if I knew then what I know now, that I'd end up in this box with you, I would have tried anyway. My life may have worked before you, Polina, but there was no magic in it. I was dead on the side of the road. You resurrected me. My second life was yours from the beginning."

She was crying now, chest aching. "There's no going back from this."

He stepped into her, placed his hands on her shoulders. "All those years, all my life, I've struggled to fill the hole my parents made. I worked for security, to create some semblance of family among my friends and my occupation. I've been hungry and lonely, loose in the world. I built Valentine's as a kind of home. A security blanket. Fuck, I'm not making any sense, I know, but just listen. Then there was you. For the first time I felt safe, not because of your power but because of your love. Your love feels endless. It feels true. It fills me. I wouldn't dream of going back." He cupped her face and lowered his forehead to hers.

"Come on, Polina. I'm as good as dead. Do what you do best. Save me. Change me. I'm not asking; I'm demanding. Change me now."

Polina closed her eyes. It was his choice and, goddess help her, she wasn't strong enough to turn him away. She needed him too much. Putting space between them, she nodded. "Last chance to change your mind."

"I want this."

She pointed one hand at his chest and, gathering what power she had left, uttered the incantation, "*Akmut ghut rae mud ed tyn.*" Caretaker of the light, always.

A forked tongue of lightning flew from her hand, plowing into his chest and sizzling as it wormed into his heart. For a moment, he looked wounded. His face begged her for relief from the pain. She cried out his name, desperate to help him, but there was nothing she could do. The spell had to run its course.

Logan collapsed on the floor seizing, his muscles rigid. Polina knelt by his side. A lock of her hair dropped from her head and fell across his chest as she leaned over him. Her bones ached from the power draining from her.

The immortality she was giving Logan had to come from somewhere. She doubted Logan had realized the implications and was glad her fate didn't play into his decision. This way, his choice to become her caretaker was about him, not her. Still, as the life force bled out of her like the release of a deeply held breath, her eyes and shoulders drooped. She couldn't give in to the fatigue. There was one last step. One last part of the spell. She had to give him an element.

A caretaker couldn't have the same element as his witch, although using the pocketknife would have been the natural solution for her. No. The rules of making a caretaker required sacrifice at every turn. Using another element would further drain her, a demanding price. But which to use? The dirt on the bottom of Logan's shoes might work for earth or she might be able to shake a drop of water from the bottom of the water bottle. Both of those options would have required her to move, a feat becoming more and more improbable. There wasn't a sliver of wood to be found. But there was one element close at hand. She pinched Logan's nose, tipped his head back. Eyes closed, she took a deep breath and blew into his mouth.

As the air filled his lungs, Polina felt the last of her immortality leave her along with a tiny piece of her soul. A twinkle of light exited her mouth and entered his. Her death seemed probable now. The only other person she knew who had done this was Grateful and her first incarnation had died, burned at the stake the day she changed Rick. Polina figured her fate was sealed, but she trusted Logan would find a way to bring her back, eventually.

Logan was quiet now, lying perfectly still on his back. Why wasn't it working? She didn't have the energy to consider the question. Instead, she lay down beside him and slipped away.

AWAKENING

Logan had underestimated the pain. When the lightning bolt from Polina's hand plowed into his chest, fire spread from his heart to his toes, searing his veins, frying his internal organs. His brain boiled inside his skull, and his skin bore the excruciating agony of being stripped from his body without actually going anywhere. His muscles seized and his body thrashed on the floor.

Kneeling by his side, Polina hunched over him as if she carried a sandbag on her shoulders. Something was wrong with her. Maybe the spell wasn't working. Maybe he was dying.

And then she kissed him. His lungs filled with her air and right at the end of the breath, a warm glowing thing advanced down his throat. It tasted of light and life with the spicy sweetness he'd come to associate with Polina. Whatever she had given him chased away the pain. It did something else, as well. It killed him.

Logan stopped breathing. His cells blinked off one by one. Those little workshops that kept his body running simply went out of business. His heart stopped beating. His stomach stopped growling. A stillness he'd never experienced came over him. And then the flashlight burned out, or maybe his vision stopped working, although his eyes were still open.

He'd been cold a moment ago. Now there was no cold. But there was a warm spot where Polina's shallow breath hit his cheek. He focused on that, in and out, in and out, the shallow flow of air that gave her life. His own lungs gave it a try. He could do it. He could breathe.

But, with marked curiosity, he realized he didn't need to.

He flexed one hand, then the other. With each blink, his vision washed in, a red wave that adjusted to his surroundings. The flashlight hadn't burned out; it had fallen over and rolled against the wall. In its current position, it gave off only a sliver of light, but Logan could see clearly.

Hinging at the hips, he sat up without the assistance of his arms and stood in a way that defied gravity, with only the slightest flexion of his knees. This was new. He'd never moved like that. Once on his feet, he noticed something else. The muscle of his bicep strained against the fabric of the jacket he was wearing. It hadn't before. Not that he needed the jacket anyway. He stripped out of the hoody and looked down at himself.

"Holy shit! Move aside, Captain America; there's a new Avenger in town." He turned toward Polina. "Hey, look at this. I think it worked."

She didn't move. A heavy ache started deep within his chest. She was still breathing, but when he lifted her in his arms, clumps of her hair fell out and drifted to the floor. "Polina? Polina?" She wouldn't rouse.

Dread turned to anger and the skin of his forearm began

to bubble ominously. He'd seen that happen to Rick. "Oh shit."

Carefully, he set her down at the far side of their prison and placed Hildegard in her arms. He backed as far away from them as he could. The pain was back, this time radiating from his bones. Boils swelled and popped along his back, and his stomach strained. He pitched forward to try to vomit and watched his jaw extend instead. His hands hit the floor, talons sprouting from the knuckles and red scales climbing up and over his arms.

By the time he noticed he'd sprouted a tail, he couldn't think at all. The roiling pain and the expansion of his body took all his concentration. He needed to get bigger, but something was blocking him, holding him in. With a roar and a stretch, the thing around him shattered and he reared up, flapping the gigantic red wings that had sprouted from his back.

Logan had no idea what he'd turned into, but if the taloned paws, spiked tail, and red scales were any indication, it was dragonlike and humungous. He practically filled the cavern they were in.

Clumsily, he gathered Polina into his paws. His talon tore her dress, but he managed to cradle her and her familiar in his scaly red palms. He used his back legs to walk them out of there. At the opening, he stepped into the snow, the icy wind coursing over his scales. The sky held the bright pink and purple hues of a recently departed sun.

The night sky invited him to be part of it as sure as if a hand reached out from the clouds to welcome him. He smiled, his lips drawing against unfamiliar fangs. She'd given him the air. The element surged in and out of his lungs, strengthening him. The night opened like a fast friend, and he spread his wings and flew.

48

MORTAL BELOVED

Polina had doubted he could do it at first. Surely flying was something that took practice, especially while holding a dying woman in your hands. But Logan slipped into the sky like he was a piece of the night. He'd transformed into a beast that could be described as a red dragon, although caretakers usually had a decidedly more doggish appearance in the face, and he was no exception. Along with tufts of golden hair that grew out between his scales, dragonlike did not equate to dragon. He was beautiful, magical, and completely deadly.

She smiled at the curve of his chest that merged into the long, graceful neck. The tips of his wings were barely visible in her peripheral vision. A flashback to King Kong came to her. She was Ann Darrow, clutched in the claws of her own personal monster.

A raucous of howls and breaking bones came from below, and her stomach dropped as Logan descended. He landed on the edge of the clearing in front of Renegade Caverns. The lack of noise he produced, his large body gracefully slipping between the trees, was almost miraculous. He set her down at the base of a beech tree and sniffed her face. With Hildegard nestled in her arm, she placed a hand on the side of his giant leather nose.

"Go save Silas. I won't be able to help you. I'm sorry." The nostrils snorted, blowing her hair back. Logan pulled away and silently coiled through the forest toward the Renegade Caverns clearing.

At first, she resolved to stay where she was, but curiosity got the best of her. She pulled herself up on a tree trunk and limped toward the clearing, using the trees to prop herself up and cradling Hildegard in one arm. After what felt like miles but was surely much less, she could see the pack.

Silas had already shifted and his black wolf lay like a sacrifice across the totem she'd seen Alex stand on yesterday night. The thick chains crisscrossed the wolf's neck and chest, threading through openings in the sides of the carved wood. Silas's black wolf seemed resolved to his fate, staring straight ahead and waiting peacefully for his end.

Alex had already shifted as well. Polina assumed this had to do with the age and experience of the werewolf, because the younger wolves still writhed in agony under the full moon. The red alpha paced the clearing, waiting for the masses to finish shifting, the amulet hanging from his neck like a dog tag. Where was Logan?

With a yelp, Alex's body lifted from the ground and twisted in the air. The amulet glowed red, and Logan appeared, hovering over the clearing. He spit out Alex like a bitter pill, his dragonlike head and body shedding invisibility as if he'd been wearing the night as a cloak. Alex lowered his growling snarl. His ears flattened against the sides of his head.

With a roar worthy of a massive reptilian beast, Logan's talon sliced through the chains holding Silas. The black wolf came to life, squirmed from the totem. He charged into the woods behind the dragon. The other wolves gave Logan plenty of room as he positioned his spiked body between Alex and Silas.

She couldn't be sure, but she thought Alex's wolfie features looked surprised. But then, there was no way the werewolf could have foreseen that Polina would have prepped Logan with the caretaker spell. A dark heart such as his wouldn't expect or understand a spell based on true love.

The amulet glowed again and Logan hopped back as if he'd been burned. Rearing, he took to the sky, flying straight up as Alex leapt and snapped and sparks flew from the amulet. But Logan's dragon scales repelled the worst of the onslaught. He circled above them, coiling like a snake with its tail in a trap, and with the speed of a rattler's bite, snapped jaws on the back of Alex's neck. The amulet glowed again, but whatever Alex meant to do didn't seem to happen. Logan's teeth severed the chain and the amulet dropped to the dirt.

Massive jaws flipped the red wolf deeper into the beast's mouth. Logan shook Alex like a rag doll until his wolf body let out a loud snap and the red wolf yelped in pain. Had he broken the werewolf's spine? It certainly looked that way. The alpha's legs dangled listlessly from Logan's teeth. And there was blood. Lots of it.

With a flurry of flapping, Logan carried the wolf away and disappeared into the night sky. Silas didn't waste a second. He scooped up the amulet in his jaws, then jumped on top of the carved pack totem. This must have had social significance among the pack because all the other wolves lowered their heads. No challengers approached Silas, but Alex had built his pack out of the weakest, most submissive pack members, whose alphas he'd murdered. As far as Polina could tell, the entire pack welcomed Silas's leadership. With thirty werewolves bowing in a circle around him, Silas dropped the amulet between his paws, raised his head, and howled.

Polina smiled weakly. She was so tired. Her pallor made the skin over her boney fingers seem to glow in the dark. She looked down at Hildegard in the crook of her arm and gasped. The owl hadn't been conscious in hours but for the first time, Polina couldn't detect a breath or a heartbeat.

"No...No... Hildie!" She shook the bird gently. The owl didn't respond.

Polina ached to her bones, but she forced herself through the woods, hooking her free hand on the trees to help herself along. The house was just over a mile from the caverns, but what used to be a short stroll felt like a jungle trek. She pushed herself, desperate to get to her spell book and help Hildegard.

When she reached Aurorean House, Nicodemus sailed down from the gables to meet her. "What has happened, my lady?" he asked.

"Help me to the door," she pleaded.

The gargoyle scooped her up and bound to the front stoop.

"Thank you." She wriggled down and placed a hand on his cheek. "Good and faithful servant, guard the house well tonight. No one but Logan gets in."

"Logan? The human male?"

"He is no longer human."

The gargoyle nodded his head. Polina navigated the house to her bedroom. She fell through the cheval mirror and stumbled to the center of her most magical space. Unable to conjure a bed, she collapsed on the floor of the room of reflection and looked up at the ceiling. She was a corpse, skeletal and nearly bald. Hildegard was featherless and motionless in her arms.

Hot tears stung the corners of her eyes.

"Please don't die, Hildie. I'm not giving up on you. It's going to be okay. Just stay with me." Her hoarse throat felt red and swollen. She laid her head on the floor, too weak to do anything more and gave herself over to the darkness.

49

THE RETURN

High above Silver Sparrow mountain, Logan accepted that Alex was dead. The werewolf hadn't moved or fought back in miles and his body hung limply from Logan's bite. He'd succeeded in snapping the wolf's neck, he was sure. He released the red wolf high over the mountain, Alex's body falling into the woods below him. Let the forest have him. He'd be nothing but bones in a matter of days.

Logan circled back to the clearing, but Polina and the wolves were gone. Her scent was like a beacon to him now. The spicy sweetness that was Polina, a faint whisper when he was human, now was all encompassing, a lighthouse that drew him to her. It wasn't just the smell. He could feel her nearby as if his heart was attached to hers by a rubber band. No, he had that wrong. It wasn't his heart that was connected to hers; it was the piece of her soul trying to find its other half. With fascination, he focused on the small light that had taken root in his chest. Her immortal soul. The idea that he now housed a piece of her inside of him made him both swell with pride and internally recoil from the weight of the massive responsibility. Was he ready? Was he up to the task?

He landed in the yard of Aurorean House. The pull in his chest told him she was inside, but there was no way he'd fit through the door in his dragon form. He paced, trying to relax, to change back to himself.

A gargoyle from Polina's north gable flapped its metal wings and soared to his feet. The twisted demon face pulled back its lips in a fanged smile that Logan would find creepy if everything about that night hadn't been so strange already. Animated copper gargoyles. Polina had mentioned them once. After the werewolves and the shifting, he just rolled with it.

"Master Logan," the gargoyle said, "Nicodemus, at your service. The lady awaits your arrival inside. May I suggest you change into your human form first?"

Logan wanted to say, *No shit, Sherlock.* All he could manage was a roar.

"Concentrate on your heartbeat, sir. The heart is key." Nicodemus worried his hands in front of his tarnished copper chest.

Logan closed his eyes and focused. *Lub dub, lub dub.* He meditated on the sound, shifting his attention to the center of himself. His head pitched forward and the pain came again, only this time the change happened faster. His talons and tail retracted, red scales shed exposing human skin, and when he thought he couldn't stand the snap of his bones breaking for one more second, he unfolded... completely naked.

"Er, thanks," he said to the gargoyle, sprinting for the entrance. He stopped short when he remembered something important. "Nicodemus, Polina's wand is missing. Can you search for it?"

"Until dawn." The gargoyle bowed low and then motioned to his friends on the roof, who swooped down and followed him into the forest.

Logan didn't waste any time getting his naked self into the house. He was aching for a shower and needed to make sure Polina and Hildegard had recovered safely. There was a cold spot at the center of his chest and he rubbed the uncomfortable feeling as he made his way down the hall, searching for her.

"Polina?" he called. When he reached her bedroom, he stepped up to the cheval mirror he'd gone through before. Of course she'd be in her room of reflections; she would need the power to heal herself. Tentatively, he reached toward the silver, breathing a sigh of relief as his hand passed through. The rest of his body followed.

Inside the passageway to the heart of her sanctuary, a million tiny reflections surrounded him from every angle. He took a step forward and smacked into polished silver. Turning, he tried again. This time he moved three steps before bonking into the next mirror. "Okay," he murmured. Holding out his hands, he skimmed the wall with his fingers, closed his eyes, and reached out with his other senses. He allowed the light behind his heart to move his body. He trusted it to guide him to her.

It didn't take long to find her this way, and he wondered if the mirrors had adjusted for him as they once had for her. When he opened his eyes, a stiff panic flooded through him. He rushed to the place she was crumpled on the floor and gathered her into his arms. Her skin was gray. Her lips blue.

"Polina? Polina?" He shook her gently.

Lowering his lips to her forehead, he began to tremble. Her skin was ice cold. He was afraid to check, but he was pretty sure the owl, tied to the crook of her arm with her bell sleeve, was dead. And what of Polina? He couldn't find a pulse.

"Come on. This isn't right. This isn't how it's supposed to be." But even as he said the words he remembered Grateful. Rick had to reconnect her soul to her body after she was reincarnated because she could die and he couldn't. The horror came to him all at once. Polina had given him her immortality, and now she was dying from whatever curse that fucking werewolf had placed on her and Hildegard before he'd boxed them up.

He hugged Polina to his chest and rocked, tears flowing. He couldn't accept this. Never. He didn't care if every witch who ever made a caretaker had died in the process, he wouldn't allow Polina to go. He'd reverse the process somehow. Give her back what he'd taken from her.

And then it came to him. Rick had given Grateful back her power through blood and sex. Polina was in no shape for the latter, but maybe, just maybe, his blood would do the trick. He cradled her in his arms.

"Polina, I need you to do something for me. You've got to wake up."

No reaction.

He raised his wrist to his teeth and bit. It was physically painful but nothing compared to the cruel punishment his emotions were drilling into him at the moment. Blood bubbled to the surface, and he pressed it to her lips. When she didn't open her mouth, he tugged her jaw down and tipped her in his arms. The blood pooled in her open mouth.

"Swallow," he begged her. "Just one swallow."

WITCH

Witches don't die easily. Polina's last thought as she passed over on the floor of the room of reflections was that, had she been human, she never would have made it this far. It was clear to her now that Alex had cursed Hildegard with a wasting disease. He knew the familiar would either die or drain Polina's energy, rendering her as good as dead in his makeshift tomb. Only Polina had done something Alex hadn't expected. When she had made Logan her caretaker, she'd given up her immortality. At that point, the wasting disease had spread from Hildegard to her.

An hour ago, she may have still had the strength to cut Hildie loose and save herself, but she was too far gone for that now. By the time she realized she wasn't just being dragged into death by Hildegard but had caught the curse and was dying herself, it was too late. Her only solace was that Hildegard would return to Hecate's garden, the place all familiars came from, and Polina would be reincarnated. She'd return to Logan when her new incarnation reached adulthood. Rick would help him until then, she was sure. She'd be with Logan again, someday.

With the image of her love firmly etched in her mind, she allowed herself to drift away. It was okay. She'd slide into the beyond and let the universe handle the particulars, her soul to join eternity. With her last breath, her soul filtered through her skin and hovered above her chest.

Unexpectedly, a glorious taste filled her mouth, and in that flavor was the song of her soul. Her spirit sank back into her body, winding through her veins to dance with its newly discovered partner. Painfully, her heart contracted in response to the flow. She swallowed and swallowed again, gasping around the tide of blood down her throat.

Strong arms cradled her body and their warmth infused her, seeping through her skin and sinking into bone.

"That's it. Drink." Logan's voice. But something was wrong. He sounded upset. Distraught. She tried to open her eyes but failed. "You're okay. You're safe. Just drink."

She did. She snuggled into his embrace, eventually raising her hand to hold his wrist to her mouth. Why hadn't she thought of this before? As the vessel of her soul, Logan's blood could heal her. It could break enchantments too. As she drank, the warmth permeated her stomach, then branched outward, worming its way through her arteries and veins, spreading to the tiny capillaries that fed her muscles and her skin.

Her strength returned slowly, but it did return. Once she couldn't hold another drop, she stopped drinking and opened her eyes. She gazed into the tear-stained face of the man who was both her love and her life.

A shaky sigh of relief broke his lips. "Thank the goddess."

"Hildegard?" she asked.

He sat her up against his chest, and together they unwrapped Hildegard's body. The bird looked dead, pale and almost featherless. But Polina had never given up on her friend and familiar, and she wouldn't now. They were bound metaphysically, which meant if Polina was alive, some part of Hildegard must be too.

Holding the bird out in her open palms, she uttered the healing enchantment she'd used on Logan. *"Reinchide velecluse moribidatae vialanium."* She didn't have her wand, but here, in the center of her element, it wasn't strictly necessary. Drawing on the strength Logan had given her, Polina fed her owl everything she had to give.

Blue light flowed from every reflective surface and plowed into the bird in her hands. Behind her, Logan turned his face from the force of the magic. The tiny body twitched, then twitched again. And then Hildegard's head rolled. Polina stopped the spell and pulled her familiar closer.

"Hildegard? Speak to me."

The tiny, bald bird blinked gigantic yellow eyes at her. "The things I go through for you. Do you know I was practically dead? And because of a werewolf I told you to get rid of weeks ago." Her beak smacked her disapproval.

"Glad to have you back, Hildie." Polina hugged the bird against her chest.

"All right, all right. Don't smother me." She flapped her featherless wings and went positively nowhere, then wiggled herself onto her own two feet. "I suppose *you'll* be around more," she said to Logan.

"I plan on it," he answered.

"You can understand her?" Polina asked.

Logan nodded. "She has a slight Scottish accent. Cute."

"I like him," Hildie said, shaking her downy stub of a

tail and looking at it forlornly. "Now what am I to do? I'm bald. I cannot fly without any feathers. You'll have to carry me everywhere. Can you fix this?" she asked Polina.

Polina frowned. "I can try. I'm sure you will recover, but it will take time. All of us need to rest and get stronger."

"What am I supposed to do until then? I can't have anyone see me like this. What about Poe?" She whispered the last as if her love affair with the raven was some well-kept secret.

Polina shrugged. "I could knit you a sweater?"

Hildegard looked positively disdainful.

"Come on, old girl. Let's see if I can recover my wand and help you out." She stood with the bird in the crook of her arm.

"Uh, Polina?" Logan said, pointing in the general area of his nakedness.

"Hmm? What, dear?"

"I'm naked."

"I see no problem with this."

Logan placed his hands on his hips and growled his disapproval.

"Oh!" Polina took a step backward. "All right, if it means that much to you." She snapped her fingers and sweats and a T-shirt appeared on the floor.

He pulled them on. "That's it? A stern look and you give in?"

"You didn't see your eyes," Polina said, sliding an arm around his waist and coaxing him toward the looking glass entrance. "I'm afraid, as of today, you officially wear your heart on your sleeve. It's become very easy to tell when you're angry."

51
GUESTS

As it happened, Nicodemus hadn't found Polina's wand before sunrise. Luckily, someone else had. No sooner had the sun broken the horizon than Silas plodded from the shelter of the branches, wearing cut-off shorts that couldn't possibly be his and a dragon amulet. In his teeth was Polina's wand. Logan held the door open for him, and Polina motioned for him to take a seat at the table. Silas returned her wand, and Polina pulled him into a quick hug.

"Thank the goddess you're safe," she said.

"I want to thank you two for stopping Alex. If you hadn't, I'm not sure if the supernatural community would ever recover."

"Agreed," Polina said, gripping her wand with both hands. "What do you plan to do with the amulet?"

"It will be returned to the Siberian dragon fae. It's where it belongs."

Logan cleared his throat. "Why didn't you tell me you were alpha of your pack? All this time and you never let me know."

Silas lowered his eyes and ran his fingers over the

table. "For your safety, Logan. The Fireborn wolves are the oldest and most established pack in the country. We rule the werewolf presence in North America. The man who was killed and stuffed in your dumpster was my decoy. He attended all werewolf events as me, just in case. He gave his life for me, but once he was dead, Alex knew the truth."

"How?"

"My pack didn't acknowledge him as their alpha. The connection between alpha and pack is metaphysical. If he'd killed me, they would have to bow down to him, no questions asked. It would have been possible for one of my siblings to challenge him for the position, but as long as he had the amulet, the effort would be fruitless."

With one hand rubbing circles over Polina's back, Logan narrowed his eyes on Silas. "Well, now you've told us, so I hope you know you can trust me."

Silas's eyes shifted between him and Polina. "And you, me. But I need to ask you something."

"Shoot."

"What did you do with Alex's body?"

Logan shook his head. "I broke his spine and dropped him on the side of the mountain. He's dead."

"Has to be," Silas said. "If he wasn't, his pack wouldn't have reverted to me as their alpha."

"My sous-chef, Jonah, was working for him. I think he was the one who actually committed the murder."

"Don't worry. Wherever he is, Jonah will find himself with new priorities. Polina, can I have your permission to recover the body from your property? It's a pack thing. There are traditions we follow."

"Yes. As long as you need."

Silas nodded. "Then my work here is done. Something

tells me you two will want to celebrate your new relationship."

Logan grinned, noticing Polina's cheeks redden. He opened the door to let Silas out, only to find Grateful and Rick on the other side.

"Oh thank the goddess! Are you all right?" Grateful eyed the shattered glass Polina had swept to one side of the kitchen. "We got your message and came as quickly as we could." Grateful pulled Logan into a hug and then wrapped her arms around Silas.

Grateful's raven familiar swooped through the door, barely evading their heads. "Hildegard? Oh my dear Hildie. What happened to you? Are you well?"

"Don't look at me, Poe. I'm hideous!"

"No, of course you aren't. You are as beautiful as a newborn chick."

"Really?"

"Oh yes." He cuddled against her on her kitchen perch. "A specimen to behold."

Hildie rested her head on his black shoulder. "You are a terrible liar, but the feathers will grow back."

Poe didn't say a word, but the look he gave Logan portrayed something along the lines of *thank the goddess.*

Logan scratched the side of his head. The others were still staring at the two birds with various expressions of mild amusement. "Refreshing when love overcomes adversity."

The others mumbled their agreement.

Polina took a deep breath and put on her most genuine smile. "Well, come on in. I'll put on a pot of tea, and we'll catch you up on the happenings of last night."

Grateful stared at Logan, her eyebrows sinking over narrowed eyes. She reached out and poked her fingers directly into the area of his T-shirt that covered the brand-new scythe-shaped scar on his chest. "Yes. I think you both have some explaining to do."

Polina lifted a teapot from the top of the stove and plunged it under the faucet.

"You may want to fill that pot," Silas said, eyes fixating on the window. There were six men standing in the front yard, each of them disheveled and wearing hastily obtained apparel. "It looks like my backup from the Lycanthropic Society finally decided to stop by."

Polina placed the full teapot on the burner and lit the fire underneath. "Welcome them in. I only want to have to tell this story once."

52

BALANCE

Once the story was told and told again, all parties agreed the young werewolves would be split up and adopted by the remaining alpha families and given more appropriate living arrangements. Silas bid them farewell and ushered the werewolf alphas to Renegade Caverns to lead Alex's remaining pack members from Polina's realm.

"I'm sorry things went the way they did, but I'm happy for both of you," Grateful said, kissing them both on the cheek. "We would have been here earlier but we were in Sedona visiting a Native American healer about Lucas."

"Whatever for?" Polina asked.

"I wanted her to tell me if he is normal," Grateful said.

"What did she say?" Logan asked tentatively.

"She said his potential is unlimited even if it is unnamed."

"What the hell does that mean?"

"It means the woman is five hundred dollars richer for telling us our child will grow up," Rick said through a wry grin.

"Rick!" Grateful nudged him with her elbow but smiled sweetly as if part of her agreed.

"I'm sure you'll love him just the same, no matter," Polina said.

Grateful nodded. They said their goodbyes and departed, along with Poe and Hildegard. The latter had recovered enough, after a few rounds of Polina's healing magic, to go hunting with Poe's help.

"That kid's definitely a warlock," Polina said once the door was closed behind them.

"Definitely," Logan agreed.

She turned to him and laughed.

"What now?" Logan asked.

"I should survey the damage to my realm. I'm sure the mountain trolls aren't happy with the happenings of last night."

Logan nodded. "I should check on the restaurant and feed Bonny. Plus, I want to pick up some groceries. You don't eat enough."

"Will you cook for me?"

"Every night."

"Will you make me chocolate cake?" Polina asked in a husky whisper. The words rolled off her tongue and across her lips in a wave that went directly to Logan's erection.

"Any time. The secret ingredient is mayonnaise."

"Will you have to kill me now?"

"Only if you tell." He stepped into her, grabbing her around the waist and pulling her against him. The move was faster than humanly possible. As light as air in his arms, he spun her around, his thigh sliding between her legs and her back arching over his arm as his chest pressed into hers. For a moment, her face registered something he wasn't expecting, the slightest degree of fear.

"What's wrong?" But as he asked he knew. His canines had dropped, the sharp tips rubbing against his lower lip. He touched his face, felt the hard bones jutting under the skin, the elongated jaw. He must look terrifying.

She placed her hands on his cheeks. "You're beautiful. And it's natural; You're hungry. Before you feed me, let me feed you."

53

CONNECTION

Polina led Logan to the bedroom and through the looking glass to her sanctuary where she commanded a bed to form at the center of the room of reflections. She would give him what he needed, and she'd enjoy every minute of it.

Logan untied her corset. His breathing hastened as her breasts spilled out of the stiff black material and strained against the thin white cotton of the shift underneath. His beast was close to the surface, his eyes dark and a hint of red scales shimmering along the skin of his shoulder.

Her fingers found the bottom of his T-shirt and pulled it over his head. As she cast it aside, she paused to run her fingers over the scythe-shaped scar on his chest. It was healed but fresh, still slightly pink. "Does it hurt?"

"No." His stare was aching, hungry. Fragile, human Logan was gone. The thing she was attracted to from the start had replaced him. The strength of will that had kept his heart beating the day of his accident now ruled his immortal being.

"You're hungry." Polina helped him out of his sweats

303

and wrapped her hand around his shaft. A swift inhale whistled through his teeth.

Goddess help her, she could feel his need. It was a living thing, a pulse between them, a connection as real as if he was in her head. Logan grabbed her around the waist and carried her to the bed. Her shift didn't make it all the way there. He tore it from her body and cast it aside.

After seating her on the edge of the bed, he crawled onto the mattress so he was kneeling behind her. His fingers trailed her back, then traced her ribs. Methodically, his touch stroked over her belly button before moving south to wedge between her thighs.

"What are you doing?" she asked.

"Let me see your reflection."

She concentrated and made it so. He met her gaze in the mirror she was facing, the reflection gave her a gorgeous view of her naked body framed in his. While she watched, he spread her knees wide.

"Logan," she said, cheeks growing hot. She closed her legs and turned her face over her shoulder, reaching for him. He gently grabbed her chin and coaxed her to face the mirror again, running his fingers under her breasts, cupping their heavy weight before pinching the nipples while she watched. She squirmed at the sight of herself, pale and thin against his massive chest. He met her eyes in the mirror and a wanting grin spread across his lips. Again, he pulled her knees apart.

With a gasp her gaze trailed down her body, from the full breasts that Logan kneaded and teased, to the curve of her waist, to her thighs, and eventually lower. She was wet with need for him. He grabbed her right hand and guided it down her stomach to her most tender flesh and pressed her fingers into herself. She moaned as his fingers coaxed hers in circles.

Eyes never leaving the mirror, Logan's lips found Polina's neck, pushing her red hair aside with his nose and chin. She picked up the pace, rubbing herself in earnest under the pressure of his hand. Logan's lips worked along her jugular. With supernatural grace, he slid his legs around hers from behind on the bed, then lifted her by the waist and lowered her onto his lap.

He worked inside her, his moan of pleasure vibrating against her neck. His hand tangled in her hair as she moved, and all the time he watched her in the mirror. She bobbed and stroked herself, arching against him in pleasure. She was close, and he was right there with her.

His reflection turned dark, teeth extending, eyes bleeding to black. He almost broke the rhythm. She could tell he was hesitating; he didn't want to hurt her. Only Polina knew what he needed. She grabbed the back of his head over her shoulder and pulled his face toward her neck.

The scent of her blood under the surface of her skin must've been too much to resist. Logan struck, his teeth sinking into her flesh. The bite wasn't painful. Her flesh moved aside just for him. Logan's pleasure echoed through Polina as he drank. Three long pulls and she shattered. Her muscles tensed and released, pulsing against him until he joined her, pitching over the edge.

Eyes open and lips sealed around her neck, Polina reveled in Logan's reflection from every angle in the mirrored walls as she writhed on his lap. He gripped her waist to keep her from falling. The orgasm went on and on, much longer than his human orgasm. The air around them grew thick with power, her skin taking on a faint purple glow.

When he'd had his fill, he closed the wound with a lick and helped her off of him and into the bed. Her limbs felt loose, worked out, and a blissful smile broke the curtain of her red hair. He snuggled in beside her.

"Do you think you can stand doing that forever?" she asked, her eyes tucked into the crook of her elbow.

He sighed facetiously. "I suppose, if I have to."

She giggled.

"Polina?"

"Yes, Logan?"

"Since we have to spend eternity together anyway, will you marry me?"

Polina removed the arm from her face. "You're asking me to marry you... now?"

He shrugged and laughed. "Seems as good a time as any. Are you holding out for a ring? I'll buy you one as soon as I get to town. I'm guessing you won't need it sized."

"Oh please. Don't waste your money. I'll make one."

"Then, will you... Marry me?"

She placed a firm kiss on his lips. "Yes. I think since you've given up your mortality for me and joined with me for all eternity, the least I can do is become Polina Valentine."

"You'd take my name?"

"You're not going to change the name of your restaurant."

"Do you think I can keep the restaurant?"

"Of course!"

"I just... I thought you'd need my help here."

"I've gotten by for almost five hundred years without a caretaker. I suspect I'll need your help on occasion, but no need to make drastic changes."

"Where will we live?"

"A witch has to stay with her cemetery."

He nodded. "Here is fine."

"I think you'll find you need much less sleep than you used to."

He placed a hand on her arm. "I'll move Bonny here right away, so she doesn't have to be alone during the day until I can sell my place."

She nodded. Rolling so that she hovered over him, she asked, "It can work, right?"

He smiled at her, eyes hooded. "It already has."

"But if you live here, you'll need a way to commute to work."

He frowned. "I have a car."

Polina straightened and took a deep breath. Focusing on the floor of her sanctuary, she worked the liquid metal like clay, creating the gift she'd wanted to give Logan for a long time. Magic and metal swirled and peaked before receding. When the fog cleared, a Harley-Davidson softail was parked in her sanctuary.

"Is that...?" Logan stiffened behind her.

"Did I get it right?"

"It looks perfect, exactly like the one I wrecked. How did you do that?"

"I pulled a piece of it out of you. I absorbed the metal. That type of thing leaves an imprint, a memory."

"Will it work?"

"I think so, but there's only one way to find out."

"What time is it?"

"Around ten, I think."

He frowned. "Already dark."

She laughed and hugged him around the neck. "You can see in the dark, darling. You have superhuman reflexes.

And even if you crash, you'll find you are more... resilient than before."

Logan stumbled out of bed and pulled on his clothes. "How do I get it out of here?"

Polina waved her wand and the bike disappeared. "It's waiting for you out front."

He grabbed her face and kissed her, hard. "You ready to go for the ride of your life?" he asked.

She grinned. "I wouldn't miss it for anything."

54

BINDING

Beneath a canopy of russet, gold, and evergreen, Logan waited for Polina at the end of a row of white folding chairs. It was September 23, the fall equinox and the day of their wedding ceremony. A witch stood next to him. Not a Hecate like Polina, but a practitioner of witchcraft. She wasn't a demigod like his soon-to-be wife, but Logan sensed magic in her, a positive energy that leached from her blood-colored robes and infused the air around them.

A chorus of hollow sounds began from behind him. His gaze darted to the group of forest fae that made up the orchestra. They were long limbed, fair skinned, and had gossamer wings that made it impossible to mistake them for human. He didn't know the names of the instruments they played. There was something that looked like a flute but was made of wood; a long, straight horn with an upturned end; a board with strings; and a drum made from a rotting stump. The melody enhanced the sense of belonging to the living mountain—earth and wind and wood coming together in unison.

His gaze wandered over the guests. Grateful and her

family, Silas and his brother and sister, Logan's restaurant manager Dustin and his wife, some folks from the restaurant. He'd invited his father, but the man was too busy to come. Just as well.

And then his heart stopped. Polina stood at the head of the aisle wearing a dress that looked like Mother Nature had sewn it for her. The material was thin and textured with leaf-shaped cutouts that revealed a shiny layer underneath. Layers of white feathers started mid-thigh and flowed outward to the runner that covered the dirt path. As she drew closer, he could make out threads of gold embroidered into the torso. That's what gave the material its texture. It was lined with gold.

Polina's red waves were swept up into a neat set of curls that proved a backdrop for the tiara that adorned her head. There was no veil. She smiled and took his hand.

Truthfully, he felt unworthy of her in his common black tux, but then he remembered that not only was he worthy, he was responsible. He was the vessel of her soul. The carrier of her light. He could heal her, make her stronger, care for her in a way no one else would ever or could ever. He was her perfect match.

"We come together to celebrate the union of Polina Innes and Logan Valentine. Do you both come of your own free will?" the officiant began. Her voice sounded older than her physical appearance, raspy as crumpled parchment.

He answered affirmatively and Polina echoed his sentiment.

"Know now that you enter into a binding of heart and soul. Come with full awareness to this table of elements, for what is done cannot be undone. You have marked each other's souls. Parting will not break this bond, nor reverse what change it brings in you today. Do you consent to this union in full knowledge?"

"Yes, we do," they answered.

The witch retrieved a cord from a small table behind her. It looked to be about nine feet long and consisted of five silken threads of different colors braided together. She grabbed his right hand and firmly placed it palm to palm against Polina's.

The officiant tossed one end of the cord over his wrist. "We call on the air, pure and white, to send new hope and dreams to this couple." Under and over Polina's wrist, she wrapped the cord in a figure eight pattern. "We call on the earth, signified by the brown, to ground you in each other." She wrapped again, the cord forming an infinity symbol around their wrists. "We call on the metal element, silver, to help you be mirrors to one another, reflecting the truth of who you are and who you will be. We call on wood, represented by green, to bless you with new growth, for that which does not grow and change withers away." She wrapped one more time. "And finally, we call on the water, represented by blue, to wash away the mistakes you've made and will make with each other, so you may begin again." This time she tied the cord.

As they'd practiced, Logan leaned forward and placed a kiss firmly on Polina's lips.

The witch turned to take up the rings, placing one in his left hand. "You may now promise yourself to the lady."

Logan held up the ring and Polina obliged, sliding her finger into it. "On this day, I promise to be your guardian in life and death, the keeper of your affections, the caretaker of your pure and lasting love. My life begins and ends with you."

The officiant handed Polina a ring. She held it between

them and he slid his finger into it. "On this day," Polina said, "I promise myself to you. I give you eternity and bind my soul to yours for all time. My life begins and ends with you."

The officiant manipulated the cords and removed them from their hands without untying the knot. "Now that you have been bound, may you strive to uphold the permanence of this commitment. May your union last as long as this knot remains tied. Blessed be."

The fae began to play again and Logan walked side by side with his bride into his new life.

THE GIFT

Polina tried to navigate the crowded rooms of Aurorean House hand in hand with her new husband. Their reception was overflowing with well-wishers and the wine flowed liberally as did the trays of hors d'oeuvres Logan had prepared for the occasion. They weren't tied together anymore, but she couldn't bear to let him go. Not yet.

"Congratulations," Rick said, appearing in front of them.

"It was a beautiful ceremony," Grateful chimed in, bouncing Lucas on her hip.

Logan reached out to rub the boy's head and noticed a stuffed black dog cuddled in his arms. "Whatch'ya got there, Lucas?"

The boy turned protectively, hugging the stuffed dog tighter.

Grateful snorted. "Don't even try to touch his pup-pup. He picked it up somewhere. Honestly, we think my dad brought it home on accident from Gymboree class. I'd return it, but he loves it too much. I had to wait until he fell asleep just to wash it. And this kid never sleeps, Logan." She kissed the boy on one chubby cheek.

"Finders keepers, right, Lucas?" Logan said.

Polina smiled. "Parenthood agrees with you two. Do I sense another child in your future?"

"How did you know?" Grateful asked.

Jaw gaping, Polina pressed a hand to her chest. "I didn't! I was kidding. Are you saying you're pregnant?"

Grateful darted a glance at Rick and smiled. "We never thought the candles would be so... um... effective."

As much as Polina tried to stay in the moment, the feeling of her short time being pregnant came back to her and she silently envied her friend. Logan must have felt it too, through their new connection, because he squeezed her fingers and whispered, "Would you like to get something to drink?"

"Before you go, Rick and I have something for you. A wedding gift." Grateful handed Polina a box wrapped in silver paper. "Best wishes for a long and happy marriage."

Polina stared at the box, the weight growing heavier in her hand. Her blue eyes flicked up to her friend's. "Are you sure?"

Grateful gave a quiet, easy smile. "Absolutely."

"What are we talking about? What's in the box?" Logan asked.

"Excuse me," Polina said. She dragged Logan by the hand toward the bedroom. Once they were inside with the door closed, she held the box out between them. She couldn't speak.

Logan got the hint and started in on the paper. "Damn, Polina. You're acting like you've never seen a gift before. This couldn't wait until after our guests left?"

She shook her head. Together, they pulled the top off.

The black candle within had the stamp of a raven in the wax. Polina stopped breathing.

"What is this? Why do you look like that?" Logan asked.

"It's a mortality candle. They are extremely rare. Grateful made six of them while she still had power over multiple elements. She can't make any more. This is how Lucas and his future brother or sister were made. If we burn this, it can make you human again."

Logan grinned. "We can have a baby?"

Polina's forehead wrinkled. "Logan, you could become human permanently. You don't have to be my caretaker anymore. You were forced into the decision. Maybe it was too soon."

Logan shook his head. "What are you talking about? We just got married."

"We can stay married, but if you'd rather not..."

"Shut up, Polina," Logan said. He placed the box on the dresser. "I'm going to tell you this once, and with our connection, you'll know I'm telling the truth. I am glad that Alex put me in a position where my priorities became blissfully clear. I want to be your caretaker. I chose this. If we burn that candle, it will be because we love each other so much, we need another person to pour the extra love into. Because we want a family."

"Truly?" Polina asked.

"Truly and forever." He slipped his hand behind her waist and pulled her against him. When he kissed her, she finally accepted it. He wanted this as much as she did, and she must never question him again.

"Would you like me to light it now?" she asked with a grin.

He shook his head. "Don't take this the wrong way," he

began slowly. "I love Lucas, and I fully intend to use that candle someday, but before we do, I'd like a few years to enjoy you all to myself."

Polina closed the box, pulled the nightstand drawer open, and dropped it inside. "You are a wise and worthy husband."

"Yeah?"

"Yes." She encircled his neck with her arms. "Now, how would you like to enjoy me?"

"Shouldn't we wait until our guests leave?"

"We should, but I've never been a patient woman."

Logan leaned into her, his lips hovering over hers. "Good, because I'm hungry, and I think we've waited long enough."

Polina and Logan didn't waste another moment. As quickly as they'd unwrapped the candle, they tore into the gift of each other. Hands bound and hearts bound, they began a long and fruitful forever.

* * *

LOGAN'S FRIEND SILAS HAS ALWAYS BEEN A GREAT friend to him. As alpha of the Fireborn wolves, he's devoted his life to the care of his pack. Unfortunately, his sister Laina, a veterinarian who'd rather avoid pack politics, is about to find her life in unprecedented danger. Safety is found in an unexpected place when she becomes entangled with a human and his dog Milo. Don't miss Fated Bonds, The Wolves of Fireborn Pack Book 1 Flip the page for a free excerpt!

EXCERPT: FATED BONDS

FIREBORN WOLVES BOOK 1

Please enjoy the following excerpt of Fated Bonds,
The Wolves of Fireborn Pack Book 1

No one comes between a wolf and their fated mate.

Werewolf Laina Flynn has been dodging pressure to mate for years. The successful veterinarian may be Fireborn pack royalty, but she's happy to leave raising pups to her alpha brother Silas. So when a human triggers her mating instinct, no one is more surprised than her.

As the face of Hunt Club, Kyle Kingsley is no stranger to doing things out of obligation and responsibility. The public demands that he uphold the lifestyle the club has come to embody, even if his playboy persona is all a lie. No surprise then that Kyle volunteers to care for his recently deceased father's dog, even if the mutt is roughly the size of a barn. But when he lands in the clinic of Dr. Laina Flynn, her presence draws out something wild and untamed within him that has nothing to do with his new pet.

An act of violence on Fireborn shifting grounds drives Laina into hiding... and into Kyle's arms. Instant attraction develops into something more when fated bonds challenge everything.

CHAPTER ONE

D r. Laina Flynn navigated to the examination room on autopilot, her stomach rumbling. Who had time to stop for lunch when you were running Carlton City's busiest and most trusted veterinary clinic? Four Paws Animal Hospital was the type of state-of-the-art facility you'd expect to find associated with a university veterinary program, not a rural town in New Hampshire. But Laina had the resources and know-how to bring the best in veterinary medicine to the area, and she had the passion to ensure her patients' unsurpassed care.

"What's going on with Milo?" she asked, shouldering open the door with her eyes fixed on the chart of the one-year-old English Mastiff her assistant, Becca, had wedged into the schedule at the last minute. Milo was not a regular patient, but it was obvious the dog needed her help. He barely raised his head to greet her as she approached the examination table where Becca easily held the 160-pound canine in place. The mastiff was clinically lethargic.

"He's been sick since Tuesday afternoon," a deep male voice said.

"Tuesday? This has been going on for three days?" Laina positioned her stethoscope to listen to the dog's heart and lungs. Typical. Too many owners let their animals suffer in hopes of avoiding veterinary bills. For Milo's sake, she prayed to the goddess it was nothing serious. She palpated his abdomen. The organs were normal, but the skin of his belly was covered in an itchy-looking rash. When she moved the assessment to Milo's head, she found dry eyes and nose, and the capillary refill rate in his gums was much too slow. "He's dehydrated. Has he been vomiting?"

"Once or twice."

"Is he eating and drinking?"

"I think so."

"What are you feeding him?"

"ButcherBits."

"Ah. Has he been scratching a lot?"

"Constantly. How did you know?"

"I think Milo has a corn allergy. Switch to something grain free. No peas or lentils, though. Avoid anything generic. Will that be a problem? I might have some samples to get you started." She scribbled some notes to herself on Milo's chart. When the man didn't say anything, Laina raised her head and looked directly at Milo's owner for the very first time.

For a second, her mind blanked, her synapses shouting in unison, *all power to the visual cortex!* The eye candy standing in her examination room was best described as sin covered in chocolate sauce, poured into a pair of blue jeans and a trendy dress shirt. Polished, she thought. More polished than the usual pet owner who graced her halls. Groomed dark brown hair, physique developed enough to pass as a professional athlete, and eyes the golden color of ripe wheat—hazel, she supposed, with uneven chocolate-

and-evergreen pigment dispersion that made her wonder if he suffered from a mild case of sectoral heterochromia. She caught herself leaning across Milo for a closer observation.

Rarely, if ever, did looks alone stir something inside Laina. As a werewolf, she was no stranger to attractive men. Her kind enjoyed genetically fast metabolisms and above-average muscle mass. Even an out-of-shape werewolf carried the appearance of a fit human. Besides, Laina was the type of woman to be attracted to brains over brawn. She'd once enjoyed a passionate affair with a height-challenged professor of archaeology during her university days. Still, one look at Milo's owner and the wolf inside her got to her paws and panted like she was in heat.

Curious, Laina took a deep breath through her nose, theorizing that perhaps he *was* a shifter, wolf or otherwise. Could the stirring in her lower abdomen simply be her inner animal sensing a playmate? But after sorting through the odors of dog and disinfectant, all her hypersensitive nose detected was the scent of human with a hint of cedar and pine needles. Had he been on a long walk through the deep forest recently?

"Are you okay?" Becca whispered, nudging her arm.

"Hmm?" Laina blinked rapidly, breaking the spell. "Oh, oh yes, of course." She cleared her throat, but her gaze snapped back to Milo's owner as if he carried a Laina-charged magnet in his chest.

He reached for her face with one knuckle in an oddly intimate way, and her breath caught. "I think you have something in your hair."

"Excuse me?" Her lashes fluttered again.

Becca ripped a paper towel from the roll they always kept on the desk and handed it to her. "Looks like you might have a leftover from your surgery this morning, Doctor," she murmured.

Laina took the paper towel and turned toward the small mirror above the hand-washing station. There, in her untamed mahogany waves, was a blob of congealed blood. How it got there, she wasn't sure. She'd worn a cap during the surgery itself. Maybe when she was cleaning up her operating room? Frantically, she wiped it out as best she could, then turned back to the owner, face blazing. Her ears had to be the color of ripe tomatoes by now.

"Had to operate on an intestinal blockage in a Rottweiler this morning." She tittered nervously. "I carry a little bit of each of my patients with me always." She laughed harder, mortified when her inhale morphed into a snort. *Crap. This is a veterinary hospital not a sports bar. Pull yourself together!* With another rapid blink, she tucked her hair behind her ear and refocused on Milo. "So...corn-free food. Will that be a problem?"

"Cost is no object," he said in a gruff voice. Oh good lord, he was sexy. *Don't look, Flynn. He'll burn your retinas like the sun.*

She exchanged glances with Becca, whose expression promised she'd position Laina on the table next to Milo if she didn't snap out of it. Why wasn't her assistant swooning at the knees over this guy?

Clearing her throat, Laina said in her most professional tone, "I want to run some blood tests to rule out other, more serious conditions. Is Milo up-to-date on his immunizations?"

"I'm not sure," the man murmured. "His last owner... had an emergency, and I agreed to take him in."

"Wait, this isn't your dog?"

"He is now. I adopted him...Tuesday. We're on our way

home. I was just worried about him and didn't think this could wait."

"Smart. It can't. How far is home?"

"A day's drive."

She rubbed the mastiff's ears and looked long and hard into the dog's big brown eyes. As a werewolf, Laina could communicate dog-to-dog through smell, sound, and body position, but those things weren't as specific as human words. For example, by the vacant emptiness behind Milo's pupils, she could tell that he'd been through a distressing experience recently. But she couldn't read his mind and had no idea what that experience was. Whatever his last owner's emergency, it had left its mark on Milo in more ways than simply adjusting to a new owner.

"Can you give him twenty-four hours here? I'll administer some IV fluids and run a few blood tests. If all goes well, he should be good to go tomorrow."

The man retrieved his phone from his back pocket and stared at his calendar app for the better part of a minute. Even from across the examination table, Laina could see he was booked solid. Would he clear that mess of a schedule for a dog he'd owned a couple days?

"If you think that's what he needs, I'll plan to spend the night in Carlton City."

"I do," she said softly, her heart warming. Attractive and an animal lover.

He stroked a hand over Milo's side. "Okay. Do what you need to do."

"Perfect. We'll get started." She helped Becca get Milo off the table and through the door to the procedure room. "If you'd like to wait out front, Becca will check you out and take your number so we can contact you when he's ready."

"Actually..." The man scratched the back of his head, the deep forest scent filling her nostrils once again.

That was definitely pine and cedar. An outdoorsy type, just like her. Well, not just like her. He didn't sprout a nose and tail during the full moon. Had he been hiking? Fishing?

"I was hoping I could take you to dinner," he blurted, shifting from foot to foot. "I don't know anyone in Carlton City, and since I'll be here tonight waiting on Milo, I thought... It would be nice to have some company if you're interested." The man tucked a hand into a back pocket in a way that was both casual and endearing. Was it possible to be jealous of someone else's hand?

It took her a second to process what he was asking. "Sorry, what?"

"Dinner. Would you like to eat with me?" He cocked an unbelievably sexy eyebrow.

"Are you asking me out?" The question erupted from her mouth with an unpleasant aftertaste. She'd blurted out the words as though his invitation had annoyed her. She wasn't annoyed; she was flabbergasted.

"I'd love to hear what you know about raising a mastiff." He gave a breathy laugh, rubbing his slightly stubbled chin.

Ah, that was it. He needed advice on the new dog. Made sense and explained his interest in her. "Sure. Why not?"

"Around seven?"

"Seven it is!" She bobbed her head awkwardly.

"I saw a place called Valentine's driving into town. Is it good?"

"The best. I'll meet you there. We can stop back here to check on Milo afterward."

"It's a date," he said, opening the door that led to the waiting room.

Her heart jumped slightly at the word *date,* and she quickly reminded herself he was just passing through town. This wasn't a *real* date. "I didn't even catch your first name," she said before he could leave. "It's not on the chart."

"Kyle." His hazel eyes crinkled slightly at the corners when he smiled. "Nice to meet you, Dr. Flynn."

"Laina." She scratched the side of her cheek, catching a glimpse of fingernails badly in need of a manicure. She stuffed her hand into her pocket.

He nodded. "See you at seven, Laina."

CHAPTER TWO

Three days earlier...

Kyle Kingsley stared at his brother Nate across their father's failing body and tried to deal with all the awkward and uncomfortable going on inside his chest. Holed up in a cabin in the middle of nowhere, Kyle had more questions than answers about the man who'd brought him into this world but had spent so little effort seeing him through it. Only, the time for questions was long gone.

"The lawyers are meeting on the Tanaka deal tomorrow. They'll want to revise the paperwork. Dad's name will be replaced by mine unless you have a problem with that." Nate's dress shirt and tie clashed with the general rustic appeal of the cabin but perfectly matched the brash ambition in his eyes.

"You mean, will I contest your claim to the throne?" Kyle shifted forward in his chair, his eyes falling on the dog who'd stayed curled by his father's side for two days now. *Fuck*, the thing was gigantic. *What the hell were they going to do with the dog?*

"Play to your strengths, Kyle. You're the face of Hunt Club. Do you think for a second that if I had the clock-stopper you wear every day, I'd want to do what I do? Hell no. You've always been the beauty. I've always been the brains. Do you think the public wants to see this ugly mug when they think of an adult lifestyle brand?" He pointed to his own face. "We need your billion-dollar abs. Leave the desk-jockeying to me and enjoy the good life as nature intended."

"The good life? Hmm. Funny, it didn't seem so great when that redhead—what's her name?"

"Kate? From the New York agency."

"She tried to set me on fire."

Nate followed up his breathy snort with a shrug. "Red-heads." He ran a finger inside the neck of his tie, loosening it a few inches. "Kyle...the deal."

"The position is yours."

Nate smiled in that lippy, gaping way he did that always reminded Kyle of a filter-feeding whale shark, only instead of krill, his gaping maw collected entrepreneurial opportunities. He had to hand it to his brother—what Nate lacked in attractiveness, he made up for in cunning. Could premature hair loss be triggered by a hot-running brain?

"I'll call the transition team and have them prepare the necessary documents for overnight delivery."

"Two things. One, Dad's still alive. Two, we are in the middle of nowhere. Unless you plan to go medieval and have the lawyer send the papers by carrier pigeon, it's going to have to wait. Relax. There's no hurry." Hell, the tiny town of Red Grove had one grocery store, and it doubled as a bait and tackle shop.

"It won't be long, though. The doctor said any minute

now." Nate's brown eyes shifted, fixing on their father's lumbering chest. "We should get the paperwork started."

Although the lip-smacking and carcass-circling didn't exactly surprise Kyle, his patience with his brother waned. Unrestrained ambition made for hasty decisions in the heat of the moment. Kyle preferred a more deliberate approach. Estranged or not, the man between them shared their DNA —one of the few things Kyle had in common with his brother. He deserved respect.

"I'd like to experience these last moments with our father minus the paperwork. It. Can. Wait." After everything, he couldn't exactly muster true grief for the loss of this man, but he did feel...something, if only regret that they'd never been a real family. He would have liked that. He wanted that.

Nate shifted in his chair. "Why do you think he chose to come out here to die anyway? I didn't even know this town was on the map. What's it called again?"

"Red Grove. I didn't know it existed either, but I think that was the point. He didn't want the public to see him like this."

"His will says no funeral. Nothing public. Does Red Grove even have a crematorium? What do we do with the body?"

Kyle nudged back his chair, the legs protesting with a rumbling screech against the wood floor. The dog lifted its massive head, brown eyes tracking Kyle as he circled to Nate's side of the bed. Despite his brother's considerable size, Kyle fisted Nate's collar and lifted him from his seat.

"I'm not going to say this again," he said in a low voice laced with menace. "Dad is still alive. As far as we know, he can still hear us. We'll handle the arrangements when the time comes. Until then, unless you want to talk about what few personal memories we have of him, shut the fuck up." He released his brother, who dropped into his chair as if his knees had gone out. Kyle returned to his own chair, his eyes shifting back to his father.

Nate spread his hands and shrugged. "Sorry." He did not sound sorry. Annoyed, but not sorry. Still, he hushed. The cabin grew quiet, aside from the deep, wet rattle of their father's breathing and the occasional whine of the four-legged beast lying at his side.

"Am I allowed to ask what we should do about the dog?" Nate tugged at his pant leg, clearly perturbed by Kyle's restrictions on the conversation.

Kyle reached out and stroked the dog's head. "His name is Milo."

"I can't have a dog. I'm allergic," Nate said. "We'll have to take him to the humane society."

"He's a 160-pound mastiff. No one is going to adopt this dog. Three-quarters of the population doesn't have a house big enough for this dog. Frankly, one fart and he could knock down the walls of this cabin."

Nate snorted. "*You* can't keep him. You're barely home. And I don't need to tell you the staff is not going to want to deal with a dog like this."

"Dad loved Milo."

"More than he loved either of us." Nate's nostrils flared. "Just another way for the old man to deliver one last jab to the balls."

"I'm keeping him," Kyle said definitively. The decision came as a surprise even to him, but it seemed right somehow.

"Don't be ridiculous. They'll never let you on the plane with that thing."

"I'll drive him back in my rental."

Nate scowled. "This is a bad idea, Kyle. You don't adopt a dog to fill the absentee-father-shaped hole in your heart."

Kyle let his eyes drift over his brother's stocky frame. "Better than filling it with peanut butter."

Nate flipped him the middle finger.

Silence settled between them again, interrupted only by their father's labored breaths. For once, even Nate had nothing to say. He crossed his arms and stared blankly at their father.

An unsettling scrape came from the direction of the front door, causing Milo to raise his head again. The canine gave one low *woof* but didn't find the noise concerning enough to leave the bed to investigate it. Kyle rubbed the tightening skin at the back of his neck. "What was that? Sounded like claws."

"Who knows? We're in the middle of the woods. Probably raccoons." Nate stood and stretched. "I'm going to grab a cup of coffee." He waddled toward the kitchen.

With a whimper, Milo laid his head back on the bed, staring at the old man with the single-minded intensity only man's best friend was capable of. Kyle scratched the dog behind the ears. "It'll be okay, Milo. I'll take care of you."

The quiet morphed into something even quieter, a silence that only came at the end of things when man and beast became equals and the last stroke on the portrait of a life was cast upon the canvas. No rattling breath filled the space between them. Kyle waited. His father's chest did not rise. It did not fall.

Kyle stood and, with two fingers, searched for a pulse.

And then he said good-bye.

CHAPTER THREE

"Becca, can you turn up the music?" Laina spread the incision she'd made in the belly of the spaniel on her operating table and skimmed the spay hook along the inside of the pup's abdominal wall. On her first two attempts, she'd caught the intestine instead of the uterus. She swore this dog was hiding its reproductive organs on purpose. Thankfully, as her assistant upped the volume on the Doja Cat tune blaring into the operating room, she found her surgical mojo. "Ah, there she is." She clamped the ovarian vessel and proceeded with the spay.

If she didn't hurry, she'd be late for her date with the mysterious Kyle. She'd never experienced anything like the moment she'd laid eyes on Kyle Kingsley. Her wolf had pressed against the inside of her skin the way it did when the full moon was about to rise, fur rubbing her inner flesh, bones stretching in his direction.

A werewolf's inner wolf was a second soul, a personality separate and distinct from her human mind, one that usually got its way only three days per month. It was common for wolves to have relationships with other wolves during the full moon, when their human counterparts were asleep. Those relationships didn't remain when the wolves were in human form. Likewise, human relationships rarely translated to wolf world. As far as Laina was aware, it was unheard of for an inner wolf to wake up and show attraction to a human. Laina had no idea what it meant, but she was bound and determined to find out.

"You seem distracted, Laina. Are you still thinking about Mr. Sexy Dog Owner?" Becca teased over the speaker. Laina caught her assistant's eye through the observation window and watched her curly brown hair bounce with her off-speaker giggles.

"Aren't you?" Laina asked incredulously, keeping her hands steady as she tied off the blood vessels to the ovaries and uterus before removing the lot. It was careful, delicate work. She prided herself on her execution of the procedure, one she'd perfected for ease of recovery.

"He was sexy if you like that chiseled, underwear-model, superhero look, but I got a whiff of stiff and pretentious. Did you see his watch? That thing cost more than my entire net worth. I bet he's warped. Rich guys are always warped."

"Maybe."

"Anyway, too clean-cut for my tastes. A man without a tattoo is like a hot dog without mustard."

"I don't want to hear about the way you like your wieners, Becca." Laina grinned. Becca's laughing face broke eye contact to answer the phone on the desk behind her. After a few heated words, she pressed the hold button before returning to the loudspeaker.

"Your older brother is on the phone. He says it's an emergency."

"Tell Silas I have a patient open on the table. I'll call him back in forty-five minutes."

"That's what I told him. He said it was a family emergency and if I didn't ask for your immediate attention, he'd see that I was fired."

Laina rolled her eyes as she continued the procedure. "You're not going to be fired. Tell my brother, if it's such an emergency, he can come to the clinic and talk to me in person. By the time he gets here, I'll be done."

"You got it." Becca turned back to the phone.

Laina continued her work. "You know," she whispered to the anesthetized spaniel, "you don't realize how lucky you are that puppies aren't in your future. Being part of a pack isn't all it's cracked up to be." She checked for bleeding, then began the arduous process of stitching the incision.

"Why the hell didn't you answer my call?" Silas said from the door to her surgical suite. *Fuck*, he must have been in the neighborhood.

"So help me God, Silas, if my patient gets an infection because you dragged your flea-ridden ass into my OR, you'll be next on my table. I'll have you neutered before you can say sepsis."

"I'm the alpha, sister. When I call, you answer." It was true that her older brother was alpha of Fireborn pack, and as such, she was obligated to obey his direct command. To be honest, it was why she regularly refused to answer the phone, instead leaving that task to Becca, whose humanity made her blissfully immune to pack hierarchy.

Until recently, despite his machismo, Silas had housed a soft heart for her and her younger brother, Jason. But Alex Ravien Bloodright changed all that. Three years ago, the rogue pack member had murdered their parents in cold blood, forcing Silas to become alpha of Fireborn pack before his time. As head of the largest pack in North America, the Fireborn alpha automatically became first alpha, the leader of the Lycanthropic Society, the council that led all werewolf packs. Grieving and orphaned, Silas was thrown into both roles overnight. He wasn't ready for either.

Alex was cruel and exceptionally deadly. Thanks to a dragon-scale amulet he'd stolen from a family of Siberian dragon fae, he'd wielded elemental magic similar to a warlock. He used it to slaughter pack leaders and force their packs to follow him. If Silas hadn't used his position as a detective to hunt Alex down and stop him last summer, all the members of the Lycanthropic Society would likely be dead, and every werewolf in North America would be forced to bow to a madman.

Technically, the threat wasn't even over. It had been more than two months since Silas had recovered Alex's body, and they still hadn't confirmed it was him and not Jonah, his Zafka—a doppelgänger used as a security detail for werewolf royalty.

Werewolves, as shifters, could change small things about their appearance at will, but with the help of the type of dark magic Alex had access to when he possessed the amulet, complete transformation was not only possible but could be permanent. After taking down Alex, Silas had wanted a DNA test to prove the body they thought was Alex's was actually his, which meant he'd needed a family member's cooperation. Alex's sister, a society member herself, was more than happy to oblige, but supernatural DNA testing took time.

Even Laina had to admit that was a good enough reason for her brother to adopt a more totalitarian leadership style. To keep the pack safe, Silas had to lead with an iron fist. It was understandable. She simply wanted no part of it. She envied the freedom of the human woman sitting at the front desk, blissfully unattached and unencumbered. Laina wanted a life free of both pack politics and Silas's over-reaching protection.

She wanted to be her own alpha.

Laina lifted her gaze to meet her brother's. "Seriously, Silas, I know you wouldn't risk the life of this sweet pup on my table unnecessarily. What is so important that it can't wait?"

"We confirmed the body we recovered from Silver Sparrow Mountain was Alex's."

Laina paused midstitch and released a relieved breath. "Alex is dead, then, without a doubt?"

A smile spread across Silas's scruffy face. "Sister was a match. It's him. He's dead."

She finished her last stitch, shaking her head. "You did it, Silas. If Mom and Dad were alive, they'd be so proud of you." She gave him a genuine smile.

"The society seems happy about it." He pushed his hands into the pockets of his blazer. "They're throwing a party in our honor tonight at Rivergate Manor, formal attire."

She groaned. "I can't go. I have a date."

"A date? With whom?"

"A guy."

"What guy? All the society members are going to be at the ball."

"Not a wolf."

"A human?" he scoffed. "Come on, Laina. Be serious. You can reschedule your playdate. This is part of your royal duty."

"You know how I feel about these things."

"Yes, I do. You hate being a princess. You think that

because I'm the alpha, your involvement in the society isn't necessary. And you would prefer to simply live your life in the human world, only joining us for an obligatory run on Rivergate Manor's protected property three days a month."

"Exactly." She cleaned Ginger's stitches and applied a sterile dressing. "You're the heir. And frankly, even if something happened to you, Jason would get the crown—not me. I'm completely dispensable, and that's okay. I prefer it that way. I didn't spend eight years in school to leave veterinary medicine behind and raise a litter of werewolf pups."

Silas frowned. He opened his mouth as if to say something and closed it again. She backed off the anesthesia and removed the intubation. Ginger whined softly. Laina whispered, "You're going to be fine, sweet girl."

"It's not all about you, you know," Silas said.

She straightened, gritting her teeth. "If my life isn't about me, who is it about?"

"The pack. Whether you like it or not, you are Fireborn royalty, which means the largest pack in North America looks to you for leadership. They also look to you to provide the future of the pack."

"You mean children."

"Royal children. You are a descendant of a primary family, a pureblood. The society is going to expect you to choose a suitor from within its ranks."

A drop of werewolf blood was enough to technically make someone a werewolf, but such a person might never shift. The greater the concentration of primary werewolf blood, the greater the chance of displaying werewolf qualities: strength, speed, ease of shifting, enhanced senses. Pureblood babies kept the pack strong and preserved the werewolf way of life. It was why mating with humans was discouraged.

"They expect the same of you, Silas, but I don't see you picking out your wedding tux. Hell, the last woman you dated wasn't even a werewolf." Her brother had dated a celestial fae for ages. Although the relationship was casual, he'd enjoyed her company regularly enough.

Silas scowled at being called out. "I can father children into my senior years. Your biological clock is ticking."

She scooped Ginger into her arms and carried her through the doors to the kennels they used for recovery. Silas followed, parking himself against the wall while she made the spaniel comfortable.

"I'm not marrying someone simply to appease society elders," she said. "I will marry who I please, and I will marry for love or not at all."

Silas drew a hand through his wild brown hair, his bushy eyebrows giving him an unquestionably wolfish appearance. "Listen, Laina, you know how this works. You can have something on the side. Marriage among werewolf royalty has often been more contractual in nature than anything else."

"No," she said.

"I could make you."

"You could, but you won't."

"I will if I have to."

"You won't because you know I'll hate you for the rest of my life. Don't risk losing one of the few people who loved you before you were alpha."

He stared at her, unblinking. "You don't realize how important you are to the pack. An alliance by marriage with another primary pack member would strengthen our numbers and our position in the society."

"Oh, I understand that."

"If you did, you'd never be this difficult."

She shrugged. "I understand. I just don't care. It has nothing to do with me. You don't need me. You are all the leader Fireborn will ever need. Alex's dead body proves that. *You* can marry to unite the packs. *You* can sire pups to fill our ranks. You don't need me."

He placed his hands on his hips, looking defeated. "You will attend the ball tonight. Seven o'clock. Formal dress. That is a direct order from your alpha."

She raised two fingers to her forehead and saluted him, ending the motion by flipping him her middle finger.

"And you will act like the princess you are." He gave her a smug grin before turning on his heel and leaving the room.

"Ooh! You asshole!" She stomped her foot. With a glance at her watch, she headed for the sink to wash up. She'd have to ask Becca to call Kyle and cancel their date. If she was going to make it to Rivergate Manor tonight, properly attired, she'd have to leave now to prepare. She couldn't be late, and she couldn't say no. Silas's direct alpha command meant she had no choice. If she tried to disobey, life would get extremely uncomfortable.

Continue the story -> Fated Bonds, The Wolves of Fireborn Pack Book 1

MEET GENEVIEVE JACK

USA Today bestselling and multi-award winning author Genevieve Jack writes wild, witty, and wicked-hot paranormal romance and romantic fantasy. She believes there's magic in every breath we take and probably something supernatural living in most dark basements. You can summon her with coffee, wine, and books, but she sticks around for dogs and chocolate. Her novels feature badass heroines, fiercely loyal heroes, and fantasy elements that will fill you with wonder. Learn more at GenevieveJack .com.

Do you know Jack? Keep in touch to stay in the know about new releases, sales, and giveaways.

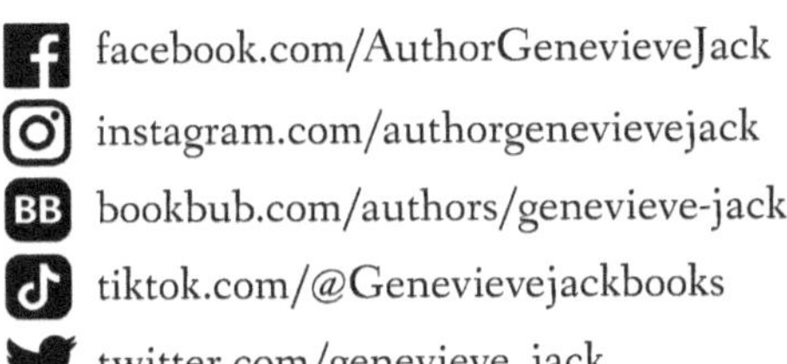

facebook.com/AuthorGenevieveJack
instagram.com/authorgenevievejack
bookbub.com/authors/genevieve-jack
tiktok.com/@Genevievejackbooks
twitter.com/genevieve_jack

Kick the Candle, Book 2

Queen of the Hill, Book 3

Mother May I, Book 4

Logan (companion novel)

The Wolves of Fireborn Pack Trilogy

Fated Bonds

Feral Instincts

Forever Mated

ACKNOWLEDGMENTS

A Game of Hearts would not have been possible without the help of a few individuals who gave their time and experience.

Special thanks to authors Brenda Rothert and L.J. Bradach for your priceless advice and bits of cleverness. You helped make Logan's story come alive.

A big thank you to my long-suffering family for your support and encouragement.

And finally, hugs to Hollie Westring, the fabulous editor who once again helped me polish this novel to a shine worthy of my readers.

www.ingramcontent.com/pod-product-compliance
Lightning Source LLC
Chambersburg PA
CBHW031312210726
48287CB00005B/1520